Goddess Good

Chris Walters

Cover design by Jaycee DeLorenzo

ISBN: 978-1-964292-03-8

Ebook ISBN: 978-1-964292-04-5

For everyone searching for love, acceptance, and a place in this crazy world.

Visit the link below to listen to the Goddess Good playlist on Spotify.

Notable Characters

Inanna: Mesopotamian Goddess of Love and War. Also, prosperity. Other names include: Ishtar, Izzy, Ayanna

Bast: Egyptian Goddess of Cats, Protection, Pleasure, and Fertility. Other names include: Bastet, Betsy, Brandi

Jesus Christ: Yes, that one. Other names include: Jesús

Sean Chambers: Human. Member of Venatores Falsorum Deorum, colloquially known as the Godkillers, a secret organization founded during the reign of Emperor Constantine and dedicated to hunting down false gods and other unnatural beings.

Annabelle Campbell: Human. Barista and artist.

Chapter 1

Dancing In The Dark
Bruce Springsteen

Izzy Thompson was a tired mess when she got home after noon. She successfully navigated the extensive series of locks on the front door and quietly entered the house. Once upon a time, she would have never dreamed of walking into her own home without fanfare, but time and caution had worn away petty concerns about pomp. Also, she had roommates now.

Dozing on the back of the worn couch was a sleek tabby cat. The cat raised her head and said, "Oh, my. Look what the *me* dragged in."

"Shut it, Betsy. It's not like you don't come in like this half the time."

"Reeking of sex and covered in glitter? You're not wrong."

Izzy watched as Betsy stood up and stretched languidly. The cat hopped down onto the floor and then in a shimmer of light and shadows was replaced by a nude young woman with bronze skin and midnight black hair. The two women could easily have been mistaken for sisters as they shared similar raven tresses and naturally tanned skin tones.

They had once been rivals, clashing over territory and ambitions, but had become friends over the years. Izzy reflected on

1

their relationship as she started to shed her own clothes. *Time has a way of changing things. Time and countless years on the run from the same enemies.*

The stairs creaked as another roommate walked down. Once he spied Betsy and Izzy's nudity, he quickly covered his eyes. They both laughed at him. "Come on, Jesús. It's natural."

"Just because it's natural doesn't mean I need to see it. Again and again."

It had taken Izzy a long time to accept Jesús as a friend. They had met in Rome and he seemed a decent sort of guy at the time. His brother was a complete asshole, though, which caused a lot of tension. With his brother's goon squads hunting both of them, she had grown fond of Jesús —plus, he was fun to tease.

Betsy purred, "That's too bad, Jesús. You'll miss watching the two of us make out, completely naked."

"Ugh, you two spin more temptations than the Devil himself. I just wanted some water!"

"Come on, Betsy. Let's give the poor guy a break. I'll take some water, too." They grabbed robes from a closet and put them on.

"Thank you, I appreciate the robes." He deliberately kept his eyes up, though, to avoid any bits that might slip out of their robes. All three sat down at the table, and Jesús set a glass of water in front of each. Betsy coughed politely, and Jesús rolled his eyes. "Fine." He touched Betsy's glass, and the water became a classy pinot noir. At Izzy's glance, he reached over, and she now had a delightfully refreshing rosé.

"Thanks, Jesús."

"I swear that's the only reason you let me live here."

"It's not the only reason, but it is a good one." Izzy gave him a playful wink. "Hey, I need to do laundry. Do either of you have anything?"

"I do. Be right back," Jesús exclaimed as he headed upstairs.

Betsy took a big sip of her wine. "He's gone. Tell me about your evening."

"Eh, work was good. I got to step into a couple of fights, which always gets me revved up. I hit a strip club afterward and left with a couple of dancers. After I exhausted them, I came home."

"Sounds delicious."

"It was. How about you?"

"Slow, but entertaining. You know how much I enjoy all the strange people who frequent an all-night diner. I need to move on, though. Been there too many years, and people will start wondering soon."

"Are you leaving Portland?"

"Nah. This city is a good fit. I'm thinking of opening a bikini coffee cart."

"Mm, I like it. Have you thought of a new name?"

"Brandy, or maybe Becky. Belle could work. Bambi, too. I'm still thinking about it."

"Tell me if you need help."

"Help with what?" Jesús was back.

"I was just telling Izzy I'm thinking of starting a bikini coffee cart. I could use a sexy shirtless guy for it. You know, to broaden my potential clientele..."

"Ugh, you're killing me," Jesús groaned.

Izzy grinned at them. Izzy wasn't her real name. Long ago, in a place now called Iraq, she had been known as Inanna, then Ishtar. For more than six thousand years, she'd used countless names and lived countless lives. Betsy was born in Egypt, and her real name was Bast, Bastet, or Ubaste, and like Izzy, she'd also had many names in the intervening years. They had been blood enemies when Assyria had been around, but Jesús' asshole brother put an end to most of their power and conflict. Jesús, on the other hand...that was his real name, but he put different accents on it now. With his dark hair and tanned skin, most people these days

3

just assumed he was from Mexico, when he had actually been born in Bethlehem two thousand years ago. It helped that he was incredibly good with languages.

Their fourth roommate wouldn't be up for a while. They went by Mortimer, but that wasn't their real name. Mortimer was the youngest by far, barely one hundred and fifty. They were a decent person most of the time, so the rest of the household didn't hold the fact that they were a vampire against them. Mortimer tended to get pretentious when DJing, but at home they were easy-going and approachable. Izzy enjoyed going to Mortimer's vampire raves when her schedule permitted, because the general mood of horniness and tension was an aphrodisiac for her.

Hiding in the shadows is certainly a far cry from my days of grandeur in Uruk and Babylon. Living a paranoid life over almost two millennia has ground me down. Having friends makes life more bearable for me. The Godkillers haven't found us yet, and just being alive is a gift.

Chapter 2

Astronomy
Blue Öyster Cult

S ean Chambers worked in a nondescript building on the outskirts of Seattle. The property was owned by the Archdiocese of Seattle, although he doubted even the Archbishop knew of its existence. A generic building in a generic office park, staffed by men wearing the generic business casual common in Seattle. It was also the nerve center for the Venatores Falsorum Deorum, although even the organization's members usually called themselves the Godkillers. From Seattle, they covered the combined territories of the Archdioceses of Portland and Seattle, known to most as the states of Idaho, Montana, Oregon, and Washington. After the near eradication of indigenous deities in the late nineteenth century, this particular posting had been a backwater for decades. The proliferation of white supremacist groups in the Pacific Northwest changed that. Most of these groups remained rabidly Christian, but some turned toward paganism—particularly favoring the false gods of the Norse.

Sean was a Diviner. The task of a Diviner was finding the evidence of a false god's presence. For centuries, the job involved travel and speaking with people; however, the growth of the internet meant that he spent most days at a computer. Once a Diviner found credible evidence that a false god was in a certain area, a group of skilled investigators and trackers called Hounds were dispatched to seek out the false god. If the Hounds found one, then they sent for a Hunter team to eliminate it.

Joining the Godkillers had given Sean a direction in life. He could best be described as smart, but not ambitious, so he was pleasantly surprised when a job offer as a researcher for a company he had never heard of arrived. Jones & Curtis Consulting was a shell company, one of the many layers of a proverbial onion whose history stretched back to the days of Constantine. Now, Sean toiled every day inside the drab walls of Jones & Curtis, unadorned save for a picture of a sternly fierce Jesus.

False gods were often difficult to find, and nearly impossible to permanently kill, as they were sustained by belief. The various versions of Odin and Thor who kept popping up in the Pacific Northwest tended to be belligerent and stupid, much like their followers. This made them relatively easy to identify, track, and kill; however, the persistent binding of racist pseudoscience and ideology with Norse mythology made for a particularly grisly game of Whack-A-Mole. Sean dreamed of the day when he might identify one of the older, trickier false gods rather than these buffoons. He sometimes idly daydreamed of becoming a Hound or even a Hunter, even though he knew that would probably never happen either.

Day after day, Sean searched news reports, message boards, and social media for the telltale signs of a false god's appearance. Night after night, he went home to his studio apartment. Sean had given up on dating a while ago, because working for a secret organization that even the CIA and FBI (probably) didn't know about was not conducive for the trust necessary for a relationship. Some guys managed to have relationships and even families, and Sean wasn't sure if they did so by breaking the silence or by being really good liars. Instead, Sean came home every evening to the one female in his life— his calico cat named Huntress.

Chapter 3

Go Your Own Way

Fleetwood Mac

Once Bast decided she wanted to start a coffee cart, she didn't waste any time. Betsy told her boss at the diner that her mom was sick in Arizona and she needed to leave to take care of her. Betsy's identity was shelved, and Bast became Brandi. As this was not one of her existing identities, she needed someone to forge a new one. The best forgers were Hermes and Mercury, and Bast used their services in setting up a new identity and a new business.

Bast/Brandi found a good location in a commercial section of Portland and secured the necessary loans and permits with Mercury's aid. She didn't actually need a loan, but having one raised less suspicion. Bast and Inanna both tried very hard to convince Jesús to give up his job as an overnight stocker at an organic market to be a shirtless latte slinger, but he adamantly refused. Teasing him about it was fun, though, and both goddesses agreed he did look really good without a shirt.

Bast decided to call her new cart "Brandi's Bitchin' Brews," and she hired some pretty local girls and one hunky guy as a crew. The business did all right, but the money really didn't matter. For all of them, jobs were simply part of a cover to keep their true nature secret. Jesús was the exception to that rule, as he seemed happy to give away any excess money he had. Inanna sometimes wondered how he had managed to evade the Godkillers for this long.

Listening to Brandi's stories about the customers and the shenanigans of the coffee cart life, Izzy started to feel bored with working security at the arenas. Sure, there were fights to get involved in and romances to watch, but it was never enough to satisfy her. As a Goddess of Love and War, it had seemed like an ideal job at first. Mostly, though, it was one monotonous evening after another.

About three months after the coffee cart opened, Izzy was preparing for another night's security work, hoping for at least some action, when Brandi stormed through the front door.

"Rough day?" Izzy asked.

"You know that idiot girl, Sasha, I told you about?" Brandi fumed. "I fired her today."

Izzy nodded. "What happened?"

"I told her at least a dozen times this was a coffee cart, not a front for prostitution. Did she listen to me?"

"I'm guessing she didn't."

"*Of course not.* Not only did she solicit a customer right in front of me, she did it when there was a *cop* in line. I knew she was stupid, but I never imagined she was *that* stupid."

Izzy chuckled, shaking her head "Wow..."

"I fired her on the spot and then I worked my ass off today. Thankfully, Annabelle was there, and the two of us got through the worst of it." Brandi sighed wearily. "Now I need to find a new barista."

"Crazy idea..."

"What?"

"I'll take the job."

"You? Seriously? If Ra could see this..."

Izzy's brows furrowed. "Do you really want to bring up ancient history?"

"No. I'm sorry. I just found it amusing. The past is the past, and you're like a sister to me now."

This mollified Izzy. "You're like a sister to me, too. Working night security is getting boring, and I could use a change."

"This actually works out. I think I might be pregnant again, and it would be nice to have someone I trust watching the cart and making sure no one else takes up prostitution."

"You're pregnant again? I am so glad I was associated with prosperity in general and not usually with fertility."

"It's such a pain in the ass. If I'm right, then I'll have the litter in a bit less than two months. I'll drop the kittens off at the shelter once they're ready."

"Is Enrique the father?"

"Ugh, trust me, I've tried. He has abs that put Horus' to shame." Brandi sighed wistfully. "Sadly, I am very much not his type. You'll get along great, though. No— I got lucky last weekend with a couple of guys, and I think a condom ripped."

"That sucks. You were on a good run, too. A whole year without getting pregnant." Izzy gave her friend a comforting hug. "Back to the cart—I'm going to go in and tell my boss this is my last night. Sick parents in Florida or something."

"Always a good excuse."

"I'll need to check my identities, but I'm pretty sure I have one that would work."

"If not, I can always get—"

"No, I'm not using either of those two dipshits. I know a vampire in San Francisco who can get me set up if I need it."

"Hermes and Mercury are faster, though."

"I don't care. You *know* how I feel about the Greeks and the Romans."

"Rome wasn't all bad. That's where we met," Jesús said as he walked down the stairs.

"Rome is also why your vicious alter ego has been hunting us for centuries."

Jesús looked crestfallen. "I know, and I'm sorry about that. My Father has always been paranoid and jealous. He might think He is infallible, but He's not."

"How are you so nice, and why does it turn me on so much?" Izzy asked petulantly.

Jesús gulped audibly. "I have to get to work," he muttered as he fled.

Brandi chuckled. "I get it, but you know neither of us will ever get him in the sack. He's too hung up on Magdalene."

"Yeah... It would be nice if we could get them back together," Izzy mused. "Any idea where she is?"

"I'm not sure, but the last rumor I heard put her in Venezuela."

"That sounds like her. Mags never could resist helping people." Izzy sighed. "I might need to rub one out before work. Unlike some people I know, I can't just transform into a cat and get serviced by every tom in the neighborhood."

Brandi smirked. "Jealous much?"

Chapter 4

Fly By Night

Rush

Sean was curious why he was being called into his manager's office late on a Friday afternoon. If he had more experience in the corporate world, he might have been nervous about this. As it was, Sean knocked politely on the door and said, "Dustin, you wanted to see me."

"Yes. Please, shut the door."

"Of course."

"Take a seat, Sean. You're probably wondering why I called you in."

"Yes, sir." Sean sat as directed in one of the uncomfortable chairs facing Dustin's desk.

"I've been ordered to send a Diviner down to Portland. So, I've reviewed everyone's files and decided you are the perfect man for the job."

"Portland, sir? There's nothing happening in Portland."

"Yes. Apparently, the Diviner General's office thinks it's too quiet. Which is why they want me to send someone in person. Someone on the ground to see what we might be missing."

"Of course, sir. For how long?"

"Indefinitely."

"Indefinitely?" Sean suddenly felt overwhelmed. "But, my cat—"

"This is a long-term assignment, Sean. Of course, I protested about losing a member of my team for so long, but orders are orders."

"I see..."

"We've arranged a place for you to stay. Pack your things this weekend and make any arrangements. You'll go down on Monday. I've emailed you the necessary information."

"Of course."

"This is a once-in-a-lifetime opportunity, Sean."

"Thank you, sir. I won't let you down," Sean exclaimed with as much enthusiasm as he could muster.

"I know you won't."

Once again, Sean's lack of real-world experience let him down. A late Friday meeting about a last-minute assignment that would uproot his life could never be a good thing. This wasn't his manager looking out for him. No, Sean was the person his manager could most afford to lose— he just didn't realize it.

Sean was excited by the time he got home. "Huntress, we're going on an adventure!"

"Rar?"

"I know! We're going to Portland! I'm a bit nervous. I hope you're not nervous."

"Rar."

"I'm going to take the best care of you. It's a long drive, but I'll bring snacks for both of us. A once-in-a-lifetime opportunity, Dustin said. Maybe this will be my ticket into the Hounds. That would be very exciting, wouldn't it, little girl?"

"Rrrrrrrrrrrrrrrrrrrrrrrrrrrrrrrrrrrr," Huntress purred.

"Aw! That's a good kitty! Who's the best cat ever? That's right! You are!"

It really didn't take long to pack up the apartment. Sean

wasn't sure whether to be relieved or ashamed. Maybe a bit of both. Looking around, he wondered if anyone in Seattle would miss him.

Chapter 5

Rebel Girl
Bikini Kill

Ayanna Somerset had her first shift at Brandi's Bitchin' Brews on Sunday. The Izzy Thompson identity was gone —her fictional life over as she was supposedly visiting her fictional parents. Ayanna's birth certificate said she was from Indiana. Supposedly, she was a high school dropout who had eventually washed up in Portland. With luck, Inanna could squeeze up to ten or fifteen years from this identity before people started wondering why she didn't seem to age.

Brandi showed her where everything was, drilled her on the menu, and generally made sure she knew what to do when the real business came pouring in on Monday. Brandi informed her staff via text that she knew Ayanna from some time in Vegas, and Brandi trusted everyone to get the job done while she dealt with a health emergency.

"You are doing me a huge favor, Ayanna. I'm so glad you offered to work with me."

"I'm happy to help. Hopefully this will be much more enjoyable, plus I love the dress code," Ayanna said, waving at the bikini she was wearing. "So much more comfortable than those itchy security guard uniforms."

"I bet. Those were definitely not flattering."

"Ugh. Speaking of not flattering, I'm guessing you'll be in sweats for a bit."

"Yeah, I probably have maybe a week before I'm showing too much to hide it. It's very hard to explain away a two-month pregnancy."

Ayanna grinned evilly. "Meanwhile, I haven't been knocked up in over four thousand years."

"Not even by Zeus?"

"He's such a pig. Zeus tried very hard to get into my linens, but I never gave him a chance."

"You didn't miss much. Most unexciting fifteen seconds of my life."

"Really, Brandi? Him? Why?" Ayanna shuddered with disgust at the thought of Zeus.

"I was in heat, all right? I didn't ask to be a Fertility Goddess. At least I didn't pop out a demigod— just some extremely aggressive kittens."

"Fifteen seconds?"

"Probably less. Thunder God. He comes and goes like lightning." They both laughed

"After we close, do you want to go out for dinner?"

"Are you asking me out on a date, Inanna— Ayanna?"

"No. I just want to hang out with someone my own age and relax. Talk about the old days with someone who remembers a time before bronze."

Brandi smirked and said, "Sweetie, I don't think there are many Gods your age left."

"Hush! You know what I mean. Yes, you're two thousand years younger than me, but I guess I'm stuck with you." Ayanna smiled at her friend. "We've seen a lot, haven't we?"

"We have. I miss the old days sometimes when I had real power. But looking at this, this bright city in a land we never dreamed of... it's incredible. Even at the height of our power, we were always constrained by belief, by *their* belief. Now they do things their ancestors never imagined and think nothing of it."

Ayanna wrinkled her nose. "Ugh, do you remember the smell? Babylon, Thebes, Rome, Alexandria... Indoor plumbing is the true miracle."

"That's the truth! I spent a century in Paris and it made those cities seem pleasant."

"I believe it. The smell of Paris drove me off before I even made it to the city gates. I went to Spain instead. It was really quite lovely before the Inquisition showed up."

Brandi chuckled. "I loved it when the Godkillers branched out to purge their own kind." Turning serious, she added, "I can never understand the incredible cruelty humans inflict on other humans. I saw the work of the Inquisition when I was in Italy. I wish I could forget that."

"Me too." Ayanna shook her head. "Okay, that took a dark turn. So... dinner?"

"Yes. Let's have dinner and enjoy the miracles these modern humans have created."

Chapter 6

Walk Of Life

Dire Straits

S ean spent much of Monday afternoon cursing wireless technology, the internet, and computers in general. Setting up his computer was easy. Getting it to connect with anything was driving him quickly toward madness.

For the life of me, I can't figure out why anyone considers these things to be miracles of human innovation. Did I say that out loud or in my head? I can't tell anymore.

After multiple conversations with someone in IT, the computer finally, blessedly, deigned to connect with the internet—and then it needed to install a critical update. To keep himself from blasphemy, Sean decided to take a walk and explore the neighborhood.

Sean walked briskly, setting a pace which provided a good amount of exercise, keeping his heart rate elevated. He had been a cross country runner in high school and could still keep up a good pace over long distances. Long, fast walks helped him keep his endurance up and stay in shape.

Block after block he walked, passing through residential neighborhoods and commercial streets. He found a grocery store close enough for a good walk, but not so close he would feel guilty if he used his car. Forty-pound boxes of cat litter were not fun to carry over that much distance. Sean also discovered a bewildering array of restaurants. He had never seen so many advertisements for vegan and gluten-free in his life, and it made him nervous. Sean was not an adventurous eater.

He'd built up a good sweat by the time the streets led him to the edge of a light industrial and commercial zone. Loading docks leading into workshops were intermingled with storefronts and auto shops. Sean was breathing heavily and seriously regretting leaving his water bottle at home in his haste to avoid smashing his computer into pieces. Just then, he rounded a corner and saw a coffee cart ahead. The name, Brandi's Bitchin' Brews, did not inspire confidence in him regarding the quality of their beverages, but hopefully he could at least purchase a bottle of water there.

Sean slowed his pace to catch his breath, and then shuddered to a full stop when he saw the barista at the window. The bronze-skinned woman was breathtakingly beautiful, with midnight dark hair. She had an eight-pointed star tattooed on one well-muscled arm, and a lioness tattooed on the other. She was wearing a bikini, which registered in Sean's head as Sinful with a capital 'S.' This woman was temptation incarnate, like Eve holding an apple. Sean desperately wanted to flee. Thirst warred with purity, with purity slowly winning the battle.

I'm sure there's somewhere else to get water. Anywhere else. Anywhere at all.

Then she saw him, and smiled. Purity was routed and fled the field, leaving thirst victorious.

I can do this. Just look in her eyes, order a bottle of water, and go. You can do this and remain pure. This is a test, and you will pass, just as Jesus did.

He kept repeating the last sentence in his mind as he walked forward carefully, deliberately keeping his eyes locked on the woman's eyes. They were dark brown, nearly black, and yet seemingly flecked with sparkling gold. Those eyes danced with unspoken laughter at the strain in his own gaze. His own eyes strove treacherously to look downward, stopped only by his straining willpower.

"I'd like some water, please."

"I have that. You look like you're having a really good walk."

"Yes, very productive. How much?"

"Hmm, water would be all right for you, but I definitely recommend our ginger green tea. Water will help with the dehydration, but I think your muscles will appreciate the tea."

"Just the water. I don't drink tea."

"Don't? Or haven't?"

"Um, haven't..."

"Tell you what. Try the tea. If you like it, then I'll only charge you the same amount as water. If you don't like it, then it's on the house, and I'll give you the water for free."

"Uh, sure, I guess." Sean's willpower was almost entirely devoted to keeping his eyes locked, and so he had nothing left over to resist the offer of tea.

It's a win-win, right?

His willpower nearly imploded when she laughed.

"It's really slow right now, and a bit chilly. Do you mind if I put on a jacket?"

Oh, thank God.

Feeling relieved, Sean said, "Not at all, you should definitely do what's comfortable."

She disappeared, reappearing a minute or so later with a jacket and his tea. "Please stay and chat for a bit, if you don't mind. I'm on my own until closing. It's a bit lonely now that the five o'clock rush is gone."

Sean felt immense relief at not having to studiously keep his eyes in one place anymore. "Um, sure. I can stay for a bit." He sipped the tea.

"How is it?" she asked.

"It's good." Another sip, this one longer. "Actually, it's really good."

The raven-haired temptress smiled victoriously. "I'm glad you like it."

"Thank you for convincing me to try the tea... Brandi?"

Her laugh was like a tinkling bell, and it sent blood rushing to uncomfortable places. "No, my name is Ayanna. I work with Brandi, but she's not here right now. What's your name?"

"I'm—my name is Sean."

"It's very nice to meet you, Sean. Do you come here often?"

"Uh, no. First time. Actually, it's my first full day in Portland. I just moved here."

"Oh. Welcome to Portland. Where did you come from?"

"A bit north of Seattle."

"That's good. Then the weather won't be a surprise."

"No, definitely not."

"If you don't mind my asking, what brings you to Portland?"

"Work. I'm doing a remote thing and I've been assigned to Portland for, um— an indefinite period of time."

"Ohh, sounds mysterious."

"On that note, I'm going to head out before I get too cold. What do I owe you?"

"Well played, Sean the Mystery Man. Let's call it two dollars. Want a refill for the road?"

"That would be great, thanks."

"Have a great day, Sean. See you tomorrow." Her smile was guilelessly inviting.

"Uh, maybe. We'll see." He knew he sounded nervous and hated himself for it. "Good night."

Sean started walking toward home, thinking about where to get food.

I'm definitely never coming back to this coffee cart. Far too much temptation.

Chapter 7

Umbrella

Rihanna

A yanna was on the "late shift" on Tuesday, getting in around nine in the morning. By then, Annabelle and Enrique had been slinging drinks for a few hours. The morning rush tended to be a long and drawn-out affair starting with early risers coming in and the night shift heading home. This included delivery drivers, cleaning crews, and all the other people who worked hard in darkness to make the city function in the light. Those folks were gradually replaced by commuters and the day shift as the sun rose. The customers were first drawn to Brandi's Bitchin' Brews by the lure of barely covered breasts, or, in Enrique's case, incredibly well-defined pecs and a six-pack that could double as a washboard, but it was the drinks that kept them coming back.

Ayanna had worked with Annabelle the day before and had enjoyed her company. She had long, wavy red hair, a garden-worth of flowers tattooed across her body—everything from orchids to roses to foxgloves —and voluptuous curves, which were currently straining her lime green bikini to its physical limits. Ayanna could practically hear the prayers of the customers in line wishing the fabric would give way. Meanwhile, Annabelle took orders and payment with an unshakeable good nature, leaving customers smiling even as they walked away disappointed that her bikini had held together.

Ayanna hadn't worked with Enrique before, but she could already tell they'd get along. Thousands of years ago, a substantial number of her priests had been gay or intersex, so his sexuality didn't bother her in the least. Early in her shift, Ayanna whispered in Enrique's ear, "Have you seen the hunk, fourth in line? He is definitely giving you the eye." Enrique started at her, then glanced at the line, checked out the hunk, smiled at him, grinned at Ayanna.

Yep, we are going to get along great.

After they established that Ayanna had no interest in actually getting Enrique in bed, and vice versa, the two reached an unspoken mutual agreement to commence flirting outrageously with each other while also directing each other's attention to customers who were overtly or covertly checking the other out.

After the morning rush died down and Enrique was on a break, Annabelle whispered to Ayanna, "You do know Enrique is gay, right?"

"Oh yeah, *super* gay. That's why we can flirt like this."

"How do you figure?"

"Love, sex... it's like war. There's layers upon layers of strategy and tactics. If I were actually trying to get him in the sack, then I might use a bold approach, or perhaps something more subtle, but there would always be a goal to pursue. With Enrique, I am one hundred percent not his type, so it's more like... sparring. We're having fun because there's no stakes involved."

"Huh, that's... interesting. I never really thought of it like that."

"It's not bothering you, is it? I got carried away with the flirting and should have checked with you."

"No, it's fine. Kinda fun, actually. Especially now that I know the two of you are having fun and not being serious."

"Feel free to join in if you want. Just, you know, keep it light and fun. Try out the stupidest pickup lines you can think of."

"Oh, I'm pretty sure I've heard every bad pickup line in existence."

Ayanna reflected on that. *It's a good thing Annabelle has never met Zeus or Jupiter. They always had the absolute worst pickup lines ever, if they even bothered to speak first. They made drunken frat bros look like Shakespeare. Too bad I never met old William. I bet I could have inspired a few sonnets. Maybe even a play or two.*

"I keep meaning to ask about your tattoos," Ayanna said. "They are incredible."

"Aw, thank you. I love flowers, and I'm an artist, so I did all of the artwork myself. One of my ex-boyfriends is a tattoo artist, so he inked most of these." Annabelle's eyebrows knitted together. "Then I found him dipping his ink into a coworker."

"I'm sorry."

The red-head sighed. "I'm not. He was an asshole. Unfortunately, I have a type, and my type is an asshole."

"That sucks, Annabelle."

Enrique opened the cart door, interrupting their conversation. Annabelle filled a coffee cup, announcing she was starting her break. Ayanna wheeled toward an approaching customer and greeted him, hearing Annabelle in the background saying, "Enrique, is there a mirror in your pocket?" Ayanna smiled and Enrique laughed as Annabelle finished the tawdry pickup line.

The rest of the morning was spent taking care of the steady trickle of customers while getting the cart restocked for the lunch rush. The banter was lively, and the time passed quickly. After lunch, Annabelle and Enrique got things ready for tomorrow and then left for the day. Ayanna settled in for what promised to be another slow and chilly afternoon.

As the day inched toward closing time, Ayanna started hanging up some festive lights on the overhanging shelter in front of the cart's window. She was mostly done when she heard movement behind her. Ayanna swung her head and saw the nice young man from yesterday standing there with a very guilty flush on his face. His eyes quickly locked onto hers, and she smiled at him.

He was definitely checking out my ass.

Ayanna hopped off the step-stool and said, "Would you like the ginger green tea again?"

"Um..." He definitely seemed to be struggling with words.

"I'll take that as a yes. I'll get you in just a minute." She picked up the step-stool and sashayed back to the cart, practically feeling his eyes straining not to watch. Ayanna grinned.

This country is full of sexually repressed men, and tormenting them can be so much fun.

"I'm so happy you came back. I enjoyed chatting with you yesterday, Mister Mysterious Job," Ayanna said after she finished making the tea.

"Um, yeah. I felt really good after drinking the tea. My muscles weren't as sore as they might usually be after such a long walk."

"I'm so glad to hear that. I'll make a regular tea drinker out of you yet." Ayanna was leaning on the counter as she chatted, subtly using her arms to squeeze her breasts and create more prominent cleavage. While she was nowhere near as well-endowed as Annabelle, this trick was enough to get Sean's eyes to pop as his willpower wavered for an instant. She kept her expression carefully neutral as she continued, "If you're ever having a rough day, I have some really good options for teas that reduce stress or anxiety."

"Um, good to know," Sean said. He looked like he was struggling to sip his tea and keep his eyes locked on hers at the same time.

"Speaking of... how was your day, Sean? It is Sean, right?"

"Yeah, Sean. You've got a good memory."

"Thank you. Do you remember my name?"

"It's... um..."

"It's right here on my nametag." Ayanna pretended not to notice Sean's eyes bulge as he instinctively looked at her name tag, which was barely hanging on to her bikini top. "It's Ayanna, and it's good to meet you again, Sean," she said as she extended a hand. He shook it, and she noted the sweatiness of his palms. In ancient times, Inanna had been associated with lionesses, and now she smiled at him in a manner reminiscent of a lioness toying with a rabbit. "If you forget again, you can always check my name tag."

"Um, thank you, and, um, it's good to meet you. Again, I mean," Sean stammered.

"Thank you so much for coming back. It gets lonely here in the evening, and it's pleasant to have someone to talk to. Now weren't you going to tell me about your day before I so rudely interrupted you?"

"Not rude at all. Um—you're very kind. And pretty."

Ayanna smiled at him.

"I'm sorry, that was inappropriate," Sean said. He stood up. "Um, sorry. I have to get home. Have to go feed my cat." Sean fled into the gathering darkness.

I hope I didn't scare him off. It really is nice to have someone to chat with. Plus, it's really fun watching him try so hard to not look anywhere but my eyes. Oops, I forgot to charge him. Although... I bet he's the type to feel really guilty about that. He'll be back.

Ayanna smiled as she turned her mind to the closing tasks.

Chapter 8

Running With The Devil –
Van Halen

Guilt nibbled at the edges of Sean's mind as he tried desperately to focus on work. This was his second day of working in Portland, and things were not going well. Looking for signs of false gods or other unnatural activity was never easy, but in some places, it was fairly straightforward. Find what didn't fit, especially on social media; once a potential target was identified, he would look for additional sources to corroborate. The white supremacist groups that embraced false gods were usually proud of this, so they often did his work for him. Portland was a different story. There was so much noise, for lack of a better word.

He came across a witch coven, and although it was possible that there might have been a genuine witch in the group, their social media pages made it clear that the most potent brew in their cauldrons was probably kombucha. Sean would need to monitor and investigate that coven, but he was faced with a deluge of similar situations. He suspected that was the reason no Hounds had been dispatched to this city for years—everything was too mundane.

Maybe that's why I'm here. The agents of the Adversary are many and devious. Perhaps they're hiding in plain sight.

Sean continued to search and identify targets, and his list grew alongside his frustration. Sean resolved to investigate a Dungeons and Dragons meet-up that evening. It was a weekly event held at a local gaming store and almost certainly not a front for something demonic, but it was fairly close, and it would be good to check it out. It was also not too far from the coffee cart.

"Huntress, am I a bad person because I didn't pay for my tea last night?"

The cat's only response was to jump into his lap.

"It means I'm a thief now, but I didn't mean to steal the tea. I was thinking such sinful thoughts, and then I told that woman she was pretty, and I ran. I mean, she is very pretty. I shouldn't see her again."

Huntress started to make cat biscuits in his lap.

"She tempts me so. The Adversary sets many traps for men, and I have fallen into one of those. Ayanna tempts me toward sin, yet she seems so nice. By trying to avoid temptation, I am now a thief, which is also a sin. If I go back to pay for the tea, then I am no longer a thief, but then she will smile at me and I risk sin again. I know she doesn't like me. She probably speaks to all men with her flesh exposed like a trollop."

Huntress was now purring loudly as she continued to make cat biscuits in his lap.

"Who says trollop anymore? Now I've implied she is a prostitute, and yet perhaps she is just a simple girl forced by circumstance to expose herself publicly to sell coffee just to pay rent. Or maybe she is a succubus." Sean was suddenly excited about the prospect of identifying a demon. "That's it. I will go back to see if there is evidence of a demon's work under the guise of paying for my tea. Then I will no longer be a thief, and I will be doing the Lord's work."

Huntress settled down into his lap for a nap.

"I'll do that when you're done with your nap. Thank you for listening, Huntress. Am I crazy because I just had a conversation with a cat?" There was no answer beyond a satisfied purr.

Sean continued to work, coming across a vague mention of a vampire ball on Friday night. This caught his eye because there was nothing else he could find. No time, no location. Just a brief mention in a social media post. Eventually he did need to leave, which required standing up. Huntress protested the loss of her nap spot with typical feline vehemence. He gave her a treat to compensate for the interrupted nap. Huntress gobbled down the treat and walked off with her tail in the air.

Once outfitted with a warm jacket, a rosary, and a pencil, Sean embarked on his quest. The coffee cart was quiet when he got there. "Hello?"

Ayanna appeared, drying her hands. She smiled when she saw him. "You're back, and you're early. Another ginger green tea for your muscles, or maybe I can tempt you with lavender or chamomile for stress?"

"Um, hi... again. I forgot to pay yesterday. And maybe something for stress would be nice."

"You did, but I figured you would be back. You seem like an honest person. I'm tempted to not ring you up again, just so you'll be forced to come back tomorrow."

Sean's ears flamed red. He wasn't used to flirting at all, and having a beautiful woman flirt with him was light years beyond his experience. "Uh, I'm sure I'll be back. You're the only person I know in Portland." Sean looked around at the empty streets. "Um, is business always this slow?"

"Nah, this cart is bonkers in the morning. The line is huge, but we clear it fast. Then a bit of a rush around late morning and lunchtime. Finally, one small push around closing time as the day people leave and some of the night people start arriving."

"Night people?"

"The night shift, the cleaners, the stockers. They are the invisible people who get things done so people who work in the day can be effective."

"I... I never thought of that before."

"You just thought your office magically cleaned itself?" There was a sharp steel edge in Ayanna's voice.

"No, I knew there were cleaners. I just... I never met them and I never thought about how what they did affected what I do."

"And what do you do, Sean?" She handed him his tea. He had his rosary wrapped around his hand, but she did not flinch or give any indication it bothered her as he took the tea from her hand.

Definitely not a succubus or other lesser demon.

"Um, I'm a researcher. I look for black swans."

"Black swans?"

"Not birds. A black swan is an unexpected event that radically changes the world."

"Like an earthquake or volcano?"

"Yes and no. For example, Kilauea in Hawaii erupts all the time, but its impact is localized. If Mt. Rainier blew similarly, the same way Mt. St. Helens went back in '80, it would take out Tacoma. *That* would be a black swan. The Yellowstone volcano is probably the biggest potential black swan of all."

"So, you're a volcanologist?"

"No, um... I look for different black swans. Not ones in the natural world. I look for black swans in the general population. Human nature is tricky, and we don't always do what is logical. So, I look for outliers and trends to try to expect the unexpected."

That should be mysterious enough. Imagine if she knew demons were real and false gods hid among us.

"Huh. Sounds interesting. So, something like the housing market crash in the aughts?"

"Yeah, like that."

Definitely nothing like that.

"It's actually not terribly interesting. Well, not yet, at least. That's kinda why I'm early today. I'm heading to a D&D meet-up nearby."

"Oh."

Sean braced himself for severe disappointment as he knew she was immediately downgrading him in her mind to nerd status, or worse. Dweeb.

Ayanna continued, "I used to play D&D... um, but not recently."

Sean was shocked at this revelation. He also mentally pictured Ayanna in a chainmail bikini, a thought which instantly redirected his blood flow to his face and groin. He tried to find his voice, "It's, umm, it's my first time playing. Do you have any suggestions?" Sean watched as she pursed her lips in thought, gently tapping them with her finger. He barely suppressed a moan.

"Half-orc barbarian. It's a classic and you don't have to fiddle with learning the magic system."

"Sounds perfect." Sean wasn't planning to do this again, so anything simple appealed to him. "Weird question, but... have you heard of a vampire ball happening on Friday?"

Ayanna eyed the rosary wrapped around his hand. "Your name isn't Sean Van Helsing, is it?"

"Sean Chambers, actually. Why?"

"Van Helsing, the vampire hunter?"

The lack of blood in Sean's brain was having an effect. "Oh, like—"

Ayanna nodded. "Yes, from *Dracula*. The guy armed with a crucifix, garlic, and wooden stakes. Because you have a crucifix in your hand and all. If it's silver, then I'm really going to start to wonder about you."

This was suddenly very dangerous territory. "Oh, right. Van

Helsing came fully equipped, didn't he? Sorry, I had a brainfart at first." Sean paused and fingered his crucifix. "I never thought to ask what metal this is." With a sigh, he added, "Anyway, I'm definitely not a vampire hunter."

I just sometimes daydream I was a Hunter, or even a Hound.

Sean continued, "I briefly overheard something at the grocery store, and it intrigued me. I'm trying to be more... outgoing, I guess... Now I'm in a new city. You know, new city, new me," Sean exclaimed with far too much enthusiasm.

Ayanna looked skeptical. "Uh huh. No, but if I hear anything, then I'll pass it on."

"Thanks! Um, I need to go if I'm going to get to D&D on time. Have a good night, Ayanna." He waved as he scuttled off.

"Bye, tell me if you find any swans playing D&D."

Sean was furious with himself.

"New city, new me," What was that? She must think I'm the biggest loser ever. Oh, and asking about a vampire ball... that was brilliant. She'll think I'm a loser and a weirdo. Probably a creep as well. I'm so stupid. Stupid, stupid, stupid! I can never go back there again. Or maybe it's not so bad—she's probably used to guys having trouble speaking around her. No, it's bad. Never going back there is good for me. I'm not a thief now, and she definitely leads me into temptation. This is better.

It wasn't better. Sean's head was filled with similar monologues, even after he made it to the game store hosting the D&D night. He settled down a bit as he learned the game. He was a bit amused that a preset character was actually a half-orc barbarian. By the end of the evening, Sean found he really enjoyed himself. He also found no evidence of false gods or demons. Just a bunch of people playing a game. He even considered coming back next week, for himself.

That night, his dreams were overrun with images of Ayanna. Sometimes she was a half-orc barbarian streaked with warpaint and blood, wearing a chainmail bikini and wielding a massive sword. Sometimes she was a bikini-clad barista with a coffee in one hand and a battle axe in the other. Sometimes, she wore white linen as she drove a chariot flanked by lionesses across a dry plain, a bronze-tipped spear in her hand, and an army at her back.

Chapter 9

Girls Girls Girls

Fletcher

Inanna watched Sean's retreat with amusement. While she was far from the peak of her powers, it was nice to know she could still transmute some people's brains into jelly. That vampire ball thing seemed strange. She recalled Mortimer mentioning they were planning one. The time she'd attended one she'd still been using her Izzy identity. Because of her previous schedule, she had attended Mortimer's events infrequently.

Once she shut down the coffee cart, Ayanna headed home to change. Mortimer was up and about, enjoying the lengthening hours of darkness.

"Hey, Mortimer! How are you?"

"I'm all right. You?"

"I'm good. Hey, are you hosting a ball this weekend?"

"Ayanna, I hope to be hosting many balls this weekend. Seriously, though, I left you an invitation over a month ago."

Oh, yeah, I think it's on my dresser. I'm pretty sure I'm using it as a coaster right now.

Audibly, she said, "I'm sorry, it slipped my mind. I'm thinking of going, since I'm not working nights. Can I bring someone?"

"Of course, darling! Make sure they're yummy."

Ayanna thought of Sean.

He's decent-looking. Not sure I would go with yummy, though.

She nearly burst out laughing when she thought of the typical pseudo-Victorian dress code of these parties, and Sean, who was obviously a khakis and polo shirt kind of guy. "I'll see what I can do about yummy. Okay, I need to get changed."

Bast, definitely starting to show, looked down from her perch on a cat tree. "Where are you going, and will it involve hot guys with a pregnancy kink?"

"I'm going out for drinks with Annabelle and her friends." Ayanna's voice went up a few octaves as she sang out, "Girls Night!"

"Ugh, I want to go, but I can't let Annabelle see me like this."

"As a cat or pregnant?"

Bast glowered at her, which was surprisingly effective since she was currently in cat form. "Inanna, please tell me you aren't sleeping with Annabelle."

"I'm not... yet. We'll see where the night takes us." Ayanna was surprised at how effective a cat frown was. "Don't give me that look. You were trying to nail Enrique. You were right, by the way—he and I get along fabulously."

"You better not cost me a good employee," Brandi said dangerously.

"Oh, don't get your eight boobs in a knot. I promise to make sure if anything happens with Annabelle she knows it's casual. Co-workers with benefits. Hm, maybe she'd work the late shift with me. It gets kinda boring. My main entertainment the past few nights is this super nerdy guy who comes for tea."

"Is he a hot nerd?"

"Kinda cute. Super repressed." At this, Mortimer was suddenly interested. With Jesús walking down the stairs, the whole house was there to listen. "It's really funny how hard he tries to not stare at my boobs." Three of them laughed, while Jesús frowned.

"It's not right to tempt the poor man."

"I'm not trying to tempt him... Okay, I'm not trying much. His refusal to appreciate what I'm showing him is his problem. I'm pretty sure your brother got his hooks in deep on this poor guy."

"That is unfortunate. I'll be sure to pray for him." As always, Jesús was looking out for people's welfare—even for someone he hadn't met.

"That's very sweet of you, Jesús. I know we all tease you... a lot. But I respect you for being a one-woman kind of guy." Jesús looked wistful. "If we ever get you and Mary Mags in your room, though, we might need earplugs." Jesús blushed furiously, but he didn't deny it, either.

Ayanna went to change clothes. She threw a bikini for tomorrow in her purse, just in case she got lucky tonight.

Chapter 10

Look What The Cat Dragged In

Poison

Ayanna made it to the coffee cart in time for her nine a.m. shift, but just barely. She had to disentangle herself from Annabelle and her best friend Tanya—which of course woke them up. Neither of those two had ever had sex with a woman prior to last night, but they seemed to be well on their way to making up for lost time as Ayanna was leaving.

She greeted Enrique and Krystal and joined the rush. Ayanna happily endured Enrique's lurid teasing and gave some back when she saw the guy Enrique had been making eyes at every morning. When that guy reached the front of the line, Ayanna made sure to take his order. When she passed the order to Enrique, she asked, "You're still single, right?"

"*Sí, chica bonita*! It's hard to find a good man."

"Write your number on this napkin."

"You're being sneaky."

"Hush and just write. Okay, thanks!" She took the napkin. When the hunk's order was done, she called out, "Order for Aiden!" She handed him the drink and Enrique's number.

"Uh, thanks, but..."

"It's not my number," she said, tilting her head toward Enrique. His eyes followed and he grinned knowingly.

"Awesome, thanks."

The Goddess of Love strikes again. Two for two in the last twelve hours.

Her matchmaking complete, Ayanna dove back into the rush. It didn't take too much longer to clear the line, and then it was back to the routine of breaks and restocking while handling any customers who came by. Ayanna also had to respond to some frantic texts from Brandi/Bast, who was worried about potentially losing a capable and extremely popular barista. Ayanna reassured her that while they had a *very* fun night, Annabelle seemed to be having an even more fun morning with her friend Tanya, and Brandi needn't worry.

Business was generally good all day long, and Ayanna was looking forward to closing as the small five o'clock rush disappeared. She kept an eye out, though, in case Sean showed. She was a bit surprised at how happy she felt when she saw him approach.

"Hey, Sean," she said breezily. "What are you in the mood for?"

"Hi, Ayanna, it's nice to see you again. Something like yesterday's tea." He was keeping his eyes tightly focused again.

"Hm, I think I have just the thing for you. Have you found any black swans today?"

"Um, no. Nothing today. Um, that's kinda the thing with black swans, you generally don't find them." He placed his elbow gingerly on the windowsill. "So... uh... how are you?" Gulping audibly, he removed his arm, holding it against his chest.

"I'm doing real good. Almost closing time."

Ayanna debated with herself. *Should I tell him about the vampire ball or not?*

"That's good to hear. Um. Ayanna? Look, I'm sorry if I've

been weird. The move and all has been stressful, and you've been super kind."

"No need to apologize, Sean. I'm sorry about the stress, but I think I have something that will help. I'm fixing up some lemon peppermint tea. It's very festive for this time of year, and it will definitely help with your stress."

"Thank you."

"Sean, can I ask you something? Please tell me if I overstep, okay?"

"Of course."

"Is talking with me stressful for you?"

I really hope his silence isn't a fight-or-flight response. He's run off before, and I suspect he might do it again. That question was too much. Then again, he's still sipping his tea. That's a positive sign.

After careful consideration, Sean answered, "Honestly, it is a bit stressful. I'm not used to... to, um, talking with, ah, women. Especially pretty women. But it's also not stressful because you're so nice and all. I guess I'm just shy." Throughout his answer, Sean seemed to be looking for guidance from his toes.

"Hey, let me put on a jacket." She was back quickly. "You can look at me now, if you want. Thank you for answering my question."

Sean raised his eyes and met her gaze, although this time without the steel focus he had earlier. "You're welcome."

"You know, it's okay to look. This is a bikini coffee cart. I mean, none of us want creepers ogling us, but part of the draw is, you know, us." Ayanna grinned at Sean. "You can always look, just be respectful."

"That's... that's hard for me. I mean, I try to be respectful. It's just I try to avoid temptation and sin."

Ayanna deliberately kept her voice soft and without the laughter she desperately wanted to let loose. "You're worried I will tempt you into sin?"

"Yes... No... It's hard to explain. You seem very nice, but I've been taught that looking upon the flesh is sinful."

The programming is deep in this poor guy. How do I say this delicately?

"That belief is shared by many people, but I'm not one of them. Your skin is natural, same as everyone else's. I think you're very sweet, and I want you to know you should feel empowered to look at me anytime you want. I know you'll be respectful." Ayanna gave him a soft smile. "I would like it if you looked at me."

"Um, okay." Sean looked nervous. Extremely nervous.

"Can I be honest with you, Sean?"

"Yes, of course."

"I can feel the strain when you look me directly in the eyes, not looking anywhere else. I respect that about you. You are trying so hard to treat me as a person, not as an object, it seems like you are hurting yourself to do so. Which makes me think you are a really good person, and I like and appreciate you. It also hurts me, too. I really enjoy it when you show up. Your visits make my day better, and I want you to feel comfortable. Comfortable talking with me—and just comfortable with me as I am. Does that make sense?"

Sean looked visibly relieved. "Yeah, it does. I'm sorry."

"Don't be sorry. I'm glad we talked about this."

"Thank you. Me, too."

"Hey, I almost forgot. There actually *is* a vampire ball tomorrow night."

"Wait? What?"

"Yeah, I'm going to go. You seemed interested before, did you want to go with me?"

"That would be... um, really cool."

"Before you say yes, I need to warn you. There's going to be a lot of people there, and some of them might be dressed—let's just say each person's ideas of appropriate attire can vary a lot, and you might consider some to be scandalous."

She could see that Sean was rattled, but he rallied. "Yes. I'll be okay."

"Great. Now let's talk about what you're going to wear." Ayanna's mind was already coming up with ideas for Sean's possible attire.

"Um, something like this?"

"Oh, sweetie. Yeah, not gonna work." Ayanna tried to find a comparison. "These are vampire cosplayers, so think anything from punk to Victorian, but heavy on black. Do you trust me?"

"Yeah, sure."

"Good. Give me a minute." Ayanna picked up her phone and made a call. "All right, meet me at this address in about an hour and a half. I have a friend who is a costume designer and part-time fashion designer. She and I will get you set up."

Sean looked very nervous, but he nodded as he took the napkin with the address. "OK, see you in about ninety minutes."

She waved to him as he walked away and then switched back to finishing her closing tasks. She was startled when she heard a knock at the cart's door a few minutes later.

"Sean, did you forget... Oh." She opened the door to see a gun pointed at her.

"Cash, now," the hooded man snarled.

Ayanna quivered, stepping back slightly, stammering incoherently, her eyes widening. The gunman stepped forward, shoving the pistol in her face. "Give me the money, bitch!" Ayanna smiled fiercely.

Idiot. Never get close with a gun.

Ayanna's sped upward like a lioness—fast, fierce, and liquid. Her fingers clamped down hard, and the gunman screamed as his wrist snapped. She caught the pistol as it fell from his limp hand.

He kept screaming as a kick shattered one of his knees. Ayanna brought the pistol around in a long arc, connecting with his head on a vicious downswing. The screaming stopped.

Ayanna quickly grabbed the body and pulled it out of the cart. There was a dark hideaway a short distance away. Once the body was there, she headed back into the cart. As she wiped and bleached everything, she called a ghoul she knew. A fresh corpse was a delicacy to a ghoul, so Ayanna knew the body would be gone before midnight and would never be found. Within minutes, there was no trace of the brief struggle inside the cart. She was thankful the bikini meant an easy cleanup for herself as well. Ayanna stripped out of the bikini and put on sweats. She wrapped the gun and bikini in the bloody towels she used and dumped them on the body. The ghoul would dispose of the evidence as thanks for a fresh meal.

From there, she went to see her friend Selina. Selina was a selkie, and after her family had been butchered for their pelts, she drifted down the West Coast from Alaska to Vancouver, then Seattle, and now Portland. Like her housemates, Selina was a kindred soul. They were all alone in a world where their very being was a death sentence if they were discovered.

Selina was able to get her new clothes, plus an outfit for the ball tomorrow.

I really want to go full-on Kate Beckinsale wearing painted-on black leather, but I should have mercy on poor Sean. Tomorrow would be traumatic enough for him with everyone else's costumes. The poor boy might not survive seeing me dressed like Kate.

Selina came up with an attractive outfit that would make Ayanna look good without causing Sean's head to explode. Hopefully.

Once Sean arrived, Selina was able to whip up an outfit for him which would pass muster at a vampire ball, although Sean looked wildly nervous. He was way outside of his comfort zone. Ayanna did her best to soothe him and build his confidence. As they parted, she told him she was on the early shift tomorrow and gave him her number so they could arrange to meet.

Chapter 11

Eat It

"Weird Al" Yankovic

S ean was having a challenging Friday. He didn't sleep well the night before, his dreams plagued by bikini-clad warriors and vampires. The alarm did him no favors, coming long before he felt ready. Much of the morning was spent preparing a report of his (lack of) progress so far.

Maybe this is a good thing. If I find nothing, then maybe this assignment will come to an end. Oddly, that thought doesn't cheer me up.

Around lunchtime, he found himself reviewing his lists of possible unnatural activity. He had broken his research into three separate categories. The first list consisted of highly unlikely leads with little or no possibility of finding false gods and other sundry agents of the Adversary. This list was filled with generally mundane items like Drag Queen Story Hour at the library. The second list took that possibility from highly unlikely to slightly unlikely. After Wednesday, Dungeons and Dragons meetups no longer fit this category, but were still worth monitoring. The final list consisted of things he thought could possibly include the unnatural, such as tonight's vampire ball, a number of local strip clubs with especially sinful themes, witch covens, nature worshippers, and alternative religions, all of which were relatively plentiful in Portland.

More than anything, Sean felt overwhelmed. He was one man alone in a city, tasked with investigating rumors, groups, and businesses which would take a team of dozens to fully cover. Sean was beginning to think he hadn't been sent to Portland because it was an opportunity for him to prove himself.

Did Dustin send me to Portland because he needed someone expendable for this assignment? Is my failure simply expected? Sean sighed heavily. *This sucks.*

Sean decided to go out for lunch, but instead found himself wandering until he reached the familiar smells of Brandi's Bitchin' Brews. He mindlessly joined the back of the line, and waited until the queue brought him up to a tattooed and voluptuous woman.

She asked, "Whatcha want?"

"Uh, is Ayanna here?"

She gave him a calculating look, but apparently decided he was harmless enough before saying, "Sure thing, gimme a sec."

The woman slid to the side. He heard her say, "Ayanna, someone's here for you."

"Oh?"

"Yeah, kinda cute, but he's gonna break his brain if he keeps trying not to stare at my tits."

"Thanks, Annabelle. I'm pretty sure I know him." Ayanna appeared quickly, "Hey, Sean!"

On the plus side, I'm apparently kinda cute. On the minus side, Ayanna recognizes me as the guy who refuses to look at women's... breasts.

"Hi, Ayanna, um, you all don't have food here, do you?"

"We do, but we're down to a couple scones right now."

"Oh." Sean's stomach rumbled. "Um..."

"Tell ya what. I'm off in about thirty minutes. Let me get you a lemon peppermint tea and we can grab lunch when I'm off."

"Thanks. That would be great."

A muscular man in the cart said, *"¡Ey, chica bonita! ¡Es guapísimo!"*

"Hush, Enrique. Don't make me tell your boyfriend you're calling other men hot."

Sean blushed when he overheard Ayanna's words. He shuffled off to the side, waiting awkwardly while Ayanna handled the last few customers. Soon enough, someone—presumably the woman she called Annabelle—passed her the tea, which Ayanna then passed to Sean. He quietly drank it and pondered what to talk about since he was about to have lunch with Ayanna. He still had nothing by the time she emerged from the cart, dressed in jeans, a crop top, and a jacket.

"Ready to go?"

"Um, yeah."

"I'm feeling Indian. What about you?"

"I've never eaten Indian before. I'm not sure about the spices."

"Thai? Mexican? Hang on..." Sean watched as realization dawned on Ayanna's face. "You've never had spicy food before, have you?"

By now, Sean was blushing furiously. Unable to speak, he shook his head.

Her voice softened. "It's okay. Do you have a medical thing, or did you just never have spicy food growing up?"

"Just never had it."

"That's fine. Do you trust me?"

I barely know this woman, and this isn't the first time she has asked me to trust her. Then again, nothing bad has come of trusting her, so I might as well trust her again.

Decision made, Sean shook his head affirmatively.

"All right, let's go. I'll help you out." She took his hand and led him over to a parked Kia. "Here, get in and pardon the mess." Ayanna drove with a confidence and assertiveness that had Sean white-knuckled for the few minutes the trip took. Between her driving, the impending lunch of spicy Indian food, and then a vampire ball tonight, Sean was beginning to doubt whether he would live to see Saturday at all.

Once they parked and exited the car, Ayanna took his hand again as they walked toward the restaurant. He couldn't remember the last time anyone had held his hand. He expected to feel uncomfortable, maybe even excited, but instead he felt soothed and comforted. Her grip was soft but confident as she led him inside.

They were seated immediately and left on their own to peruse the menu. Once the hostess left, she looked at him and said, "Do you mind if I order for you? Tell me if you have any food allergies or other restrictions."

"Um, sure, that's fine. I don't know of any allergies."

"Awesome. I'll be gentle as I introduce you to the wonderful world of spices." She grinned and then perused the menu. When the waiter returned with water glasses for each of them, she quickly rattled off an order. He couldn't understand what she was ordering, but he did understand when she answered questions about spice level. Once the waiter was gone, she looked back at him and smiled. "Don't worry, the hot one is just for me, but you can try it if you want."

"How hot is it?"

"It's pretty hot. There's another level called Indian hot. That's what I like, but they always ask me three times if I'm sure. This is fine for today."

I have no idea how to respond.

She continued, "I do hope you like this."

"Um, I hope so, too. I never tried tea before I met you, and that's been good. Maybe this will be the same sort of thing."

"Look at you. Taking all sorts of bold steps. I'm excited for you," Ayanna gushed.

Bold isn't how I picture myself, but I like that she thinks so.

"Yeah, maybe I needed a fresh start, along with a friendly person to help me out."

"New city, new you, right?"

"Oh, you remembered that... Probably the single stupidest thing I've ever said."

She laughed. "It does sound corny, but you know what? It's honest, and you're making it true. That's a good thing. You also mentioned a cat..."

"Oh, yeah. I have a cat."

"No, your cat has a human. That's how this really works."

"Truth." He grinned, thinking of Huntress. She would agree for sure. "Her name is Huntress. I got her... um, she chose me a few years ago."

"I love her name. From a shelter?"

"Of course. Do you have, um... live with a cat?"

"I do. Her name is Bast, it's—"

"The Egyptian cat goddess."

"I'm impressed, not many people know Bast. She was... a stray. But she prances around like a little goddess." Ayanna's grin was mischievous. "Hm, I should get one of those laser toys."

"Huntress *loves* her laser toy. We have a lot of fun with the red dot game. You know, cats get a bad rap for being aloof, but Huntress isn't like that at all. I'm not sure what I would do without her in my life." Sean sighed and grinned at thoughts of Huntress playing or snuggling.

"Amazing how that happens." Ayanna smiled happily.

"It is. I never had pets growing up. Never had much of anything, really. I mean, like, we had stuff. My parents were... distant, I guess. They did their own things, not with me, not with each other. Like I was the unfortunate accident they had but didn't want, so they didn't know what to do with me and didn't want to be with each other... Oh, no... I'm so sorry! I can't believe I told you that—"

She grabbed his hands before he could get out of his seat and flee. "It's okay... Sean... It's okay."

"It's not. I shouldn't have burdened you with my issues."

"I'll admit... That's... a lot. I mean, for a first date when we haven't even gotten the appetizers. Definitely a *lot*."

"I should go."

"No, you should stay. You obviously really needed to tell someone that, and I'm honored you shared it with me."

"Really?"

"Yes. Family trauma can be hard to talk about, and you definitely have a lot. We've only known each other a few days, but I'm happy you trust me enough to talk about it. Have you ever talked with anyone about this?"

"Like therapy? No. That, um, really isn't something I've thought of."

"Let me guess. Someone in your life probably told you therapy is for the weak, or some similar nonsense."

"Something like that. Dad always said therapy was 'mumbo jumbo' and it's all a scam. And the guys at work... they're definitely in the 'real men don't need therapy' crowd."

"Wow... I believe the modern term for that is 'toxic masculinity.' And it is some really dumb shit." Ayanna shook her head irritably. "You definitely don't need toxicity in your life. Oh, let me guess... did they also say therapy would make you into a pussy?"

Sean chuckled. "Actually, yes. Pretty much all of them, including my father."

Ayanna grinned assertively, "They're right, you know. And that's a good thing."

"Huh?"

"Do you know why? Because pussies are strong, flexible, and

nurturing. Meanwhile, dicks are weak, fragile, and really funny looking when you think about it."

Sean chortled. "I never thought of it that way, but you're right. I'm okay with being a pussy." Of course he said that right when the waiter arrived at the table with food. Sean saw the waiter's surprised look and blushed, while Ayanna giggled.

"All right, Sean. Are you ready?"

"I think so..."

"These are samosas. Think of it like potatoes and peas, wrapped up in a pancake, and then baked or fried. They have a mild amount of spice. Not spicy hot, just spicy flavorful." She speared one with a fork and offered him the other.

He took the samosa tentatively, then watched as she expertly cut hers up with a fork and knife. He copied her motions and then lifted a bit of samosa toward his mouth. She watched him intently as he brought the piece into his mouth. He bit down. It was hot and crunchy, yet also soft, the potatoes and peas contrasting with the crispy shell. Sean expected a rush of spices, but instead found it was more subtle. There was a gentle tingling on his tongue as he chewed. This was like nothing he had ever eaten before, and it was amazing.

"It's good, right?" Ayanna asked before taking her own bite.

"Ish oo ood," he replied, covering his mouth with his hand as he savored a second, larger bite. Sean really wanted to make the samosa last, but he quickly found his plate was empty. "Can we get more?" he asked as he stared wistfully at his plate.

"Maybe to go. We still have the main course coming. I guess you liked it then."

"I did!" Sean said ecstatically. "I never had anything spicy growing up. Maybe barbecue sauce on chicken nuggets."

"Let me guess. Straight out of a bottle and loaded with high fructose corn syrup."

"Yep, exactly."

"You poor thing. That stuff is serviceable if you're desperate. The real thing, though... I passed through the Carolinas a while ago, and it's just so good. There's this huge debate about what the best base for barbecue sauce is, vinegar, mustard, or tomato. Ignore the nonsense and try them all until you find what *you* like best."

"You make food sound amazing. When you said, a while ago... How old are you?"

That was a really stupid question. She looks a bit pissed with me.

Ayanna's voice was quiet, sweet, and dangerous when she stated, "I'm a bit older than you might think, but sweetie, just a hint. Never ask a lady how old she is."

"I'm sorry! I'm really sorry! I didn't mean to offend you," Sean apologized frantically.

"I'm not offended. I'm going to go out on a limb and guess you haven't had too many conversations like this with women." He nodded, and she continued, "I suspect you probably didn't get much advice from your parents. I'll bet the toxic morons you work with either didn't offer any advice, or they probably gave you really bad advice."

"You're correct," Sean admitted sheepishly.

"You made an honest mistake, right?"

"Yes, definitely."

Her voice brightened. "That's okay, then. Now, you just need to learn from your mistakes. If you improve, then everything is forgiven."

"Of course, thank you. Um. Earlier, you said something about a first date, and... uh."

"I did? Hm, yes, I did. This doesn't have to be. Doesn't have to be a date, I mean. I guess, it wasn't a date when I asked you to lunch, and then you shared... a lot."

"I'm okay with this being a date. It's been a while."

"Do you mind if I ask how long is a while?"

Sean blushed and suddenly found his napkin to be very interesting. His voice dropped to a near whisper. "Probably about seven or eight years. Maybe more."

"So, you're a bit rusty."

"And, um. I didn't tell any of those girls, you know, the stuff I told you. They weren't as pretty as you, either." Sean felt himself blush even harder at his last admission.

"I'm very flattered. I will definitely keep that in mind in case you ask anything else you shouldn't." Ayanna smiled kindly.

Sean was saved further embarrassment as lunch arrived, borne by two servers. The smell was overpowering, intoxicating. Visually, it was a stunning mix of colors. The server set down two heaping bowls of long, thin rice first. Those were followed by a creamy green dish which Ayanna directed to the center. Their waitress placed a bowl filled with a brownish-orange sauce and chunks of what he presumed was chicken closer to him. She set a similar bowl, less saucy and much more brown, closer to Ayanna. Finally, a plate of some kind of flat bread completed the feast before them.

Ayanna spoke first, "Let me give you the tour of what we're eating. This is jasmine rice. It's a bit more flavorful than the standard rice you are likely used to. In the middle here is Aloo Saag, which is potatoes cooked in spinach and greens. It is a great meal on its own, but also makes a phenomenal side dish. This is mildly spicy. In front of you is Chicken Makhani. It's boneless chunks of chicken, cooked in a spicy butter sauce. Again, I asked them to keep the spices mild, so it should be flavorful but not hot. Speaking of hot..." She gestured at her own dish. "This is Chicken Vindaloo. It is chicken and potatoes in a sauce that is definitely hot. Finally, this is Naan. It is an Indian flatbread. Never say naan bread, because you're essentially saying 'bread bread.' You can use naan to scoop up your food and eat it that way, or it's also good to use it to mop up the sauces. Sounds good?"

"Yeah, it looks and smells incredible." Sean spooned some rice on his plate, then watched as Ayanna did the same, then spooned vindaloo on top of hers. He copied her with his makhani. Both served themselves aloo saag toward the side. Once his plate was loaded, he took a deep breath, inhaling the scent of the food. Sean then got a forkful of rice and chicken makhani. His mouth erupted. The creamy sauce blended perfectly with the soft rice and chicken, delighting his tongue with the texture. The spices, already aromatic in his nose, lit up his taste buds in a bewildering yet pleasing array of flavor. It wasn't hot, but it was definitely more than he was used to; Sean coughed after he swallowed his first bite.

"Are you all right?"

"Yes, I'm just not used to that. It tastes amazing!"

"Good, I'm glad you like it. The offer stands to try the vindaloo, but it is definitely hot."

"I'll think about it." Sean dug into the rest of his meal like he hadn't eaten in a week. He did eventually try the vindaloo, and promptly downed a full glass of water immediately. "That's a bit much. I'm going to have to work up to vindaloo."

Sean finished his meal by wiping his makhani bowl clean with pieces of naan, which was the perfect finish.

"Wow... I had expected leftovers. You clearly liked it," Ayanna exclaimed.

"Yes, everything was incredible. I feel like I've missed out so much over all these years. I'm never eating mac and cheese again."

"Hey! Let's not go too far. I know of a mac and cheese food cart that will blow your mind."

"Really?" Sean asked incredulously.

"Oh, yeah." Ayanna's grin was both knowing and tantalizing.

I wonder if she would want to go there with me.

Chapter 12

Black No. 1 (Little Miss Scare-All)
Type O Negative

After splitting the bill, Ayanna drove Sean back to his place, then headed home. They would meet up later for the vampire ball. In the meantime, she had a lot to think about. Lunch was... a lot. Definitely a lot.

Sean was obviously inept with women. As the kids might say, Sean had no game.

Eight years without a date, so probably not since college. Almost certainly no sex during that time. Would he have used a pro? No, he can barely look below my nose, there's no way he used the services of a professional. I can't imagine him being less awkward in college. Oh... He's a thirty-year-old virgin. Has to be. That complicates things. And we just had a first date. I just took a thirty-year-old virgin on a first date. What was I thinking?

Horns blared as she cut through traffic. Ayanna tried to focus on the road, but it was a bit of a struggle as her mind raced faster than her car ever could.

To be fair, I didn't ask him on a date. Then, he drops his whole story about growing up on me. That was a surprise, and I slipped up. Going on a date was nice, though. Except I can't date mortals.

He thinks I'm older... Sure, by about six thousand years. With modern medicine, Sean has maybe five or six decades left while I'll live forever or until the Godkillers finally hunt me down. You really messed this up, Inanna. And we're going to this ball tonight. Maybe I can tell him my parents are sick in Florida and skip town. Denver might be nice. I've never been to Wichita. I could spend a couple decades in Wichita. I really don't want to leave, though. Spending time with Bast has been great, and Jesús is a really good guy. I even like Mortimer.

Inanna was torn over all of this. She was actually coming to like Sean a lot. Well, Ayanna was, but Ayanna was Inanna and the experience of going out to lunch with someone new and cute was very pleasant. For being six thousand years old, she actually had not been on many dates. One of the downsides of being a goddess is that your identity and life are often bound by your worshippers. She had been married, more than once she thought, but the memories were hazy. Inanna had a son in a later incarnation, but he was long dead. The Shepherd God that was her husband, or one of them, spent half the year in her sister's underworld realm as punishment for not missing Inanna. Or at least that was how their worshippers explained why winter happened.

She could remember so much, the battles, the lovemaking, but at the same time remember so little. So much of her long life was shrouded in fog. Inanna thought it was ironic that her clearest memories were from when her power started to fade. As her worshipers dwindled, perhaps they could influence her less. She could remember fending off the lewd advances of Zeus and later Jupiter. She recalled dalliances with other gods and goddesses, although none of them had ever taken her on a proper date. She had slept with mortals beyond count, but those were brief, purely physical affairs. Sean was different, though, and this was starting to frighten her.

He moves around due to his job. Perhaps we can go out on some dates. It could be fun, and maybe I can help him open up to love. After some time, when his job takes him to another city, we will say tearful goodbyes. Or I'll move to Wichita.

It wasn't a great plan, but then again, she wasn't much on plans. Which her last long-term lover had reminded her again and again. Athena was much better with plans, and they had both shared a strong sense of disgust regarding the males of the Greek pantheon. Their affair had lasted a good century or so, until Constantine came along. She hated him with a passion.

Inanna got home without a car accident, which was good, given how distracted she was. She did her best to be quiet, as Jesús and Mortimer were likely sleeping. Being quiet would do no good with Bast and her feline hearing, but thankfully Bast was out.

Probably getting some from Mr. Mittens down the block. I wouldn't mind talking to her at some point about Sean, but not right now.

Deities don't necessarily require sleep, certainly not like mortals do, but it felt good. Inanna took a nap and then got up and got dressed for the vampire ball. As she slipped into her clothes and Ayanna's identity, she smiled at the outfit Selina had created for her. It was more steampunk than Victorian, but it worked. She wore black above-the-knee boots, held together with a series of buckles, and a black below-the-knee skirt with a slit on one side providing brief glimpses of white lace stockings. Above the waist was a frilly, nearly opaque white blouse, topped by a lightweight black leather jacket with a wildly over-accessorized belt. To complete the look, she had a black cap with aviator goggles. The effect was very over-the-top, but lots of fun.

Ayanna met Sean at the designated time and place, and she gave him a once over and a whistle. Selina had geared him up with a tailed tux, top hat, and a golden pocket watch that was almost certainly once a prop for a science fiction TV show or movie. The look was completed by a black sword cane, likely also a former prop. She had to admit, he looked pretty good—and pretty nervous. He laughed at her whistle and said, "I feel really strange wearing this."

"I bet. You're more of a khakis and polo guy. You look good, though." With a flirtatious wink, she added, "Good enough for a vampire to eat." Somehow, he managed to look more nervous.

Ayanna walked up and put an arm through his. "Hey, we're going to have fun tonight. It's a fun party, you look great, and I look..." Ayanna was a bit annoyed, but took into account Sean's inexperience with flirting. She said gently, "Sean, I'm not fishing for compliments, but this is the part where you tell me how great I look."

"Oh, um, sorry! You look beautiful, and your costume is amazing."

"Thank you. Nicely done. Now let's get inside."

Once through the doors, they entered a maelstrom of humanity. Ayanna kept a close grip on Sean, maneuvering him through the crowd. The poor boy was clearly starting to go into shock, trying to look everywhere and nowhere at the same time. As she'd expected, the state of dress ranged from nearly complete body coverage to lots of skin. Given Sean's challenges, she figured he might need a minute. Ayanna found a table for them in a corner as Mortimer started spinning Type O Negative's Black No. 1.

"Hey, Sean. Are you doing all right?"

"Um, maybe?"

"Look, I know it's a lot. We don't need to stay if you don't want to."

"Thanks. I just wanted, you know, to see some vampires."

Ayanna laughed. "You're too funny. You know it's all pretend, right?"

Sean looked around the room. "The red drinks?"

"Bloody Marys, mostly. Or vodka with red food coloring."

"I saw a couple people with fangs."

"You mean, like those..." She pointed at fake plastic fangs on the neighboring table.

"Oh."

"Vampires aren't real, you know?"

She laughed to herself. *Except for the DJ, of course, but no one here besides me knows that fact.*

Ayanna continued, "People like to pretend, and some of them get really, really into it."

"You mean, like drinking blood?"

"Yeah, there are a few who actually drink real blood. Which is very unsanitary."

"I didn't know that."

"This is all just fun. Relax and enjoy. If you want, I can get us Bloody Marys."

"Um, I don't drink."

Wow... I'd say he's a monk, but most monks drink.

"Just to clarify, won't drink, don't drink, or just haven't had a drink?"

"Um, I got drunk once in college and threw up all over my bed. I haven't had anything with alcohol since that night."

"I get that. I can get us a couple of very light Bloody Marys, or I can get water for us."

"I don't want to ruin your fun, I'm sorry. I trust you, so—I'll try one."

She grinned at him. "Okay, light Bloody Marys it is."

When she returned to the table, she found Sean nervously eyeing the guy at the next table with plastic fangs and an overly loud voice telling an obviously unimpressed woman about how much he enjoyed drinking blood.

Ayanna handed Sean a drink and whispered, "What a poseur."

Sean laughed and sipped his drink. "This isn't bad."

"I tipped the bartender well, so it should be light. You can still get drunk on these, but you'll likely turn into a tomato first." Out of the corner of her eye, she saw the blowhard at the next table get something out of his pocket and reach toward the drink of the bored woman he was at the table with.

Ayanna reached with feline speed, grabbing the bastard's arm and twisting. His arm hit the table with a bang, and his bored companion looked back at them.

Blowhard shouted, "Ow! What the fuck, bitch?"

Ayanna looked at the woman and said, "This asshole was about to spike your drink." Her eyes indicated the drug that fell out of his now limp hand. The woman kicked Blowhard square in the nuts. Ayanna force-marched Blowhard toward the door and told the bouncer what had happened. He grinned like the Cheshire Cat and grabbed hold of Blowhard, propelling him toward the door.

Sean was staring at her as she strutted back to the table. "Wow. You're amazing. How'd you know he was spiking her drink?"

"I'm a woman living in a world where assholes get away with that shit all the time. It pays to keep an eye on my drink and every other woman's drink as well."

Sean looked ashamed. "I'm sorry about that. Where'd you learn those moves?"

"Lots of self-defense classes."

And close combat on a thousand battlefields. I wish I knew how to break a wrist with a simple twist back when Zeus was sniffing around.

"That makes sense."

"Forget about him. Let's have fun, maybe dance a bit." Sean looked panicked at her mention of dancing. "I'll introduce you to Mortimer at some point. They're the DJ and my housemate."

The remainder of the evening went well. Once Sean relaxed and stopped looking like everyone might bite him, they settled in and watched people. His naivete was mildly amusing, although she tried not to show that. Ayanna even did manage to convince him to dance a bit. They left far earlier than most, but she felt all right about that. She even gave Sean a ride home.

For a mortal, he is nice.

Chapter 13

Weird Science
Oingo Boingo

Sean's head was still spinning when he woke up on Saturday.

She is way out of my league. Like a T-ball team playing the Yankees. Ayanna is smart, worldly, incredibly gorgeous, and a total badass, and I'm... me. No one would believe me if I told them. She called lunch our first date. Oh, God... what if there's a second date? I mean, I'd like a second date. Should I call her? Text her? I'm supposed to wait three days, right? If I call now, it will seem like I'm desperate. Okay, I'm probably desperate. If I wait a few days, she might think I'm not interested. Of course, she knows I'm interested. She must have a mirror! I'm interested in her for more than her looks. I mean... The way she took down that asshole last night. She could definitely kick my ass. If I wait too long, then she'll definitely kick my ass. Or worse, find someone else. She can definitely do better than me. Not helping yourself. The crazy thing is, I think she likes me.

Sean couldn't remember if any girl or woman had ever been interested in him. Maybe some unspoken high school crush, but none he ever knew of. This was like *Weird Science*, except Ayanna was even more badass than Kelly LeBrock, and he didn't frankenstein her with a computer while wearing a bra on his head. Of course, the nerds didn't end up with Kelly LeBrock at the end.

Perhaps 80s movies aren't my best choice for comparisons. I'm going to have to do something. But not on an empty stomach.

After feeding Huntress, Sean grabbed a bowl of Raisin Bran and pondered what to do next.

Up till now, Ayanna has been calling the shots. I asked about the vampire ball, but she was the one who got us in. She arranged appropriate attire for us, although I suspect she has plenty of clothes she could have worn. Ayanna suggested Indian food and then guided me through that, even ordering for us. It's time for me to take some initiative.

Sean was at a distinct disadvantage in dating. He lacked experience and confidence; however, there was one thing he was really good at. Research. He dove into what to do and where to eat in Portland. The options were vast and overwhelming. He separated the searches. For what to do, he concentrated on something romantic and then culled that by finding something that was also casual and potentially non-romantic. As for what to eat, it was still fairly early in the day, so maybe brunch. Now he had a plan. The hardest part was yet to come, though. Sean grabbed his phone, debating calling or texting.

Text. Has to be text. Calling is too personal.

He typed, "Hello, Ayanna. Would you like to go on a date with me?" He erased it immediately.

Again, he typed, "Want to hang with me today?" Also immediately erased.

Sean tried at least a dozen more texts, erasing them all. Finally, he decided he had to send something if he ever wanted to break his long date-less streak.

> Sean: Yesterday was awesome. Can I thank you with brunch?

His heart raced as he sent the text. Nothing happened. His anxiety ticked up as each minute passed. After fifteen agonizing minutes, a response came.

> Ayanna: I could eat.

"I could eat?" What does that mean? I guess it's a yes. She's being casual. Okay, Sean. Be cool. Be casual. You got this. What would someone who has gotten a date in the last decade say?

> Sean: I saw this place called Jam on Hawthorne.
>
> It looks like a good place to broaden my horizons.

Sean looked at the last text and instantly regretted sending it. *Broaden my horizons? That wasn't cool. This is a disaster...*

> Ayanna: It's good food but there can be a wait, especially on the weekend.

He wasn't sure what to make of her response. *Um, is that a "No"? What do I say back? I'll tell her a wait is fine because I enjoy her company. No, that's awful.* As he dithered, Ayanna texted again.

> Ayanna: I'll meet you there.
>
> We can walk around if there's a wait.

> Sean: Sounds perfect! See you soon!

Sean dropped the phone and raced to his closet to change clothes.

Wow. Ayanna was right. I really am a khakis and a polo guy.

Um, let's go with jeans and... a polo shirt. I just need a pocket protector and tape on my glasses and I'll nail the nerd stereotype perfectly. What do cool people wear, anyway?

He pulled on a sensible jacket and went to meet Ayanna. As she predicted, there was a wait for a table, so they put their name on the list. With time to kill, she asked, "What would you like to do now?"

"Um, you were right, you know. My closet is nothing but khakis and polo shirts."

"And jeans." Ayanna gestured to his legs.

"And one pair of jeans. Any chance you want to do some shopping?" He smiled wanly.

Ayanna roared with laughter. "I love it! C'mon, Ken, let's go."

"Ken?"

"Like Barbie and Ken? Wow, you didn't get out much, did you?"

"Um..." He was blushing furiously.

"Don't sweat it, Sean. We can't change all of this..." Ayanna gestured at all of him. "...within the time we have, but let's start. I know just the place."

She dragged him up the street to a haberdashery. He picked up a Stetson and was raising it toward his head when Ayanna said sternly, "*Sean. Put. That. Down. Now.*"

"But, I..."

"Look, Roy Rogers, cowboy isn't your look. Nope, put that down, too. You're not Sherlock Holmes, either. Here, try this..." She handed him a black beret.

"Okay, but—"

"You're right. We'll skip the berets."

There followed a flurry of trying on various hats, followed by immediate critiques from Ayanna. Eventually, they settled on a wool fedora for him. "This works for you. It's practical in rain or shine, but it has style."

"What's the difference between this and the Stetson?"

"Are you getting on a horse anytime soon?"

"Definitely not"

"Fedora it is. You don't look as good as Bogey, but it works." Ayanna flashed him a grin before picking up a red beret.

"Thanks, I think. Hey, I thought we were skipping the berets?"

"This is for me, silly. I wonder if they have this in raspberry. I used to have a raspberry beret... It was inspirational," Ayanna said with a smile that was half lascivious and half wistful. "Oh, here's a raspberry one. Okay, let's get these and go."

They walked out arm-in-arm, wearing their purchases. Sean actually felt something akin to dapper, and Ayanna looked incredible in her beret. They had to wait for a few minutes when they got back to the restaurant, but they were soon seated. Ayanna ordered the loaded hash browns, and Sean decided on the French toast. As they waited, Sean implemented the next phase of his plan. "If you're free after this, would you like to go to the Japanese Garden?"

"You realize the Gardens are on the other side of the city, right?"

"Um, sort of?"

"You're really cute."

"Um..."

"And you have quite the way with words." Ayanna's eyes sparkled as she smiled at his confusion. "I see what you're doing. Brunch is casual, yet intimate. It says you're interested, but if I'm not interested back, then it's just a chill meal between friends. Then, the Japanese Garden. Romantic, but it can also be a pleasant place to go with a friend to enjoy a peaceful respite from the city. Very smooth, Sean. Well, except for the distance between these two places. I'm very impressed."

Despite her encouraging words, Sean felt despondent. *Appar-*

ently, I am completely transparent. I thought I was being so clever, and she just read the whole thing perfectly. I really wish I had more experience with dating.

"Did I sum this up correctly?" Ayanna asked.

"Yes, you did. One hundred percent accurate." Sean felt like everything was crashing down in flames until he saw Ayanna reach a hand across the table.

"I'm not going to say I'm interested, but I am intrigued. You have a very good plan, by the way. Something is missing, though."

"What's that?"

"Phase three. You have one, right?"

"Uh, no."

"Too bad, because I know a really good ice cream place that would be perfect for phase three."

"Would you like to go out for ice cream after the Japanese Garden?"

"Oh, you charmer!" Ayanna laughed. "How can a girl say 'no' to that?"

Feeling elated, Sean took her hand and joined in her laughter.

Chapter 14

Good Times Roll

The Cars

Ayanna was having a surprisingly good time with Sean. She almost said no when he texted about brunch. Of the many strange things humans had come up with during her long life, brunch was one of her favorites. She almost declined his invitation because she worried she was enjoying spending time with a mortal too much. His text was just so innocent, though, and so she had agreed to meet him.

Once she'd deduced his plan for a deniable date at the Japanese Garden, she was genuinely impressed. Sean was clearly inexperienced at dating, yet she found him disarming. Every time Ayanna reminded herself that dating a mortal was a horrible idea, Sean would do or say something, and her concern would fade.

What impressed her most was that he'd taken the initiative and planned something for her. She had led this figurative dance so far, and was quite enjoying having him take lead for a bit. In her very, very long memory, she couldn't recall the last time someone had asked her out in such an unobtrusive manner. Her experiences, particularly with men, fell into two general categories: charmers and assholes. She preferred the former by far, but neither really made her feel good. Sean wasn't either of those.

Instead, he was kind, clueless, and gamely trying his best. She was finding his irrepressible guilelessness irresistible.

"Why me?" Ayanna asked.

"What do you mean?"

"You came back to the cart, day after day. Our tea is good, but..."

"Oh, got it." Sean paused. And paused some more. "That bet. On Monday, when we first met. You essentially bet me to try tea. I don't gamble—no one has ever dared me to do anything unless they were making fun of me—and yet I tried the tea. It was this tiny step that was somehow so different from everything else in my life."

"Okay, maybe the tea *is* that good," Ayanna teased with a lopsided grin.

"I'm being serious. I've lived a risk-free life. I've always dreamed of something better but never had the will, or the courage, to do anything. And then, the most beautiful woman I've ever met dares me to try tea. And it was good. It's like... it's like my entire life has been lived behind this dark curtain, and for a brief instant, light shines through. I didn't mean to come back to the cart. I didn't *want* to come back, but somehow I did. I couldn't even look at you. I still can barely look at you, because I think sinful thoughts."

I am sorely tempted to ask him to elaborate on that particular tangent. Sean's sort of repression is unnatural, albeit all too common.

"Every time I saw you, there was a little more light coming through that curtain. I don't care that you're beautiful... I mean, I care... You intimidate me. You're an eleven and I'm like a four."

I despise ranking. It's just so dehumanizing. Also, in my experience, most men who consider themselves to be a "ten" are usually incredible assholes. I don't think Sean is being humble here. That screams low self-esteem.

He kept going. "You're smart and confident, and you have this aura of experience about you. Like with the Indian food or taking that guy down at the ball. You've shown me there's so much of the world I've been missing." Sean smiled shyly. "I really like discovering it with you."

Sean actually gave a really good answer. A bit all over the place, but certainly better than the usual, "You're hot, and we should totally bone" I usually hear.

"Now I have a question for you."

Lost in her own thoughts, Ayanna was startled by Sean's reverse. "Huh?"

"Why me?"

Not cool, reversing my question back on me. Totally fair, though. Because you're the first mortal in decades who hasn't bored me to tears. No, that's not true. You're the first mortal in decades intriguing enough that I want to get to know on a level beyond flirting and sex. Which scares the shit out of me. Of course I can't tell him any of that.

"You pose a good question. You're different—mysterious, yet not. You're a khakis-wearing guy who has never had spicy food before and who is completely predictable. Even without you telling me your life story, I almost knew it." She watched his face crumble. "Underneath your facade is a complex and remarkable person. Take today, for example. Asking me to brunch and then a date that doesn't have to be a date. You're not predictable at all." Ayanna paused briefly before adding softly, "Not just unpredictable, you're also nice."

"I feel like nice is a bad word."

"For ignorant people, it is. Sean, nice can be a really good word, too. Another positive word is considerate. You've asked me to brunch, the garden, and ice cream, which all combine into a fantastic date, but they are all really great things to do with a friend, too. I feel like you are hoping they will be a date, but at the same time, you are giving me space to make my decision without pressure. You're both nice and considerate. I'll be honest... I'm not used to that. It's very refreshing, actually."

"I'm sorry." He looked ashamed.

"Why?"

"Because someone being nice and considerate to you is unusual for you. That just seems wrong."

Ayanna heard a hint of anger in his voice and liked it.

"You're very sweet. I do need space to make my decision about what this is. We've known each other for less than a week. I'm enjoying getting to know you. I do know you're a good guy, and I appreciate you. I also really like this." Ayanna squeezed Sean's hand for emphasis. "Holding your hand, exploring the city with you, introducing you to new foods. It's fun. If you're okay with it, let's just keep things slow and casual like we're doing right now. I'm honored you don't want to pressure me, and in turn, I don't want to pressure you, either."

He squeezed back. "Thank you for talking with me and being understanding, Ayanna."

"I also like that you're angry because men aren't usually considerate of me. It tells me you care about justice and kindness."

"I do," Sean responded quietly.

Before Ayanna could say more, she saw their server approaching. "Oh, I think this is our breakfast!"

Chapter 15

Paradise

Sade

Breakfast was really tasty. This wasn't Sean's first time eating French toast, but it was by far the best. He paid the check and they headed out for the Japanese Garden. Ayanna suggested they take one car, so they piled into his. Once they parked and paid, she took his hand. Together, they walked up the long, curving path to the Gardens.

At any other time, Sean probably would have been a bundle of nerves, but the calming effect of the wooded slope helped immensely. As they slogged up the slope, he could feel the city disappearing and the forest asserting itself. Each step brought them further into an enclave of rich greens and browns. It felt like the only evidence of humanity was the gravel path under their feet.

At the top, Ayanna guided him past the cultural center, suggesting they return there later. They walked arm-in-arm toward a white gravel space filled with small islands of stone, moss, plants, and a large pavilion beyond. After a few minutes there, Sean felt a gentle tug on his arm, and he followed Ayanna to the right, down a path to a small pond. They slowly continued around, past a small tea house. Sean paused there to admire the simple yet elegant architecture of the structure.

Ayanna leaned in close, almost confidentially. Her voice was soft and wistful. "I've always wanted to host a tea party here. It just seems cozy and peaceful."

"This is a perfect spot. I mean, I only experienced tea a few days ago, but I can imagine sipping a cup here would be peaceful."

"True, but it's different. You've enjoyed drinking tea, but experiencing real tea is more than drinking. Some cultures, like the Japanese or English, have a very deep connection to tea and developed a formal... almost like a ceremony, around tea. You're not just imbibing a drink, you're getting a window into a culture and mindset. It's a true experience you need to take part in to understand fully. A real one, not a tourist trap version, obviously."

"I've heard of things like high tea, but when you talk about it, I understand it better and really want to have the experience."

"Maybe someday we can go for tea."

"We," she said. "We." As in, we as a couple might do that in the future.

"I'd like that. Speaking of things I like, this garden is amazing. Look at the stone pathway surrounded by moss—it's like islands of gray in a sea of green."

Ayanna took his arm and snuggled close. "It's beautiful," she murmured. "When you're ready, there's more good things ahead. There are so many cool things to discover here. This is one of my favorite places in Portland. It's especially beautiful in spring. You can feel the good spirits inhabiting this place."

Sean started at that. "What do you mean?"

"A place like this, peaceful, serene, harmonious... It attracts a positive energy. It feels like a place kind beings would inhabit."

This was a new and disconcerting thought for Sean. As a member of the Godkillers, even a lowly Diviner, there was a fundamental assumption there were two teams, spiritually speaking. There was his side, i.e., God, Jesus, the Holy Spirit, and the angelic host. Then there was the other side, and it was all bad. Ayanna seemed to be suggesting something outside of that framework.

"Like, angels?"

"Not really... more like spirits of nature. To vastly oversimplify Shinto, from prehistoric times, the Japanese believed divine spirits inhabit the world around them, manifesting in mountains, trees, and water." She paused, then continued, "Can you feel them?"

Sean watched as Ayanna closed her eyes, lifted her face toward the cloudy sky, and smiled. She seemed peaceful and joyous. For his own part, he was torn. What she said was blasphemous, and yet how could anything that inspired such feelings be wrong? He could almost feel some spark of divinity in the towering trees above them and the gently running water beside them, leaving him in a state of unease.

"Maybe? I don't know."

"I really hope you do." Ayanna opened her eyes and smiled at him. When he looked into her eyes, he no longer saw weariness. Her eyes practically gleamed with innocence and delight. Sean desperately wanted to share Ayanna's feelings, but he was also terrified of what that might mean for his beliefs.

"Close your eyes," she murmured. "Now breathe in... hold... breathe out... hold... breathe in... keep breathing and let the Garden in. Keep your eyes closed and experience what you hear, what you smell, what you feel."

Sean felt a gentle breeze on his skin, heard trickling water and a knocking sound in the distance, smelled moss and the faint scent of decaying leaves. More than anything, he felt peace. He opened his eyes to Ayanna's beaming face.

"How was that?"

He felt... "Amazing."

They strolled down the path, once again arm-in-arm until they came to a zig-zagging wooden walkway that bridged the stream and part of another pond. In the reeds underneath the bridge were massive fish in colors ranging from orangish-gold to charcoal to a pearly white or some combination thereof. Some of the fish lurked under the bridge, but the zigzags meant they were still visible. Others swam in the stream or in the pond.

Sean pointed at some of the lurkers under the bridge and said, "Do you know why they are hiding there?"

Ayanna looked puzzled. "Um..."

Sean broke into a huge grin as he said, "Because they're playing *koi*!"

Ayanna groaned at the pun, but she smiled, too. "I should have seen that coming the moment you asked the question."

"So... you suspected something *fishy*..."

Ayanna lightly punched him in the arm, but she smiled as she did it. "Okay, that one was bad, but the first one had me *hooked*."

"Huh?"

"Fish? Hook?"

Sean groaned.

"Oh! So it's okay for *you* to make puns, but *I'm* not allowed?" Her mock indignation was hilarious, and Sean couldn't help but laugh.

"Sorry, I guess I just wasn't expecting that."

"Just so you know, I have more fish puns! More than you *cod* imagine." Ayanna grinned impishly.

"Really now? Is that the *bass* you've got?"

"No, but I want to save some for later. Right now, though, let's walk to the end of the bridge and ex-*salmon* the waterfall."

She's smart, beautiful, and funny—and she can trade puns. I don't understand why she's here with me, but I'm not arguing, either.

Sean reached over, taking her hand and acceding to her suggestion to look at the waterfall. It wasn't a large waterfall, and the gentle tinkling of the water was soothing. Ayanna's hand in his only enhanced the experience.

After some time there, enjoying the scenery, the serenity, and each other's silent company, they strolled up the slope and then down into the Natural Garden. A burbling brook ran next to and sometimes through the path. Sean slipped once when he wasn't paying attention, but Ayanna caught him before he fell. He gave her a grateful smile as he recovered his balance. As they walked, they pointed out things to each other and commented on them quietly. Eventually, they reached the Sand and Stone Garden at the end and they sat together in silence there. Sean felt peaceful and centered in that part of the garden—so peaceful he forgot to be nervous.

In all, they spent over two hours in the Garden. On the trail down to the parking lot, they chatted about how relaxed they felt. At the car, Ayanna said to Sean, "I seem to recall a phase three. Something about ice cream." She waggled her eyebrows emphatically.

At the ice cream shop, Sean looked at all of the possible flavors and settled on chocolate.

Ayanna gave him a flat stare and announced, "Nope. Not happening."

"But, I *like* chocolate."

"Of course you do. It's chocolate. Everyone likes chocolate. Do you trust me?"

"You keep asking me that," Sean pointed out.

"True. Have I steered you wrong yet?"

"No—"

"Great." Ayanna beamed at him before focusing on the person behind the counter. "Okay, he's going to have a waffle cone, double scoop, one scoop of sea salt caramel and the other... triple chocolate fudge. I'm going to have a waffle cone, double scoop, one scoop of chocolate peanut butter and the other will be the Kahlua fudge brownie." Ayanna spun around and hugged him, adding, "And of course you're going to share, right?"

Sean had never shared ice cream in his life. It seemed highly unsanitary. Then again, his lips would be going where hers had been, which seemed like a good thing. "Definitely, so long as you share as well."

"Deal!"

The ice cream was fantastic. Four flavors Sean had never been willing to try before, and then the combinations as the ice cream scoops mingled... Perfection. Looking at Ayanna smiling at him with smudges of ice cream at the corners of her mouth and a tiny speck on the tip of her nose... also perfection.

Chapter 16

High Hopes

Pink Floyd

After the ice cream, Sean drove Ayanna back to her car, and from there she went home. When she got there, she found Jesús puttering around, cleaning the kitchen.

"Welcome home."

"Thanks, Jesús. How are you?"

"Wonderful, you?"

"I'm all right."

Ayanna wheeled to head upstairs when Jesús said, "You seem much more than all right. Come and talk with me, Inanna."

She pivoted back, joining him in the kitchen. "What's up?"

"Something's going on with you. Something good, I think."

"It's probably nothing."

Jesús' eyes twinkled. "Oh, it's definitely more than nothing. You're seeing someone. Mortimer mentioned a man with you last night."

"Mortimer talks too much."

"True, but they see a lot, too. They saw you manhandle the roofie guy. Well done, by the way. Mortimer saw you drink, chat, and dance with, as they said, 'a tasty morsel of a man.' They even said you introduced this Sean person to them."

"I did."

"Well, now I'm interested in meeting your new, apparently mortal, boyfriend."

"He's not my boyfriend."

"Really? Mortimer said you both smelled of Indian food. You know... when you escorted this Sean fellow to the vampire ball."

"Damn vampires..."

"And then you left without breakfast this morning and came back late in the afternoon with a spring in your step, and what appears to be some sort of chocolate ice cream on your lips."

"I could have been out with friends, having a girls day."

"Possible, but I suspect not. So, what did you and your not-a-boyfriend do today?"

"We had brunch over at Jam on Hawthorne, then strolled through the Japanese Garden."

"The Garden is clear on the other side of the city."

"I *know*, that's what I said," Ayanna exclaimed. "Anyway, the Gardens were nice, and then, as you surmised, we had ice cream."

"Well, that definitely does *not* sound like a date with your definitely-*not*-a-boyfriend."

"You know, Jesús, teasing people isn't very nice."

"You and Bast tease me all the time. And don't get me started on how the two of you enjoy prancing around naked in front of me."

"Well, sure. That's fine for us. But you're... you know... you. Prince of peace, turn the other cheek, blessed are the meek, and all that other stuff. You're not supposed to tease us. As for the naked thing, well... I'm a love goddess and she's a fertility goddess, so it's normal for us to prance around naked."

"No, you just enjoy tempting and teasing me."

"Okay, fine. Yes, we enjoy that, even though you're a spoil-sport who has no interest in us."

"You know why."

79

"I do." Ayanna paused and smiled sadly at Jesús. "The love goddess in me really wants to find her for you and reunite you two."

"That's actually very sweet."

Ayanna continued, "Provided, of course, you don't screw it up. Seriously, how have you gone almost two thousand years without telling her you love her?"

"I did tell her I love her."

"No, you told her you love her. You didn't tell her you *love* her. Not like you love everyone else."

"Maybe one day I'll get my chance. In the meantime, I'd like to make dinner for you and your *not*-a-boyfriend."

"Wait, what?" Ayanna was aghast.

"Yes, invite him over for dinner."

"You want to invite a mortal into this house? What if Bast walks in naked and pregnant?"

"Is that really your concern, or are you more concerned about how you might feel about this mortal man?"

"Ugh! Why do you have to be you?" Ayanna threw her hands into the air. "Fine. I'll invite him over for dinner. Tonight?"

"Of course."

"Dinner better not be loaves and fishes," Ayanna said sternly.

"I was thinking of shrimp scampi with a nice salad, and garlic bread."

"I knew it. Loaves and fishes. And salad. Hey, what about the whole thing about not eating shellfish because it's an abomination?"

"What's really important is what's inside a person, not what they eat. Besides, the whole issue with shellfish was because a prophet was allergic."

"What about pork?"

"Trichinosis."

Ayanna nodded. "Makes sense."

"So, are you going to invite Sean over for dinner?"

"Ugh, fine! I just saw him, though. He's going to think I'm weird."

"You are weird, and we both know he will say yes to you." Jesús grinned.

"I'll text him in a bit. Apparently I have ice cream on my face."

She waited about an hour, then texted Sean to ask him about dinner. After he accepted, she texted him their address.

Sean showed up around six with a bottle of wine. He had on jeans and a flannel shirt. Ayanna cocked an eyebrow at his outfit. "Hey, at least I'm not wearing a polo shirt."

"I'm not sure I like it on you, but maybe I'm just used to the polos. Hey, come on inside. This is Jesús. Jesús, this is Sean." The two men greeted each other warmly and shook hands.

Jesús welcomed Sean in, saying, "Here, let me take your coat. I like the hat, by the way."

"Thanks. Ayanna helped me pick it out."

"She did? Mhmm. She failed to mention that." Ayanna glowered at Jesús from behind Sean's back. "Since Ayanna seems to be withholding information, I suppose you will have to tell me everything about how you two met and all of the fun you've had up until today. Before you start, you aren't allergic to shrimp or gluten, are you?"

"Um, no. Not that I know of."

"Excellent! So, how did you two meet?" Ayanna was glaring daggers at Jesús, but he seemed completely unmoved by this, smiling along as Sean related the past few days. Jesús interjected occasionally with clarifying questions. As Sean went on, Ayanna started listening with interest, as she was now getting some of Sean's perspective.

I know my appearance in a bikini caused Sean discomfort, but Jesús effortlessly draws out just how challenging that was for Sean.

It's no secret Sean is very inexperienced with dealing with women, but the extent of his inexperience is shocking. Especially how his inexperience was overlaid with intense programming that viewed women in a rigid and binary way. Jesús simply asks a few questions and Sean just opens up. Sean is fascinating. There's a version of him that is timid and sheltered, but there's the much more relaxed man who made fish puns and braved the dangers of Indian food, brunch, and sea salt caramel ice cream. I can't help but wonder just how deeply entrenched his negative programming is. He's certainly comfortable talking with Jesús, but almost anyone is. Sean's probably more comfortable around me when my boobs are fully covered. That's something to work on. Wait, why did I think that?

Ayanna pondered the different aspects of Sean as his tale drew to a close. After he finished, Sean asked Jesús, "Do you always invite Ayanna's... uh, friends over for dinner?"

"Oh, no. It's been a very long time since anyone has held Ayanna's interest this long."

"Jesús!" Ayanna hissed. "That's not for you to say!"

"I apologize. You are right."

Sean looked stunned, as if his mind was racing through dozens of competing thoughts simultaneously. "Is that true?"

"I'm not sure how to answer."

Jesús picked this moment to jump in and save her. "I'm very sorry, Sean. My words were indelicate. What I meant to express is that while Ayanna is a vivacious and outgoing person, she does not form close bonds easily. I invited you over because I sensed a recent change in her and wanted to meet the person who has put such a glow in her smile."

Thank you, Jesús, for saving me from that awkward exchange, even if you caused it. That might be the nicest way of describing my slutty lifestyle that I've ever heard.

Sean's shoulders and expression seemed less tense than

before, although perhaps not fully soothed. "That—makes sense. I appreciate the invitation more now."

"You must be a remarkable person, Sean. I feel as though you are a man of many hidden depths. Speaking of hidden things, do you spend much time in front of a computer?"

"Ah, yes, I am at a computer a lot, for work, you know, not personal stuff. I mean, some personal stuff, but just normal personal stuff." Sean was blushing harder the more he rambled.

In other words, you don't want us to think you watch porn, which now makes me wonder if you are one of those Christians who says they hate porn yet watches tons of it.

Jesús cut him off, saving all of them some embarrassment before Sean could explain normal personal stuff in further detail. "Ah, I thought so. When we shook hands, I felt some tension in your hands which might be an early indicator of carpal tunnel syndrome."

"Wow, that's bad."

"It's still early and easy to fix. I have a balm that will help greatly if you use it regularly." Ayanna felt her eyebrows involuntarily climb toward her scalp. Jesús' good nature sometimes didn't lend itself well to the secrecy required to avoid the Godkillers.

"Is the balm safe?" Sean asked warily.

"Of course. I've used my hands all of my life and this balm has helped me greatly. Here, let me go get some for you." Jesús stood up and left them alone.

"That was strange."

"Don't worry about it. Jesús always wants people to feel better. It's his thing, and honestly, you'll probably appreciate it."

"How did you two meet?"

In Rome, eighteen hundred years ago. Perfectly normal. Seriously, I need to say this very vaguely, yet believably.

"We bumped into each other while traveling. We got along well, and then happened to end up in the same city. We bumped into each other again here in Portland, and now we're renting a place together."

I don't think that answer satisfied Sean's curiosity. He looks like he wants to delve further.

Jesús returned with a small bottle in hand, forestalling Sean's inquiry.

"Here, Sean. Try this."

"Now?"

"Of course."

Sean looked dubious, but he dutifully rubbed some lotion onto his hands.

"No, no! Let me show you." Jesús took hold of Sean's hands and rubbed them vigorously. Sean looked more than a bit uncomfortable, but was unable to resist Jesús' enthusiasm. After rubbing the lotion deep into Sean's skin, Jesús released him. "There, how do you feel?"

Sean flexed his hands experimentally. "Actually, I feel really good. Like kinks in my hands I didn't even feel before are now gone. Thanks, Jesús."

"*De nada!* Come now, dinner must be ready."

"I should wash my hands before dinner, right?"

"The bathroom is right over there."

As Sean closed the door behind him, Ayanna whispered, "What was that?"

Jesús shrugged, saying, "He was going to be in pain soon, so I helped him."

"You mean you healed him," Ayanna said flatly.

"Helped, healed, what's the difference?" Seeing Ayanna's glare, Jesús mumbled sheepishly, "I can't help myself sometimes."

"Ugh, I can't even be mad at you."

Sean rejoined them and they sat down to eat. The look on Sean's face as he chewed his first bite was rapturous. "Wow! This scampi is divine," he exclaimed.

Ayanna nearly choked. *You don't know the half of it.*

When she recovered enough to speak, she simply said, "Jesús is an incredible cook."

As they slowed down, Sean asked Jesús, "How long have you and Ayanna known each other?"

"I've known her for many years, but it feels like I've known her for most of my life."

"And you met while traveling?"

Jesús gave Ayanna a knowing look. "That's right. We didn't really like each other at first, but once we got to know each other we became friends."

"So, you two used to date?"

Both Ayanna and Jesús laughed uproariously.

Ayanna recovered first. "No, nothing like that. Only one person holds the key to Jesús' heart, and I'm definitely not her." Once again, tension seemed to ebb from Sean's shoulders and posture. His expression shifted from a tightly controlled neutrality to something akin to relief.

Sean was jealous of Jesús. Interesting to know.

Jesús added, "Ayanna and I are strictly friends and nothing more. That's one of the reasons we are such good housemates. I am completely immune to her charms."

"Your girlfriend must be really special, then."

"She is," Jesús said longingly.

"Which is why you need to tell her you love her if you ever see her again!"

"I know, Ayanna. I know."

"What?" Sean appeared baffled.

"It's a long story," Jesús murmured bleakly.

"Oh, sorry. I didn't mean to bring up something painful."

"It's all right, Sean. You meant no harm," Jesús said soothingly.

"I still feel awful."

"And that is a credit to you. Sadly, too many people lack empathy. I understand more why Ayanna is attracted to you."

Ayanna choked on her wine.

Sean spluttered, "Wait, you're serious?"

"You two clearly like each other. I'm not sure why you both insist on denying the mutual attraction that is obviously there. Oh, Ayanna. Don't give me that look." Jesús looked at Sean and said, "She's pretty when she's apoplectic, isn't she?"

Jesús, I could happily strangle you. Is he right, though? Am I really attracted to Sean? To a mortal? There's certainly attractive things about him, and I really do enjoy spending time with him. He's giving me space, and we talked about that. I wanted to take things slowly, but am I doing that because I'm worried I might like him too much?

"Um, I'm not sure I should answer that." Sean's face was flushed.

"Smart man."

"In fairness, Ayanna did say she wanted to take things slowly and get to know each other."

"Very sensible. Speaking of sensible, you'll really need to get comfortable seeing her boobs," Jesús grinned playfully.

This time, Sean was the one choking.

Ayanna shouted, "Jesus Christ!"

Chapter 17

Shot Down In Flames

AC/DC

L ater, as he lay in bed, replaying the day in his head, Sean had to acknowledge the hard truth of what Jesús had said. If he was to continue seeing Ayanna, then he needed to overcome his reluctance to actually look at her. Sean felt like the two of them had had an incredible day together, talking, laughing, and at times simply being with each other silently. Ayanna's intelligence and sense of humor were immensely attractive to him, and while they'd been together today, he'd almost forgotten that her day job involved wearing a bikini while slinging lattes. He imagined himself as her White Knight, riding in to save her from a lifetime of debauched drink making.

As he drifted off to sleep, his dreams were burdened by more images of Ayanna. The old images of her as a chainmail bikini-wearing barbarian or leader of a vast army were now joined by dreams of Ayanna in a bikini swimming in a gigantic coffee cup, or Ayanna with nine foxtails scampering through a garden. The dream of her as a vampire clad in black leather woke him with a start. He felt something move against his legs, and was only partially relieved when he realized it was Huntress, not a sexy leather-clad vampire.

Sean fell back asleep, and the rest of the night was blessedly dreamless. He still didn't feel fully rested, but he at least felt better. The early morning was spent doing some cleaning, unpacking, and rearranging of things he hadn't gotten to during the previous week. Sean then went to mass.

Mass had become an integral part of Sean's life since he first started going during college. Growing up, his parents had been ambiguously religious. They never went to church as a family outside of Christmas and Easter; however, his parents were enthusiastic about using the prospect of eternal damnation to keep Sean in line. His formative years were filled with the sure knowledge that teens who drank alcohol or smoked cigarettes were definitely destined for Hell. Sexual activity of any sort was the most certain path to Satan's doorstep.

For Sean, going to mass was a different experience. Mass was less about a sure path to Hell and more 'you have questions, well, we have the answers.' Being given the answers, usually without having to ask questions, was comforting. Any spiritual inquisitiveness Sean possessed had been brutally repressed by his parents, so he accepted what he was told in church.

Now, though, he was starting to have questions.

Today's homily, during the lead-up to the holiday season, focused on the "True Spirit of Christmas." It was a sermon Sean had heard a dozen variations of before, all decrying the commercialization of the holiday and urging parishioners to focus on family, church, giving, and, oh, by the way, we're having a fundraising drive for the parish.

Sean sat in the pew, pondering the True Spirit of Christmas and thinking about things that had come up with Ayanna and Jesús. He reflected on how Jesús had sensed an injury he hadn't even been aware of and then offered to heal his injury. Sean had sensed nothing but kindness from Jesús all evening long. Even when he made them both uncomfortable with his talk about mutual attraction and Ayanna's boobs, he seemed intent on guiding them past their own hang-ups and toward a deeper relationship.

I really shouldn't be thinking about boobs in church, even heavenly boobs.

He thought of Ayanna and her talk of good spirits being drawn to places like the Japanese Garden, or the Shinto belief of divine spirits all around.

I've been trained to seek out false gods, spirits, and unclean creatures. That's my actual job. What if some of these beings, deemed unholy by the Church, are actually benevolent? Ayanna probably didn't mean actual spirits, but still, the point remains. Who can I talk to about this? Could I talk to Ayanna about this? I bet Jesús would have answers. Or, now that I think about it, he probably wouldn't, but he might lead me to some deeper questions.

Sean was still considering this when the homily ended, sending him back into the flow of the mass. As he exited, he checked the church schedule to see when confession was available. Sean felt he had a lot to confess, particularly impure thoughts, yet he was also starting to question sacraments as well. The impure thoughts he could at least talk to Ayanna about, especially since both she and Jesús indicated he needed to get over some of his issues about women.

I should invite her to dinner.

A quick text exchange later, Ayanna agreed to dinner at his place. Sean immediately regretted asking her over. His cooking experience was limited to boxed mac and cheese. Take out was an option, but he really wanted to impress Ayanna. Sean raced home and did what he was good at—internet research. He didn't want anything too basic, but he also didn't want to get in way over his head. He settled on chicken parmesan. It was Italian two nights in a row, but he was anxious, and chicken parm seemed to be not too far out of his comfort zone.

Sean quickly ran to the store to get the necessary ingredients. Online videos showed him the necessary steps, although the video he used assumed he would know to preheat the oven, so there was a slight delay as he did that. Ayanna came over at the appointed time, and Sean went down to greet her rather than buzz her in. They walked up the stairs to his floor and into his apartment. The tour of the apartment and its spartan furnishings took less than a minute.

Huntress seemed very happy to meet Ayanna, and she cheerfully twined herself around his guest's legs. For her part, Ayanna seemed perfectly happy to have a cat impeding her steps, and once the tour was over, she squatted down to properly greet the mistress of the apartment. To Sean's astonishment, Huntress plopped over and let Ayanna rub her fuzzy little tummy unimpeded. Whenever Sean tried to rub Huntress' tummy, he received the claws of doom.

I'm a bit jealous. Does Huntress like her more than me?

"Wow, she never lets me do that," Sean grumbled.

"You mean rub this soft, warm, fuzzy tummy?"

"Yeah," Sean sighed.

He watched as Ayanna buried her face in Huntress' soft fur, petting and murmuring to the cat. After a bit, she stopped and Huntress walked over to him and headbonked his ankle, then plopped on her side. He squatted down and for the first time ever rubbed her soft belly without having blood drawn. After a few seconds, she grew tired of this and went back to Ayanna for more petting.

"Did you tell her to let me rub her tummy?"

"Eh, not really. I've always been a bit of a cat whisperer. I think she sensed you might be feeling jealous and went over to reconnect with you. Cats are very sensitive. Some of them, at least. There are a few interesting documentaries about cats. Did you know cats are the only animal that regularly lives with humans that we didn't domesticate?"

"What? Really?"

"It's true. Every other domestic animal is some variant of a herd, pack, or flock animal that humans inserted themselves into their natural hierarchy. There are some scientists who posit that not only did we not domesticate cats, but they domesticated us."

"No, that can't be right."

"Think about it. When humanity first figured out agriculture, they had to store food. Those food stores attracted rats and mice. Humans provided cats with a regular source of food, and humans benefited because the cats kept their food safe. Over time, cats learned how to train humans."

"Train us?"

"Yes, train us. Did you know cats have certain purrs designed for humans? As in, there's an 'I'm hungry, feed me' purr."

"Wow, that's crazy. So, it's like I'm Huntress' servant."

"Yeah, pretty much."

"I never thought of that. I wonder if Huntress laughs at me because she knows she's the smarter one."

"Trust me, Huntress already knows." Ayanna looked at his computer monitor. "What's on your screen?"

Sean responded merrily, "That's the otter cam at the Monterey Bay Aquarium. I like watching them. It's soothing and they make me laugh."

"Wow... They are otter-ly adorable!" Ayanna grinned at her pun, and Sean laughed.

"Why don't you watch the otters for a few minutes while I check on dinner, okay?"

"Sure, sounds good. Everything smells great, by the way."

Sean puttered away in the kitchen area, desperately hoping everything was going to taste good. Meanwhile, Ayanna sat and watched the otters. Huntress jumped in her lap, and she absently scratched the cat's head. Sean's brand new food thermometer indicated the chicken was indeed done, the spaghetti seemed cooked, and the garlic bread was hot. It was time to bring the food out to the table.

Here goes nothing.

"What have we here?" Ayanna asked.

"Chicken parmesan, garlic bread, and a salad. Plus, the wine you brought."

"Very nice! It looks tasty."

"I hope you like it."

"I'm sure I will."

"I'll be honest. This is my first time making anything that didn't come out of a box. If it's awful, then we can get take out."

Ayanna laughed. "So, you brought me here under false pretenses to experiment on me. I guess, since I'm here, I'll just have to partake and be your guinea pig."

Sean rubbed his hands together menacingly and gave her an evil stage laugh, "Muwahaha!"

I'm glad she seems positive about this.

Once everything was set, Sean briefly bowed his head in prayer before saying, "Here goes nothing!" As they dug into their meals, they discovered it was actually good, especially for a first effort.

After they were done eating, Sean transitioned to the conversation he'd wanted to have all day. "Have you thought about a different job, because I would be happy to help you with online job searches, resumes, or stuff like that?"

"Why? I just started working at the cart a week ago."

"It's just that you're so smart, I... I know you can do better."

"Better?" There was an edge in Ayanna's voice warning of danger ahead.

Completely oblivious to impending danger, Sean forged ahead. "You know, a job where you're not, you know, showing yourself to everyone."

"You're actually being serious right now?"

"Of course! I really want to help you, because you can do—"

"What the fuck, Sean? You want to *help* me? Because apparently, I need a *man* to save me from working in a coffee cart with my tits out? Is that it?" Ayanna was standing now, clearly furious.

Uh oh. This isn't going how I expected. She seems really upset.

He weakly uttered, "Yes?"

"*Fuck you*, Sean! I've only been at the cart for a week, and I'm liking it. I've worked a lot of shitty jobs in my life, and maybe this isn't a phenomenal job, but you know what?"

"What?"

"People like coffee. For a lot of people, it's a necessary part of their day that brings them joy. And I like delighting people. It makes *me* feel good. You know what else brings a lot of people joy?"

Sean barely managed to whisper, "What?"

"Boobs. Breasts. Tits. Sure, I don't have Annabelle's twin Zeppelins, but I have fantastic boobs, and they exhilarate a lot of people. And again, I *like* bringing people joy. Oh, and another thing."

Sean was by now cowed into silence.

Ayanna was shaking with fury. "You don't get to tell me what to do with my body. You don't get to comment on it. It's my body and I can show it off or not show it off as I choose. I don't need to be saved. Not by you. Not by any man. I was a night security guard before this, and I mostly hated it. Now, I get to chat with losers who have never heard of tea before and change their lives for the better, which pleased me, or at least it did until a couple minutes ago. So, once again, Sean, thank you for a lovely dinner and go fuck yourself."

Ayanna stormed out, leaving Sean bereft and bewildered.

I saw that whole conversation going very differently in my imagination. Now Ayanna is angry with me, and I'm still not entirely sure why. The only thing I am sure of is that I've ruined everything.

Chapter 18

Fuck You

Lily Allen

Ayanna's rage dissipated slightly by the time she got home, but not by much. The door rattled as she slammed it shut, drawing stares from Brandi and Jesús. Brandi shifted from cat to woman and walked over to give Ayanna a hug.

"Dinner didn't go well, then?"

"Want to talk about it?" Jesús added.

"He's such an idiot," Ayanna snarled.

"Uh oh," Brandi and Jesús uttered simultaneously.

"Dinner was actually nice. He made chicken parm. His first meal from scratch, or so he claimed."

Brandi asked, "Then what happened?"

"He decided he needed to 'save me' from the horrors of serving coffee in a bikini."

"You're right, he's an idiot," Brandi agreed.

"Well—"

"Shut it, Jesús. Let the woman vent first."

"Thanks, Brandi. He wanted to help me find a new job because I'm smart and can do better."

"Then what?"

"Then I ripped him to shreds."

"Literally or figuratively?"

"Figuratively." Ayanna sighed. "But literally would have been cathartic. I told Sean I don't need to be saved, and it's not his place to comment on what I choose to do with my own fucking body."

"If you still want to literally tear him to shreds, then I can get my coat."

"Brandi—"

"Stuff it, Jesús. You know I'm joking. Mostly—you know, unless Ayanna wants to."

"Thank you for your support, Brandi." Ayanna hugged her. "You're the *Bast* friend a girl could ask for."

"Ugh, don't you ever get tired of that joke?"

"Nope."

"I'm guessing it's okay for a man to speak now?"

"Fine. Out with it, Jesús."

"I'm sorry, Ayanna, that he caused you so much pain."

"Thank you. I really liked him, too."

"He really likes you as well. You said yourself he is very inexperienced with women and with people in general."

Brandi interjected, "I gotta say, I never pictured you and Super Virgin together."

Jesús sighed. "Not helping, Brandi. Ayanna, I know this might be painful to hear, but perhaps Sean's incredibly stupid blunder tonight was coming from a place of love."

"Dammit, Jesús! Why do you always have to go looking for the good in people?"

He shrugged. "It's who I am."

"Sometimes it's a really annoying trait. He still should never have said those things, and maybe it's *not* coming from a place of love. Maybe it's because he's got these rigid values of right and wrong with no gray. Or what is okay for men but not women.

Maybe he's just an uptight prick who thinks only loose women wear a bikini at work." Ayanna worked herself toward fury.

"Loose women? Queen Victoria would like a word," Brandi snickered.

Jesús followed up with, "You may be correct, Ayanna, but I hope you are not."

"I'm not sure why I'm so upset anyway. I'll probably live for another six thousand years and he'll be dead in sixty. What does one mortal matter anyway?" She grumbled, anger retreating.

Jesús looked crestfallen, and brought her in for a hug. "It hurts because you grew to care for him, even if he is mortal."

"Jesús, if you are using a hug to heal me, I swear you'll be out of cheeks to turn."

He laughed at her remark. "I wouldn't dream of it. All right, I need to go to work. Brandi, please look after Ayanna, and don't do anything I wouldn't do."

"Like have fun?"

"Hush." Jesús grabbed his coat and headed for the door.

"Hey, now that he's gone, you wanna go out and get laid? I know some guys who have a thing for pregnant chicks, but I'm sure they'd make an exception for you."

From the doorway, Jesús said, "I heard that, Brandi."

Chapter 19

Purple Rain
Prince

I feel totally lost, and there's no one I can talk to about this. Well, if I can't talk directly to someone, there is one place where answers are always available. The internet.

Sean started doing some searches.

Well, I just discovered that asking the internet about whether it was acceptable to try to save a woman from an objectifying job was a horrible decision in its own right. What the hell do I make of this?

The answers ranged from 'Yes, and she should be thankful you saved her,' to 'No, you shouldn't touch dirty women at all,' to 'Don't save her, just enjoy objectifying her,' to, "No, it's none of your damn business.'

When I imagined his conversation with Ayanna, I definitely thought it would fall into the first group. Clearly, I was very wrong, and Ayanna was in the latter group.

Reading through posts and blogs in the 'none of your damn business' category was still frustrating and confusing. There was a lot of discussion around feminism, a word Sean had been groomed to believe was nearly akin to the worst swear words. What Sean found most confusing was a split between some who felt feminism meant not objectifying women at all and some who felt it was a woman's choice to do with her body what she pleased. Much of the discussion centered around pornography, but Sean figured the primary themes applied just as well to bikini baristas.

Here is a totally new concept for me. The "Male Gaze." I never knew how much of... everything was affected by the male viewpoint. Certainly my idea to "save" Ayanna was all about viewing her not as a real person, but this objectified version of her. I know I'm inexperienced in relating with women, but I had no idea just how much there is to learn. This is going to be a lot of work, but if I am going to have any chance with Ayanna, then I have to put in the effort. I need to keep researching feminism, the male gaze, patriarchy, and the myriad other parts of this puzzle.

He fed Huntress and dove in. He spent a few hours before bed reading a lot of theory and criticism around feminism. Sean's sleep was troubled again. He was finally getting used to the Ayanna as a vampire dream, but now he had a new dream featuring Ayanna in a classroom, dressed as a teacher straight out of a Van Halen video.

Talk about the male gaze. Ugh, that dream wasn't helpful.

Monday was a slog, churning through potential supernatural activity in Portland, most of which was easily explainable as just everyday life. There might be a few possible sightings in Forest Park, but those were most likely racoons or something similarly natural. The best thing Sean could say about work on Monday was that his hands felt amazing. Whatever Jesús had done worked really well. Sean hadn't even been aware his hands needed any care, but after three days of using Jesús' ointment, he felt renewed.

As the day came to a close, Sean thought about going to Brandi's for tea. Ayanna would be working then. He desperately wanted to see her, but he didn't think she would want to see him. Sean also thought he needed more time to think about what he'd done wrong and how to be better in the future.

After work, Sean spent more time reading and thinking,

taking breaks to feed Huntress and himself. He was really struggling with the whole concept of the male gaze, particularly as it related to his lurid dreams of Ayanna. Sean felt like he grasped the idea for the most part, but now he was feeling guilty about what his subconscious mind was envisioning in the night.

As the evening ticked closer to bedtime, he started to research dream control, but that subject made his head hurt. Sean felt like his brain was already stuffed with the deluge of information and opinions on feminism, patriarchy, sex positivism, and capitalism. Anything else might make him explode.

Monday night again found Sean awash in a kaleidoscope of imagery as all of the previous night's dreams returned. Once again, there was a brand new dream to add to the mix. This time, Ayanna was clothed in white linen and seated on a massive throne atop a ziggurat where she watched as a similarly clad priestess rode a king to an ecstatic climax atop an altar as the residents of an ancient city cheered them on.

Sean woke in the morning, sweating like that king and wondering what was going on with his dreams. He had rarely remembered his dreams for most of his life and now suddenly he could remember them every morning in excruciating detail. After getting ready and feeding Huntress, he dove into his work, hoping to bury the memories of his dreams.

Chapter 20

I Can See Clearly Now
Jimmy Cliff

By Tuesday, Ayanna's mood had improved a bit. After a night of meaningless sex with some random guys on Sunday night, she was still out of sorts on Monday. Annabelle and Enrique did their best to cheer her up while they were all together at the cart. It was hard to feel angry with those two around. Ayanna was pleased to hear Annabelle and Tanya were now officially dating, and Enrique and Aiden were going to have dinner that evening.

Monday afternoon was a slog. The hours dragged toward closing time, and Ayanna noted Sean hadn't appeared for tea for the first time. She told herself this was for the best, but somehow she didn't quite believe herself.

When Ayanna arrived at the cart on Tuesday, she dove into the rush with Annabelle and Krystal. Once the rush hour crowd was cleared, they settled into the familiar routine of restocking and chatting. Annabelle regaled Krystal with a tale of her tryst with Tanya the night before. Krystal asked Ayanna to find her a guy since her track record with Annabelle and Enrique was stellar. Ayanna of course agreed, but felt depressed about the recent implosion of her not-a-relationship with Sean.

After the five p.m. mini rush cleared, Ayanna spotted a familiar form approaching. She drew her face into a carefully neutral expression. "Sean. What can I get you?"

His face flushed as he stammered, "Hi, Ayanna. Do you have any tea to help someone sleep?"

"Guilty conscience catching up to you?"

"Uh, not exactly…"

"I see." After her flat response, Ayanna disappeared into the cart.

When she returned, Sean said, "Ayanna, I am so sorry about Sunday night. I am an idiot, and I made a gigantic mistake."

"I agree completely."

"You were right. Your life is your business, and I overstepped badly."

"Uh huh."

"Look. I've been doing a lot of reading and thinking. I tried to learn about feminism, and I'm still very confused about some things, but I do know I was imposing my own patriarchal beliefs onto you, which is wrong. Um, I also learned about sex positivity and while that makes me pretty uncomfortable, I understand that's a growth opportunity for me."

"A growth opportunity?" Ayanna snickered at the double entendre. "Don't move."

She walked out of the cart a couple minutes later, carrying a coffee cup. She strutted up to Sean, clad in only the bikini. When she stopped, she put one hand on her hip and raised the coffee cup to her lips with the perfect sensuality one would expect from a six thousand year old love goddess.

For the first time ever, Sean looked at her. It wasn't a leer, it wasn't objectifying, it was… almost worshipful.

Interesting. Sean is making progress. He's been thinking, and he actually looked at me. I don't want to be pleased with him making progress, but I have to admit I am.

"So?" she demanded.

"Wow. Thank you?"

"Mhmm. Thank you for what, Sean?"

"Um, thank you for not cutting my head off with a giant barbarian sword?"

Ayanna laughed out loud at his absurd statement. "*What?*"

"Um, you know how I asked for tea to help me sleep? I've been having strange dreams lately."

"You've been dreaming of me with a giant sword? I've never heard that before."

Sean's face flared a brilliant shade of scarlet, and he whispered, "While wearing a chain mail bikini..."

"You're serious?" Ayanna's grin went ear to ear. She twirled around, giving him a full view with a calculated dose of jiggle. "Does this match your dreams? Besides the chain mail of course..."

Sean gulped and said, "Yes."

"Hm, maybe I should get a chainmail bikini made. I bet the customers would love that."

"I bet they would. Um... I would, too."

Did he just express a sexual desire? Sean is coming out of his shell.

"Well, it seems like you are actually making progress. That's interesting."

"Ayanna, I'm really sorry. I screwed up so badly. I know you're angry with me, and you should be. I know I don't deserve your forgiveness, but I really want to earn it. You're very important to me, and I'm willing to do the work to be more enlightened." Sean ended his deluge of words with, "You're worth the effort."

"Intriguing. That may be the most heartfelt attempt at forgiveness I've ever heard from a mor... a man." Ayanna paused.

I almost said mortal. That would have been bad. Also, I did kind of miss him.

She continued, "You haven't earned forgiveness, but perhaps

maybe a second chance." With sharp steel in her voice, she added, "Provided what you said wasn't bullshit."

"I meant it, I swear. I can't promise perfection, but I do promise to learn and do better."

"That's good. Now come and sit." Ayanna indicated a low bench set against the side of the cart.

When they sat, she sipped her coffee, then turned to him and asked, "So, was that the only dream of me you've had?"

"There's the dream of you as a half-orc barbarian facing off against the horde of ogres. There's also the dream of you as a vampire in skin-tight black leather."

He dreamed of me in Kate Beckinsale's Underworld leather outfit? On the one hand, that's weird since I thought of wearing that for him. On the other hand, if I were a guy, then I would dream of me in that outfit.

Sean continued, "Ah, and there's one of you here in a bikini with a coffee in one hand and a battle axe in the other. There's another one in a beautiful garden where you have nine foxtails. Oh, and the one with you in a bikini swimming in a giant cup of coffee..."

"I'm sensing some themes here. Apparently you really did have a good time at the Dungeons and Dragons thing. And the vampire ball. Oh, and you like my bikinis. Not sure about the foxtail one."

That last one isn't strictly true, although me with a Kitsune tail is very strange.

"Yeah, bikinis are a theme. And then there are the weird dreams."

"Wait, those *weren't* the weird ones?"

"No. I keep dreaming of you, riding a chariot, dressed in white linen, with lionesses flanking the chariot. You have a bronze spear in your hand, and there is an army following you."

Ayanna suddenly felt extremely tense.

"And then there's the new dream from last night. I see you sitting on a huge throne on a ziggurat towering over a city. You're in white linen again. This time, there's... a priestess or something wearing the same white linen clothes as you, and, um, she's riding a king on an altar. To make it weirder, there's this vast city below and everyone in the city is cheering them on as they have sex on the altar."

Ayanna tried to hide the shock and the chilling grip of terror she was feeling. "Yep, those are some weird dreams. I'll make sure to get you more tea before you go." Internally her mind was racing. *How is he dreaming those dreams? He's dreaming of me, thousands of years ago when I led armies into battle or blessed the sacred rites for a bounteous new year. It was so long ago I can barely remember these things. Even archaeologists have only gleaned indistinct glimpses of what once was. Sean could be Enki or Marduk in disguise, but that's bloody unlikely. Which takes me back to the first question. How is he dreaming of me when I was a goddess in all of my glory?*

"Hey. Thanks for stopping by. I need to close up soon, but I'm okay to see you again."

"Great, thank you, Ayanna. You look beautiful, by the way."

"Thank you. Let me get you more tea." *About an ocean's worth of tea to drown those dreams.*

Chapter 21

Somebody's Watching Me

Rockwell

Ayanna raced home after closing up the cart. The door slammed behind her as she hustled inside. She breathed a small sigh of relief when she saw Brandi and Jesús staring at her.

Brandi asked, "Is the cart okay?"

Jesús chimed in with, "Ayanna, are you all right?"

"No... uh, the cart's fine, but I'm not. Sean stopped by."

The couch groaned as Brandi shifted from a cat to a lioness. "Do you need me to rip his throat out? Because I will."

"I appreciate that, but it's not necessary. He actually apologized to me."

Jesús smiled as he asked, "Really now? How did that go?"

"He was sweet, actually. He said he's been reading up on feminism and stuff."

"I'm not surprised. He clearly likes you a lot. I'm glad he's putting in the effort to learn about feminism. Changing people's worldviews isn't easy. I certainly failed when I tried two thousand years ago. Women were critical to my ministry."

Brandi giggled as she shifted from lioness to human. "We know. Especially one of them."

Jesús blushed.

Ayanna continued, "There's a problem, though. Sean has been dreaming of me."

Brandi interrupted her with a whistle. "Of course he's been dreaming of you. Look at you—you're a goddess."

"Yeah, that's the problem. Along with the kinky sex dreams, he dreamed of me as a goddess."

"Not seeing a problem," Brandi said lecherously.

"No, he dreamed of me leading an army across the land between the rivers and also of me observing the sacred rites to bring plenty to the city and land. He dreamed of me as Inanna—as I once was, thousands of years ago."

"Oh... shit."

"For once, I agree with Brandi. That isn't good," Jesús added. "Are you certain?"

"Yes, he described in detail what I was doing, what I wore, what was happening around me. Brandi, what do you remember of the wars between us—when we fought?"

"Bits and pieces. I remember you leading armies in your chariot. I can see you in combat against Ra when his chariot crashed, and he fell. I blocked your spear before you could finish him. Our lionesses fought each other at our sides. I held you off for hours while Ra slipped away. You were so beautiful and deadly in battle."

"That's what Sean dreamed. Not our fight, but me as a goddess, going to war. It's not possible. I barely remember those times. Somehow he is seeing them with perfect clarity. Jesús, do you have anything to add?"

"Father once dealt out many dreams and prophecies, but He would never have one of His worshippers dream of you."

"No, he definitely wouldn't. He always resented our very existence."

"Very true. This is fascinating to me. I assume you haven't

inspired any other dreams or prophecies recently."

"Not that I know of. I don't recall inspiring anyone for two thousand years."

"Same here," Brandi added.

Jesús turned to Brandi and asked, "Are you still in touch with Thoth?"

"Yes. Do you want me to ask him about this?"

"Yes, please," Ayanna and Jesús said simultaneously.

Jesús added, "Hopefully Thoth can help. This is out of my area of expertise."

Brandi snickered, "So true, but if we ever need a statue to cry blood, we know who to call!"

"Very funny. Can you please put on a robe or something?"

Brandi pouted, but got up from the couch to put on a robe, then grabbed her laptop and started typing. Meanwhile, Jesús offered Ayanna a chair and sat down as well. "Do you want to talk about Sean?"

"Yeah, I think so. He really was sweet. He knew he screwed the proverbial pooch with his little speech on Sunday." Ayanna smiled. "Jesús, he said I was worth putting in the effort to change for."

"Sean's sweet. He's learning about feminism for you?"

"Yes, and the patriarchy and sex positivity." Ayanna patted Jesús on the arm. "Look at you. You didn't even blush when I mentioned sex. Oh, apparently patriarchy is intertwined with capitalism, which I had no idea about."

"That's definitely the other Jesus' fault. I've always been more of a feed the hungry and heal the sick kinda guy."

"We all know your feelings about money corrupting religion. It's nice to know you actually can lose your shit on someone. Sometimes you're are too nice, you know."

"You always tell me that. Back to Sean, though. I'm very impressed he's willing to grow and change. That shows a lot of character and gives you an idea of the depths of his feelings toward you. Not many men will admit when they are wrong and then do something to fix it."

"He looked at me, too. Not disgusted at the fact I work in a bikini or in a gross or creepy way. More of an accepting and appreciative way. I still think he's nervous about it, and I wonder how much is going on in the back of his mind, but it was nice."

"You are beautiful... Please sit down and keep your clothes on. You and Brandi have teased me enough that I am quite familiar with both of you." Ayanna pouted at Jesús, but the effect was ruined by her hint of a smile. "And before you say it... No, I won't become intimately familiar."

"I wasn't going to say that... All right, I was. Next time I run into Mary Magdalene, I will be sure to tell her how you steadfastly resisted my wiles."

Jesús sighed but then smiled impishly, "Now, I get my revenge for all those years of teasing me—Ayanna, since Sean is willing to grow and change for you, how are you going to grow and change for him?"

"I'm a Goddess, I don't change for mortals," Ayanna said haughtily.

"Are you sure? Millions of mortals have shaped us over the years. In your case, it's now just one mortal. Who do you want to be now?"

"I'm me."

"Think about it, Ayanna. You may only have vague memories of your past, but your worshippers once made you the Supreme goddess of your lands. They told tales of who you loved, who you fought, who you married. They gave you a son and then took him away. You died and then rose again from your sister's realm three days later. All of your choices—the entire tapestry of your life for thousands of years—was woven *for* you, not *by* you. Your followers have been dead for centuries, though. Maybe this is your chance to make a new fate for yourself. For once, maybe you can decide who you are."

"Wow... I never considered that."

"You could even become just a Goddess of Love."

Ayanna snorted derisively. "I'm not going to do to myself what the Greeks did to me when they created Aphrodite. I *enjoy* being Queen of the battlefield as well as Queen of the bedroom. You do make some good points—that's a lot to think about. I'm going to meditate on this, and you need to get to work. Organic kombucha doesn't stock itself."

That's crazy, right? I can't pick who I am and what I want to be. Sure, I've made my own decisions, lived my own life since the days of the Abbasids, but I've always been a Goddess of Love and War.

Chapter 22

Dream Weaver

Gary Wright

Sean practically skipped home that evening.

Ayanna doesn't hate me. Seeing her had actually gone really well, considering how things ended on Sunday. Clearly, I'm not out of the doghouse yet, but there is definitely reason for hope. Things are looking up.

On the way home, he stopped at the store to grab a few things. Tonight, he was going to try making stir fry. Maybe, someday, he might have Ayanna over again, and he wanted to expand his repertoire. Huntress was pleased to see her human, and more pleased when he fed her. The stir fry turned out pretty well. He did more reading that evening before turning in.

Sean got some good sleep, untroubled until the effects of the tea wore off. After midnight, Ayanna once more invaded his dreams. The same dreams as the nights before, and once again, a new one appeared. Sean dreamed of Ayanna kneeling at the feet of a man, an ancient general of some kind. Her head was bowed in submission and her clothes were torn. Behind the general were arrayed twelve tall figures he thought looked like the Greek gods. The images left him despondent and disturbed.

When he woke, he did his best to shake off the disturbing

dream as he prepared for the day. As Sean began his usual research, he recalled a dream reader and fortune teller on his lists. That particular business was filed in the almost certainly harmless category, as it was most likely a scam. Given his sleep lately, Sean decided to do some personal investigation.

After lunch, Sean headed deep into southeast Portland to find the shop. He actually missed it the first two times he walked down the street, but he did eventually spot it out of the corner of his eye. A narrow staircase took him to a second floor shop, which was an unusual arrangement as every other shop nearby was street level. The shop itself was about what he expected, full of crystals and occult symbols to fool the unwary. The air was warm and smelled heavily of incense. A heavily tattooed woman greeted him with a dry and accented voice. Sean figured this was all part of the con, but he decided to stay.

After a few minutes of aimless browsing, Sean approached the woman he presumed was the proprietor.

"What can I help you with?"

Sean was struggling to place her accent. Definitely foreign, but he didn't know where.

"Um, yes. I saw you are a dream reader, and I have been troubled by very vivid dreams lately. It's the same dreams every night, plus one or two new dreams added each night. I'd like to know what they mean."

"I may be able to help, but interpreting dreams can be difficult. I will do my best to divulge their secrets to you."

"Thanks, that sounds great."

"One hundred dollars for the first hour. If more time is needed, it will be sixty dollars per hour. You can pay one hundred now. Cash or app."

"Oh, uh... sure." This was going to be expensive. Sean paid using an app, wondering if he could get reimbursed. *Probably not.*

"Excellent, take a seat on the couch in the back room. I will be in to see you shortly."

The back room was somehow even warmer and more incense-filled than the front of the store. As he sat, Sean considered leaving, but stayed since he had already paid. He jumped when he heard the proprietor's voice directly behind him. "Do you consent to me touching your skull? It will make the process easier."

"Sure, whatever."

Her hands were surprisingly strong yet gentle as she dug through his hair to his skin. She began gently rubbing her fingertips in patterns. "Tell me about your dreams. Describe them to me in as much detail as possible. Everything is important."

Sean began to recount his dreams. The warmth in the room and the hypnotic tracings of her fingertips made him drowsy as the session drew on.

He woke up with a start to see the proprietor scribbling in a notebook. She lifted the notebook and turned it toward him, where he saw the images from his dreams sketched out perfectly. She asked him, "Is this what you see in your dreams?"

"Yes! That's it," Sean exclaimed.

"You are clearly obsessed with this woman."

"Ayanna? Yes, I suppose so."

"But you knew that already. She is very beautiful, so I understand that. The imagery, though, is phenomenal in its detail. You say each dream is exactly the same, every night?"

"Yes."

"Fascinating." She held the 's' for an extended time, almost a hiss. "You might think I say this to every client, but I assure you, your dreams are different from most. Some of your dreams are innocent, but others are a window."

"What do you mean my dreams are a window?"

"Dreams as vivid and detailed as yours sometimes provide a window to another time, or perhaps another reality."

"So, I could be dreaming of Ayanna in different worlds? What does that even mean?"

"I said different times or different realities. You could very well be dreaming of this woman's past lives."

"But—that doesn't make sense. There's no such thing as reincarnation."

"Says who? Your Christian god? There are so many gods and so many different concepts of what happens after death. Who is to say which is correct, if any of them?"

Talk of other deities made Sean uncomfortable; however, he forged onward. "Which is it, then? Am I dreaming of her past lives, or some alternate reality? Why am I having these dreams?"

"That knowledge is beyond my abilities. My best interpretation is that most of your dreams are simply fantasy; however, a few have some connection with your Ayanna's past."

"You're being vague."

"Dream interpretation is not an exact art. This is my best interpretation, but your situation is extraordinarily rare. Now, it is closing time and you must go."

"What time is it?"

"Half 'til five now. You have been here for three hours."

"Impossible."

"You fell asleep, and I chose not to wake you as I sketched your dreams. Now go, so I may close up the shop." She ushered Sean to the door and locked it after him, closing the blinds as well.

Sean felt bewildered and groggy, so he wasn't surprised when he eventually found his way back to Brandi's Bitchin' Brews. "Hi, Ayanna."

"Hi, Sean. Welcome back."

"Thanks. Um, do you have any tea to clear my head?"

"Straight coffee might work, but I also think I have some tea that would do the trick. What's up with your head?"

"You know those dreams I was telling you about? Well, I went to a dream reader today, and my head is feeling really foggy right now."

"A dream reader, huh? You know that stuff is fake, right?"

"I dunno. I thought so, too. She kicked me out after three hours after saying most of what I dreamed was just fantasy. Maybe it was a scam, but somehow I feel like she gave some things to consider."

"Huh. Three hours. That's a lot of time to talk about your dreams of me. Unless you're dreaming of other girls now..." Ayanna grinned at him.

"Oh, no. I'm a one girl dreamer for sure. Speaking of, I had a new dream last night. It was really disturbing, and I didn't like it."

"I guess the anti-dreaming tea didn't work, then."

"It worked really well, then maybe around midnight it wore off."

"Sorry. Dare I ask what your new dream was about?"

Sean was reluctant to speak about it, but inevitably acceded to her query. "I saw you kneeling in submission before a great general. Your clothes were torn and your spear was broken. Behind the general were twelve figures. I think they were the Greek gods."

"What makes you say that?"

"In the middle was a man with a thunderbolt in his hands. There was another man with braced legs. A beautiful woman with no weapons at all. Another woman with a hunter's bow standing next to a man whose face shone like the sun."

"Yep, sounds like the Greeks."

Why does she sound so bitter? It's not like she ever met the Greek pantheon. Maybe she just doesn't like mythology.

Sean tried to sound soothing. "Any idea what it means?"

"Let me fix your tea. Um, no clue. Maybe your dream reader can figure it out."

She sounds off. It can't be because she's hiding something, right? Maybe she's just had a long day and is mentally fatigued. There's no reason for her to hide anything about my dream. I'm being selfish just talking about me. We should talk about her for a bit.

"Hey. Do you have a couple minutes to chat? It's okay if you don't."

"Sure. I would like that. Want me to come around?"

"Only if you won't be too cold."

"I'm good, I have a high tolerance for temperatures, plus it's really warm in here, so the cold will feel good."

"Okay." Sean waited for Ayanna to exit the cart and then they sat down on the little bench. "What are you drinking?"

"Mm, hot chocolate."

"That sounds good. How come you never suggested cocoa for me?"

"Because you always have some malady that tea would be better for. Oh, you're warm." She proceeded to arrange their positioning so his left arm and part of his coat was around her.

"I thought you said you have a high tolerance?"

"Yeah, I do, but you're warm. Ergo, it's your job to help keep me warm."

Sean had never been in close contact with a nearly naked woman before, so his ability to think straight was beginning to degrade, but he did manage to ask, "How was your day?"

"It was good. Enrique and Krystal were in this morning. I'm trying to see if I can find her a date."

"With a customer?"

"Maybe. I hooked Enrique up with a customer and that seems to be going well. They've been on a couple of dates so far."

"How does that happen?"

"I saw them making eyes at each other. He seemed like a decent sort, a bit too muscle-bound for my taste. Anyway, I gave him Enrique's number and things have been heating up since."

"Oh, Enrique is—"

"Gay. Is that a problem?"

"I'm going to be honest with you. If you had asked me that question this time last week, then I would have said yes. But I've have had certain eye-opening experiences since then, so I'm going to say no. I will admit, I might still be uncomfortable if they were hanging out with us, but I'm working to be better."

"Not a great answer, but a fair answer. I appreciate your honesty about your growth process. What about my co-worker Annabelle? She's dating her friend Tanya."

"Um, pretty much the same."

"But maybe less discomfort because they're two women?"

Sean was beet red, but gamely responded, "Yeah, kinda."

"*Men.*" Ayanna's tone was a mixture of exasperation and resignation.

"Sorry. I'm just trying to be as open and honest as I can be. So, did you set up Annabelle with Tanya or something?"

"Um, we had a girls night out, which led to a girls night in, and I, ah, facilitated getting them together."

"As in, you saw they had a spark and got them together—" Sean's eyes widened as realization struck. "Or the three of you had sex and they figured it out?" He felt stunned.

"The second one."

"So, wait—you're a lesbian?"

"Actually, the term you're looking for is pansexual."

"Oh... I have no idea what that means," Sean admitted.

"Pansexual means I am attracted to all people, regardless of gender identity and sex. Does that bother you?"

"Yes and no. Partially for the same reasons as before—trying to grow. Also, I figured you were a lot more adventurous and experienced than I am, because it's almost impossible not to be. It's just a bit weird to hear you say it out loud."

Ayanna was about to say something, when Sean said, "Sorry,

let me finish. I know I've got my hang-ups, but I also understand your body is yours and it's not my place to comment or judge because it's not my business."

Ayanna paused briefly before responding, "I get that you're trying, and that's sincerely appreciated. So long as we're communicating, then we should get along just fine. Maybe we can do a double date some night with Annabelle and Tanya. Would that work for you?"

"I would be happy to be on a date with you in whatever form I can get it."

She laughed. "I'll check with her, then."

"After last Sunday, I'm grateful you're willing to go out with me again." Sean was awash in relief and trepidation. "Hey, Ayanna. I know it's none of my business but, um, have you had any serious relationships before? Sorry, I shouldn't have asked—"

"It's okay. I get it." She paused, took a deep breath, and blew it out. "I was married once, and I had a son. They're both dead now."

"I'm so sorry, Ayanna."

"It's fine. You didn't know. I don't like to talk about it. It's been a while, but it's still painful. Maybe you can just hold me like this for a bit."

"I can do that."

They sat in silence for a few minutes, until Ayanna spoke up. "Thank you, by the way."

"For what?"

"I custom ordered a chainmail bikini. I have a friend named Bridget who is good at that sort of thing. I had Jesús take my measurements. She said it wouldn't take long to forge because there was so little material."

"Why Jesús?"

"Seriously? I'm ordering a chainmail bikini straight out of your dreams and that's your question? I could have had Brandi do it, but teasing Jesús is way more fun." Ayanna flashed him a grin before levering herself up. "All right, my feet are starting to get cold. I'm gonna go inside and close down the cart. See you tomorrow?" Ayanna asked hopefully.

"Yeah, I think so."

"Are you going to D&D again?"

"Ah, I hadn't thought of it. The last group was on a Wednesday. Lemme check. There's a Thursday meetup, too. And a Saturday one."

"Well, how about this? I'll check with the others and see if they'll swap shifts with me. If I can get someone to take the closing shift, then I'll go with you to D&D."

"A D&Date would be great."

Ayanna groaned, but still smiled. "Cool, I'll text you as soon as I know."

"Awesome. Bye, Ayanna."

"Later, Sean."

Sean headed home, where he was fiercely greeted by Huntress. They had some good petting time. He fixed dinner for her, and ate his leftover stir fry. Sean's dreams were again all of Ayanna. This time he dreamed he was a tailor, fitting her in a wedding dress to match her beauty. No matter what dress she tried, the white always turned blood red.

Chapter 23

One Way Or Another

Blondie

Ayanna's good mood dissipated as soon as she walked through the door. The tension in the house was palpable. Brandi and Jesús appeared to be in the middle of an argument, and Mortimer was up and about, a rarity on non-club nights.

"What's going on?"

"A werewolf thinks she spotted Godkillers near Brentwood Park," Brandi answered brusquely.

"She thinks she spotted?"

"She glimpsed four men with buzz cuts, silver crosses, and the smell of old blood. She didn't think they looked like Hunters, maybe Hounds, but she didn't want to get close enough to find out."

"Huh. I get that. Silver crosses? Not crucifixes?"

"She said crosses, I assume that's what she saw."

"Maybe it was a bowling team or something?"

"It's possible, but that's why I want to go check it out."

At this point, Jesús interrupted, "And I keep telling her it's a bad idea. She's pregnant right now, and not as agile as she normally is. What if she falls out of a tree and hurts her kittens?"

Brandi rounded on him, "I'll land on my feet! Are you really worried about my kittens when there might be Hounds in the city?"

"I'm just saying it's not safe for you. Mortimer is already listening through the ears of local bats. Let them scout and you stay safe."

"Jesús, have you ever heard the term, 'blind as a bat?' We need eyes on the ground, or better, in the trees. No one is going to notice or care about a cat."

"But, I worry about you."

Ayanna decided to intervene. "Jesús, it's very sweet how you care about Brandi, but she will be fine. I'll drive her down there myself. She can look around, and I'll stay nearby. If she gets in trouble, then those Godkillers will get to meet a Goddess of War."

"Ayanna, you have to be careful," Jesús pleaded. "You have no believers. You're as vulnerable as a mortal."

"True, and I appreciate your concern. I may be as vulnerable as a mortal, but no mortal has my six thousand years of combat experience. Brandi, go get changed while I go and gear up. Jesús, we're doing this."

Jesús looked crestfallen. With sadness in his voice, he said, "I know. Please be careful. Even if they are Godkillers, they might only be using Portland as a base for raids into coastal or eastern Oregon, or maybe Idaho. Let's not attract any unnecessary attention. Also, if anything happened to either of you, then I would be devastated. You two are my best friends."

"Aw!" Suddenly, Jesús was getting double hugs from the two goddesses. Brandi and Ayanna each gave him a big kiss on the lips, leaving him spluttering and blushing. Ayanna broke the hug and flounced away. Looking back over her shoulder, she said, "I'm totally going to find Mary Mags, and buy her a one-way ticket to Portland!"

Fifteen minutes later, Ayanna was ready. She wore a black

trench coat over a bulletproof vest. A bandolier strapped across her chest held a half-dozen throwing knives. There were two more combat knives sheathed on her hips. More knives were secreted around her body, in her boots and at the small of her back. She carried a sheathed sword she could throw over her shoulder in a pinch.

"Holy fuck, you're hot!" Brandi breathed.

"It is impressive, but Ayanna, please remember, those who live by the sword—"

"Die by the sword. So, I've heard. Don't worry, Jesús, I plan to sit in my car and let Brandi scout. With any luck, no mortal will ever know we're here."

"Come back soon and safely. I'll be waiting here until you get back. If Mortimer's bats hear anything, then I'll pass that information on to you."

"Thanks, Jesús." Ayanna gave him a smile as she and Brandi headed for the door.

When they got in the car, Ayanna plugged in her phone. "Let's assume this werewolf was right about silver crosses. There's a couple of Protestant churches near Brentwood Park. We can start there."

"Good idea."

It was a fairly quick drive to get to the park. Ayanna found a place where she could roll down a window and let Brandi hop out as a cat. She whispered, "Be careful."

The next few hours were tense as Ayanna waited and listened.

I hope there are no coyotes in the area, as that would be very bad for Brandi. She could easily survive a coyote attack by turning into a lioness, but a brawl between a coyote and a lioness would attract a lot of unwanted attention.

Ayanna was startled when Brandi hopped through the open

car window, into her lap, and then into the passenger seat. "Let's go," Brandi said. Ayanna started the car and they headed home.

"So..."

"Let's wait until we get home, all right? That way we can fill everyone in."

"Sounds good. Why do you smell like cat sex?"

"It's not my fault every tom in the neighborhood wants a piece of this. Besides, while Loki was having his way with me, I got the info we needed."

"Loki? As in..."

"Nah, not that one, although he's pretty good in the sack. Or she. Gotta love shapeshifters. Anyway, this was just a normal cat whose humans liked the name. Definitely would have preferred banging the god, though. Did I tell you about the month we spent together in Constantinople? It was so hot. The city and the sex..." Ayanna listened to Brandi's bawdy tales with lecherous interest as she drove them home.

Brandi had barely recounted the first day of her debauched month by the time they got home. Once there, they sat down with Jesús to go over what Brandi had found out. "I can confirm, they are a Pentecostal Hound squad. From what I could see and hear, they are in Portland because of a tip that you're here." She pointed at Jesús before continuing, "Thankfully, these dimwits don't seem to have a clue about what you are doing or even what you look like."

Jesús considered this information. "How did anyone know I'm here? I haven't been doing anything likely to draw attention."

"Well, you did heal Ayanna's boyfriend."

"He's not my boyfriend!" Brandi and Jesús stared at her dubiously. "He's not... Anyway, Sean's almost certainly Catholic, so he wouldn't have told Pentecostals."

"What makes you so sure he's Catholic?"

"Because he always feels guilty about something, and no one does guilt like the Catholics."

Jesús shrugged and said, "You're not wrong, at least among Christians. Do you think we're in danger?"

"There's a Hound squad in the city, so yes. Plus, they may attract competition, which would be bad. Based on what I observed, they don't seem to be looking for a Mexican stock clerk named Jesús, so we're probably fine if you keep your head down."

"I will. We should probably get the word out to be careful in Southeast Portland for a bit, particularly around Brentwood Park."

"Yeah, don't need Hounds running into someone by accident."

Ayanna chimed in, "I'm on early shift tomorrow, but I'll run the register and pass the word to any of our people I might see. I'll try to subtly ask Sean if he has told anyone about Jesús' healing ointment."

"*Ah ha.* You *are* seeing him again," Brandi squealed triumphantly.

"We're meeting up to play Dungeons and Dragons tomorrow."

"Hold me, Jesús! My best friend is turning into a nerd. What happens if she doesn't want to go out trolling for dick anymore? Please, Ayanna, don't make me take Jesús along as my co-pilot."

"Wingman, Brandi. Not co-pilot."

"Well, I want him to be my co-pilot so he can cum in my *cockpit!*" Brandi and Ayanna collapsed in laughter at her raunchy pun while Jesús just shook his head at their antics. "Seriously, though," Brandi continued once she caught her breath, "don't make me take Jesús as my wingman. I'll never get laid."

Jesús ignored her, saying, "Ayanna, it's good to know you and Sean are getting along again. I think you two will be good for each other."

"See! Imagine trying to pick up a couple of studs and having that kind of commentary." All three of them laughed.

Chapter 24

Tease Me Please Me

Scorpions

Sean was very pleased to wake up Thursday to a text from Ayanna stating that she was on the early shift and would be able to meet him for D&D in the afternoon. After feeding Huntress, he decided to walk over to Brandi's Bitchin' Brews for coffee and one of their new breakfast sandwiches. The line wasn't too long and moved quickly. Ayanna's smile deepened when she saw him in line, and she gave him a nod.

Eventually, it was his turn. "Good morning, Ayanna. I'd like a breakfast sandwich with egg and bacon, and, uh…"

"Let's get you a mocha. How about some pepper jack on that sandwich?"

"Ah, sure. I've never had a mocha before."

"You'll like it. Trust me."

"I trust you. You haven't led me astray yet."

"We'll see about that!" Ayanna gave him a suggestive wink and turned to her voluptuous, fire-haired co-worker. Sean observed a brief conversation between the two before Ayanna returned. "Okay, I've got your name for your order. Just tap or insert here to pay, and we'll call you in a couple minutes."

Sean did as instructed and walked to the pick-up window. Normally, he might have checked his phone, but instead, he just watched Ayanna. She had an effortless way of interacting with each customer, always smiling genuinely, putting them at ease. Ayanna danced with grace and purpose, subtly teasing and titillating the customers with provocative looks at her bikini-strapped breasts, but never crossing a line into crass. She was amazing.

His reverie was broken when someone called out, "Order for Super Stud Sean! I've got a mocha, and an egg, bacon, and pepper jack sandwich for Super Stud Sean!" Sean saw Ayanna's co-worker holding his order with a giddy grin. He blushed as he went to take it from her.

"Um, that wasn't the name I gave."

"That's all right, sugar. It's just the name on the order. I'm Annabelle, and it seems like we'll be having a double date tomorrow night—*Super Stud.*" She gave him an exaggerated wink and then stood up in such a way her bouncing bosom brought her bikini almost to its breaking point. There was an almost audible sigh of disappointment from those in line when the fabric held.

Sean looked at Ayanna and silently mouthed, "Date?" She responded with a wink and a slight smile. He remembered her smile well from their day in the Garden, and he smiled back.

He could have left, but instead Sean stayed to watch for a bit while he ate his breakfast sandwich. Before taking the first bite, he looked dubiously at the molten pepper jack oozing from the edges of the sandwich. As he chewed his first bite, he savored the crusty and clearly freshly-baked bagel, the crispy and salty bacon, the mild, almost buttery taste of the scrambled egg, and the tangy spiciness of the pepper jack. It was glorious.

His sandwich, along with the delicious bittersweet mocha, was probably the best breakfast Sean had ever had. Previously, Sean had eaten eggs, bacon, and toast, but that was a poor cousin to this delicacy. Also, like most Americans, Sean was at least a bit of a coffee addict, but the mocha was a step beyond. Once again, Ayanna had opened his eyes and led him into a new world of experience.

Sean used his walk back to check out a couple of potentially suspect businesses, but closer inspection indicated they were purely mundane, if a bit eccentric. More and more, his being stationed in Portland to identify potential supernatural activity seemed to be a bust, and yet, he wasn't disappointed by this. Next Thursday, there was something called a "secret roller disco," which didn't seem very secret as it had a social media presence, but he wondered if he should ask Ayanna to go with him when he investigated.

Once home, he sat down to work, after which the day seemed to drag. The only thing he really wanted to do was play D&D with Ayanna, or honestly just spend time with Ayanna. Every minute between now and then seemed to drag on endlessly. After an interminable slog, his day finally came to a blessed end. Ayanna asked to meet him at the cart before the meetup, to which he readily agreed. Sean arrived a bit early and found Ayanna already there, chatting with the pretty brunette working the cart.

"Hi, Sean, come meet Krystal. Krystal, this is my... This is Sean. Sean, this is Krystal."

I'm your what? Did she almost say friend? Boyfriend? Acquaintance?

They exchanged greetings, then Ayanna asked Sean, "Do you want anything to drink? Tea? Or something else?"

"Ah, something else this time."

"Cool. Krystal, can you whip up two hot chocolates for us?"

"Wow, are you sure you two nerds can handle the hard stuff?"

Ayanna laughed. "Yeah, I think we can, right?"

Sean stumbled out an, "Uh, yeah," as Ayanna wrapped an arm around his waist.

"Oh, my god! You two are so cute. Y'all have fun playing with your dice tonight."

"Yeah, we will. You'll blow on my dice for luck, right, Sean?"

"Uh, of course."

"Who knows, maybe you'll roll a natural twenty tonight, and then I'll blow on your dice." Ayanna giggled and waggled her eyebrows suggestively at him.

Sean really wanted to say something, but he found he was having a hard time breathing. He was having a hard time thinking as well. Sean was saved when Krystal returned with two cups of hot chocolate. Krystal gave them a smile along with their drinks and wished them a good night. Ayanna let go of his waist and instead took his hand as they walked toward the game meetup, sipping their drinks. Sean released her hand when they arrived so he could open the door, but she quickly reclaimed it once they were inside. He felt like everyone was looking at them, probably wondering what she was doing with him. He was doing his best to not wonder that, too.

He had his character sheet he had used the previous week, and got himself situated at the table. While he was settling in, Ayanna browsed around and purchased a set of dice and a chain-mail dice bag.

"Sean, do you have your own dice?"

"Uh, no."

"Come here. Let's find you a lucky set."

"Um, sure. What did you get?"

She opened up the bag and showed him a set of hot pink dice.

"Wow, those are pretty."

She batted her eyelashes at him. "I'm glad you think so."

They perused the options, each of them pointing at various options and critiquing the possibilities. As game time approached, Ayanna steered him to a set of bronze metallic dice with rune-inspired numerals. "These are your dice."

"I dunno. Those are pretty pricey."

"Get them," she purred. "Trust me. I know these are perfect for you."

"Uh, sure. You still haven't steered me wrong."

"Yet!" Her eyes twinkled. She turned to the clerk. "He'll take these dice. Oh, and that fuzzy dice bag as well!"

"Um..."

Ayanna leaned in and he could feel her breath in his ear as she whispered, "I like a man with a fuzzy sack full of heavy dice."

Sean's brain stopped working again. Before he could stop himself, he whispered back, "You can hold them any time you want." He was horrified that he'd just said something like that to a woman.

To Sean's immense surprise, Ayanna giggled and smiled coquettishly. "What kind of a girl do you think I am?" she asked with glee in her voice.

"Uh." Sean struggled with words.

She leaned in again, now cheek-to-cheek. Her lips brushed against his ear as she whispered again, "If those dice are as lucky as I think, then maybe I'll take you up on your offer."

The clerk coughed delicately, saving Sean from complete and total brain lock.

"Oh, right! I gotta pay for this."

"See you at the table... sweetie," Ayanna said as she dragged her fingertips down his arm, leaving trails of incandescent fire on his skin.

Is this actually happening? Please don't let this be a dream.

He wasn't sure whom that prayer was directed to, but it definitely wasn't directed to any deity he had ever prayed to before.

When Sean arrived at the table, he found Ayanna already seated between two other players. His seat was across from her. Sean sat down and said, "Since this is your first time here, you'll need... oh."

"I got it." Ayanna had her phone out and was copying information onto a character sheet in a precise hand, taking up minimal room on the sheet while still being easily readable. "Meet Onyxia, a tiefling paladin."

One of the other players spoke up, saying, "Uh, I was going to play a—"

His friend elbowed him in the side and said, "Shut up, Gene. You're playing a cleric now."

The Dungeon Master got them going shortly thereafter. For about ninety minutes, they progressed through the premade adventure. Players at most nearby tables were doing the same, although a couple of tables with non-beginners were in a different adventure.

They were now at a climactic battle, their characters wounded and tired. The foe's henchmen fell one by one, but each victory drained the party's resources further. Finally, only the penultimate villain of the adventure was left, and everything hung on this one final round of combat. Sean's barbarian had the next attack in the initiative order, right before the villain. Success or failure hinged upon this next roll.

"*Stop.* Let me blow on your dice, for luck." Ayanna half stood and leaned over the table. Sean cupped the twenty-sided die in his hands and held it out to her. Her breath was warm and humid as she pursed her lips and blew. She placed her hands around his, and held them as she gently kissed his closed fingers. "Now roll."

Sean did, and his twenty-sided die bounced across the table, coming to a stop and teetering briefly. For an instant, the result hung in the balance between a '7' and disaster or a '20' and victory, then the die fell over and the table erupted in cheers. The Dungeon Master coughed and said, "You still have to roll damage, but that is a critical hit."

Once the damage was tallied, the day was saved and the party emerged victorious, even though the cleric was still grumbling about how unfair it was that they weren't a paladin.

As they left, Ayanna once again took Sean's hand. "You wanna get dumplings?"

"I've never had dumplings before."

"Let's fix that, then!"

Chapter 25

Kiss

Prince

Ayanna watched Sean's face as he dug into the first dumpling of his life. She enjoyed the progression of his expressions as they went from dubious to intrigued to delighted.

This is fun. Sean is really cute. And he's really good company. I like this. A lot. He's so much fun to tease, too.

Ayanna pensively chewed her own dumpling, meditating on her last thought.

Am I teasing him, or am I serious about this? Maybe I am serious about this... Oh... shit... I don't just want to ride him like a horse, do I? I want more than that.

"Hey, Sean. Are you enjoying the dumplings?"

Of course she asked the question immediately after he took a big bite, so the response was a vigorous nod and a muffled noise which sounded vaguely like, "Yes."

"I wanted to say sorry about how I acted earlier tonight. I shouldn't have teased you like I did. That was unfair to you, and I shouldn't have done it."

"What do you mean?"

"I'm really enjoying spending time with you again, and like

I've said before, I appreciate how you are trying to change and grow. I was talking to Jesús about how amazing that is, and then of course he asked me what I'm going to do to change and grow."

"Ayanna, you don't need to change. You're already incredible."

"I really appreciate that, but as annoying as it is to admit, Jesús was right. Look, Sean... you're very special. You seem to like me for me, and not just because you think I'd be a pretty trophy for you."

"You're definitely not a trophy." Sean nodded his head vigorously.

"Also, I mean, we haven't talked about this really, but I'm assuming when you mentioned you don't have much experience with women, that included sex. Am I right?"

Sean looked mortified as he nodded his head in silent assent.

"There's nothing wrong with virginity. Nothing to be ashamed of. I like that about you."

"That I'm inexperienced?"

"You are willing to learn and are open to new things. Like with the dumplings tonight, or going to play D&D with me. Let me tell you something. There are plenty of people who would have never considered a pen and paper role-playing game to be a good choice for a date, especially an early date."

Sean looked less somber. "Are we on a date now?"

"I want to talk to you about it. I would like to consider this a date, but only if you are comfortable."

"Yes, of course." Sean had flipped from mortified to elated. "Who wouldn't be?"

"I'm sure plenty of people wouldn't be, and that's fine. Okay, so this is a date. And tomorrow night, we'll have a double date with Annabelle and Tanya, right?"

"Yeah, it should be fun."

Ayanna laughed. "I think so, too."

"Is this what you mean by changing and growing? Dating a... dating a virgin?"

"Sort of... There was a time in my life when, um, when I would have jumped on that, ah, figuratively speaking. I would have twisted you around my finger, taken advantage of your innocence, and ruined you for life."

"That doesn't sound so bad. Well—except the ruining part."

"It is. It's selfish and manipulative. It certainly doesn't benefit the other person—discarding them like trash once you've wrung as much pleasure as you want out of them."

Sean looked shocked at this revelation. Lust and revulsion warred on his face.

Ayanna continued, "That's not what I want for you. For us. Like you, I want to be different. I want to be better. We both deserve better."

"Why are you telling me this?"

Because for some insane reason, I'm taking relationship advice from the two-thousand-year-old virgin.

"Because you deserve to know. When I was teasing you earlier, I was leading us toward a bad path."

"I kinda liked it, though."

"So did I. I enjoy teasing and flirting with you."

"I like it, too, although I'm a bit embarrassed about it, and kinda nervous."

"Thank you for being honest. We should have fun dating, and flirting is part of that, but I don't want to make you uncomfortable."

"Ayanna, can I admit something to you?"

"Of course."

"When you were flirting at the store, I felt... Everyone was looking at you and you were with me. The most beautiful woman in Portland, and you were flirting with me, and everyone could see, and I felt good. I felt like another person."

"Did you feel like you were better than everyone else?"

"No, not superior. I felt grateful... happy... joyous."

"That's good, Sean."

"Ayanna, why me?"

She chewed a dumpling to buy herself some time and then chased the dumpling with a drink to stall a little more. "You pissed me off so much with your white knight bullshit on Sunday. We were having a really nice time and then you pulled that shit. I was fucking done with you, but somehow I didn't want to be. Then you show up on Tuesday and you apologize, tell me you're learning, and I'm worth it. *I'm worth it.* No lover has ever told me that."

"Really?"

"Yeah." She sighed. "Sean, you are putting in the work, so I'm going to put in the work, because I think you are also worth it. And, I like you a lot."

"I like you, too, Ayanna. You challenge me, push me, and I really enjoy spending time with you. Every day, I am excited at the prospect of something new with you."

"Well, we've done some new things tonight, but I have one more thing in mind."

"What?"

Ayanna scooted around the little table they were sharing at the food cart pod until she was seated next to him. "Sean, if this makes you uncomfortable or is too much too fast, then you can be honest. I won't be offended, I promise." Ayanna leaned in close, her body twisting as she reached over to lightly touch his cheek. His skin felt hot under her fingertips, and she exerted a light touch, gently pulling him toward her. Ayanna closed her eyes, and her mouth hovered mere millimeters from his. All he had to do was follow her gentle pull, and he did. Ayanna felt Sean's lips touch hers, and she rejoiced.

Chapter 26

Like A Virgin

Madonna

In that moment, Sean's fears, anxieties, and misgivings were temporarily banished as his entire being focused on where his lips touched hers. Ayanna's lips were warm, pliable, soft, and tasted faintly of dumplings and sauce. He wanted this moment to last forever, but it did end. Sean felt her pulling away and he watched her eyes open as the kiss faded. All he could see of Ayanna was her face, framed by waves of dark hair, her eyes shining with delight, and her mouth slowly forming into a smile.

"Are you okay we kissed?" she asked.

"Yes, definitely. Was it good? I mean, good for you?"

"It was, Sean. I thought it was perfect. Was it good for you, too?"

"It was. Are you sure it was good for you? I feel like I'm bad at this, and I'm sure I'll get better with practice." Sean's insecurities were racing back. He felt a touch on his hand. Sean looked down at her hand on top of his.

"Hey, when I said it was perfect, I really meant it." Her smile broadened. "But just because it was perfect doesn't mean I don't want to practice with you."

"Ayanna, since we both want this to be a date, then does this mean I'm your boyfriend now?"

"Wow, you are keen to define the relationship, aren't you?" She paused and smiled before continuing, "Yes, you are officially my boyfriend now. *But.* Just know I'm still a bit stung from Sunday and don't want you to take your new status for granted. Got it?"

"Yes, of course. This is still new."

"I guess that makes me your girlfriend, then."

Sean's heart leapt at the idea of having a girlfriend. He'd had a few first dates in college, but no second dates. This was new territory for him, and now fear and insecurity were stalking him. Sitting next to Ayanna bolstered his confidence, but he knew it wouldn't last forever.

"I need to confess something."

"Go for it."

"You're my first girlfriend. I mean, I've gone on dates before, just never any second dates."

"Well, by my count, this is our third date, so you're improving. Plus, we'll have our fourth date tomorrow." Ayanna dropped her chopsticks and clapped her hands together. "Oh, I get to introduce you as my boyfriend. Hey, are you gonna finish those dumplings?"

Sean saw the predatory gleam in her eyes and covered his remaining dumplings with his hand. "Speaking of improving, maybe we should practice kissing some more."

"Maybe, but only if you stop distracting me with your dumplings."

Eating gave Sean time to think about their conversation prior to the kiss. Ayanna's revelations about her past and how she'd manipulated and hurt people disturbed him. He was already insecure, and he felt jealous of her prior lovers.

How many lovers has she had? What if I bore her? How do I

know she'll be faithful to me? What if I'm just terrible at all of this and she decides I'm not worth it?

As he chewed his last dumpling, Ayanna said, "You look pensive. Is everything all right?"

Once Sean swallowed his final bite, he responded carefully, "I appreciate you being honest about your past. I feel I should be honest in return. It really bothers me that you manipulated and hurt people. It worries me as well—you know, about us and our future. Then again, this is something you confessed to me, so maybe it bothers you, too. Since I'm saying all of this, I might as well confess that I'm also somewhat jealous, too. I don't like that about myself."

"Thank you for your honesty. Yes, I am bothered by how I mistreated people in the past, and I want to be better. Like I said, you deserve to be treated better than that. Going forward, we should be as honest as we can be with each other."

"I agree."

"The other important thing is being comfortable with the word no. As in, different forms of no. Saying, 'I'm not comfortable' or 'can we stop' is another way to say no or not right now. Your feelings are just as valid as mine, and as we go forward, either one of us might need to slow or stop things."

"Do you mean my virginity?"

"That's definitely part of it. As you said, I'm your first girl-friend. We may hit a point where one of us isn't comfortable, which is perfectly acceptable. I mean, do you want to lose your virginity?"

This definitely wasn't where Sean had thought this conversa-tion would go. He felt blood rushing to his face, and his groin. "Here?"

"No, definitely not here." Ayanna laughed, then became serious again. "I guess I meant the question in a general sense, but

I was also wondering if you're planning on saving yourself until marriage or if it just hasn't, um, come up before."

The double entendre there was not helping Sean's blood flow issues. "I always thought about waiting until marriage, but now I'm thirty-one, and I just want to get it over with." His eyes and mouth widened in surprise. "Wow... That sounds bad."

Ayanna touched his hand to comfort him. "I get it. It seemed like a good idea once upon a time, and now it feels like a burden, but you still want it to have meaning or else you would have hired a professional to take care of the problem."

"Oh—that's about it, although I feel like hiring a... prostitute would be weird. Like, how would I even do that?"

"Actually—you know what, never mind. So, I'm going to guess you would like to lose your virginity with me, but my past both makes you nervous and also jealous."

"And anxious as well. I also don't want to be bad at it. I want to take care of your needs." Sean's palms were sweating.

Ayanna smiled at him. "If you feel anxious about anything, just say something, all right?"

"I will, I promise," Sean responded earnestly.

"Good."

"Since we're talking about promises, I seem to recall a promise of a kiss once the dumplings were gone." His voice was optimistic.

"That's right. Just one kiss, though. I was up very early this morning, and you have a cat to feed."

Sean leaned toward Ayanna, pursing his lips. He watched Ayanna smile and reciprocate, leaning toward him to bring her lips to his. Once again lost in the moment, Sean kissed her for as long as he could, but eventually he needed to breathe.

"Mm," Ayanna purred. "I like practicing kissing with you. Now, though, I really do need to get home, and so do you."

"I wish you weren't right. We could practice more tomorrow," he added hopefully.

"Yes, we can."

They parted soon after, and Sean went home. Huntress greeted him at the door by happily rubbing against his leg.

"Huntress, you'll never believe it, but Ayanna called me her boyfriend tonight." Huntress responded to this epic news by falling over and rolling on the carpet. "We kissed tonight, too. It was amazing." Huntress scootched herself forward on the carpet and then rolled over again. Getting the hint, Sean squatted down and scratched her head and butt. "I know. This is very exciting news. I would scootch and roll on the carpet, too, if I could. Okay, let's feed you now."

Sean struggled to get to the kitchen due to the feline leg weave. He got a reprieve once he made it to her bowl. Huntress jumped onto the counter as Sean was opening a can of food for her. "Chicken stew for you tonight. Doesn't that sound delicious? I had dumplings tonight. Those were delicious, too. You know, it would be easier to get this in your bowl if your head wasn't in the way. I could taste the dumplings on Ayanna's lips when we kissed. You don't care. You just want your dinner."

As he watched Huntress gobble down her dinner, he kept talking to her. Sean needed to talk to someone, and Huntress was at least a good listener.

Chapter 27

Venus

Bananarama

The door opened before Ayanna could get her keys out, and Jesús exited, dressed for work. He held the door for her as she approached. "Hi, Ayanna. Dungeons and Dragons with Sean must have gone very well then, because I sense a certain glow about you. And the smell of dumplings."

She smiled. "It went really well. I really hate this about you, but you were right. I do need to change and grow. I told him about my past, I mean, not all of it, of course. I told him how I manipulated and hurt people, and I don't want to do that with him. I want to be better because he is worth it."

Jesús mostly succeeded in not looking smug. "That's great to hear. I suppose this means you'll be seeing him again."

"Yes, we have a double date tomorrow with Annabelle and Tanya. That will be a good opportunity to see how much he has really grown."

"Good plan. But that's not all that happened tonight, is it?"

"Seriously, how do you know this stuff? You never used to care who I dated or fucked, and now I kiss Sean and you can just tell."

"You did what?" Brandi came flying to the door, hastily fastening a robe around her pregnant belly.

"Ayanna kissed Sean."

"I heard. My hearing is really good. I'm just shocked, that's all."

"Twice."

"You kissed him twice? We need to talk. Jesús, don't you have to go to work?"

"Of course, you two enjoy your girl talk."

Ayanna looked at Brandi quizzically. "Is he allowed to smirk?"

Brandi pulled Ayanna inside and shut the door behind them. "Probably. Sometimes it drives me crazy how incredibly nice Jesús is. He's just so accepting and tolerant."

"That's because the other Jesus attracts all the negative qualities. We get to live with the super nice one while his evil twin hunts us." Ayanna sighed dramatically. "I guess you want to know how my date went."

"Yes, *nerd*. Dungeons and Dragons followed by dumplings and face sucking. You might as well wear glasses and put your hair in a ponytail now, Laney Boggs."

"Um, it's been a while, but you might be mixing up movies."

"Ugh, shut up and tell me about your date."

"Wait, am I supposed to shut up, or tell you—"

"Ayanna, if you don't tell me about your date, I swear when I have these kittens, I will let them rampage in your closet."

Ayanna laughed, holding up her hands in mock surrender. "Okay, I'm sorry. Don't unleash the kittens on me. We met at the cart for drinks beforehand and then walked to the game store. I bought some dice and a chainmail dice bag. Did I mention I ordered a chainmail bikini from Brigid?"

"Ayanna, the fury of the kittens awaits," Brandi threatened.

"Sorry, where was I? Oh, then I got him to buy some dice and flirted with him."

"Flirted how?"

"I told him I liked a man with a heavy set of dice in his fuzzy bag, but I said it in a super sexy way. Don't laugh. When I did it, it was *really* hot. Anyway, then he said I could hold it anytime I wanted to." Ayanna was trying to appear nonchalant about it all.

"Wait. Super dork dropped that line on you? Was he super sexy like you when he said it?"

"I might have gotten a bit wet, actually. Brandi, he's... Okay, he's a nerd, but he's a really cute nerd, and I like him a lot. I'll admit he wasn't super sexy when he flirted, but I actually preferred that. He was genuine, which made it really attractive. If some arrogant prick like Apollo had pulled that line on me, then I would have bitch-slapped his ass back all the way back to Delos. Anyway, so then we played for a while and it was so much fun. We got into this huge boss fight at the end and Sean's character had to get a hit to give us a chance. So, I blew on his dice, kissed his hands, and then he rolled a natural twenty."

"Pretend I don't speak nerd." Brandi said sarcastically.

"A natural twenty means you automatically hit and do critical damage. He won us the fight on that roll, and we all cheered."

"I can't believe we used to go to clubs and pick up the hottest people there and now you're fighting imaginary monsters with your boyfriend."

"Aw, it's okay, Brandi. I'll still be your wing-woman whenever Jesús isn't available."

"It's a good thing I like you, Ayanna. All right, hurry this story up. I have a bunch of preggo chasers coming over to rail me in about ten minutes."

"You are always horny, but pregnancy really sends you into overdrive, doesn't it? Anyway, back to my night. We went out for dumplings at that food cart pod you and I went to fairly recently. We had dumplings and a good conversation and then I kissed him. The second time, he kissed me."

"Was he good?"

Ayanna smiled wistfully. "Yeah, he was really good. I think he was too shocked to overthink it, which worked out well. I mean, he's inexperienced, so he'll get better, which is great for me."

"So, you're going to mold him, deflower him, and then dump him?"

"No, I'm being a better person. Jesús was right. I need to change and grow. I'm going to treat Sean like a real boyfriend. He is inexperienced, but I'm not rushing him into sex. He needs to be comfortable, and we're going to talk and be okay with consent. It's time to be a Love Goddess again, not a date 'em and dump 'em goddess."

"Wow. I'm really impressed, Ayanna. I give you a lot of shit because we're friends, but underneath all of that, I am happy for you. It's so nice he makes you happy. You deserve that. Jesús was right. You do have a certain glow about you."

"You have a certain glow about you as well."

"That's because I'm pregnant and with any luck, at least three guys are going to be here really soon to drown my raging hormones—there's the doorbell. Make yourself scarce and grab some earplugs. Unless you want one of these guys for yourself."

"Ah, thanks for the offer, but I think I'll be passing on random hook-ups for a bit." Ayanna headed upstairs to her room where she put on noise-canceling headphones and loud music.

In the morning, Ayanna was up just before Jesús came home. She met him with a glass of water as he entered. "Thank you. I appreciate the water, but I am wondering why you are doing this for me."

"I could tell you it's just what thoughtful housemates do, but we both know that would be a lie. I want to talk to you."

"Of course. What would you like to talk about?"

"Do you have any new information on the Hound squad that's searching for you?"

"So far, nothing. They are out and about during the day, which makes them difficult to track. At night, they are buttoned up in their safehouse, at least so far. There's no indication they have found any real evidence of my presence here in Portland. That isn't what you really want to talk about, is it?"

"No, it isn't. I want to know why you are suddenly so interested in my love life. Like I said last night, you haven't paid any attention before, even on the rare occasions when I've brought someone home."

"Well, you said it yourself. You haven't had a love life until now. You definitely have had a very long and extensive catalog of sexual encounters, but you didn't really have feelings for any of them. You might as well have been using your vast stockpile of sex toys for all the difference it made emotionally."

"I'm not sure if I'm supposed to be insulted; you're insinuating I'm a slut."

Jesús shrugged. "I'm not judging you."

"Wait, are you saying you're interested in my relationship with Sean because you think I love him?"

"Ayanna... Inanna, is love such a strange concept for you? You are, after all, a Goddess of Love. I am also a God of Love, although my purview is, shall we say, more emotional and spiritual than physical."

"Of course it's a strange concept for me." Ayanna was struggling to keep her temper in check. "He's a mortal, and I haven't been in love with a mortal since before Cyrus took Babylon." She grunted angrily, "It probably wasn't love anyway, just something my worshippers cooked up. I haven't loved *anyone* since Athena, and our relationship ended well over a millennium ago. Why would you think this is any different?"

"I don't mean to upset you. I know he loves you, although he has not made that discovery himself."

"What the—how could you possibly know that?"

"I told you, I am a God of Love, and Sean is one of mine. My brother has deep hooks in him, but those hooks do not reach his heart. Because of my connection with Sean, I can see a bit into his mind, at least for now."

Ayanna felt confused. "For now? What do you mean by that?"

"I'm losing my connection with him."

"To the other Jesus?"

"No, that would be awful. I'm losing him to you."

"I... I don't want Sean to be a worshiper."

"You want him to be your lover."

"No... well, yes." Ayanna glared at Jesús. "You really make things difficult sometimes. He's my boyfriend and—wow, you are the first person I've said that to, besides Sean, of course. I *like* having him as my boyfriend. I like going on dates with him and discovering new foods and experiences with him. After six thousand years, life gets stale. Being a part of Sean's discovery of new things makes me feel younger. I want to be his *girlfriend*, not his goddess. And yes, I do want to make love to him, but again only as his lover and not as his deity."

"Why can't you be both?" Jesús raised a hand before Ayanna responded. "Wait—hear me out. Remember my idea about reinventing yourself? This is your chance. Your previous nature is long lost to history. Only a handful of scholars today debate what your rites were, what your story was—in other words, who you are. None of those scholars worship you. Let's say you have one worshiper. One true believer. His beliefs shape who you are, but because you are part of this as well, then you will be recreating yourself."

"Are you suggesting I manipulate him?"

"No. Far from it, actually. Because then that also becomes who you are. Instead, be the person you want to be. Let him see the beautiful new you blossom in all of her glory. Then maybe that is who you will be. Ayanna, Goddess of Love and Tea."

"What do you mean, maybe? You have no idea if this insane idea of yours will work, do you?"

"I confess that I am speculating. You do realize how special your situation is, don't you? There are no groups of mortals actively trying to restore your worship. There are no Christian saints to corrupt people's ideas of you. To the best of my knowledge, you are unique."

"Wow. That really is fascinating—and completely crazy. I'm not sure if I like the idea of reinventing myself or if I'm terrified of it. Both, probably." Ayanna shuddered as she remembered her discussion with Sean. "Oh, no... I told Sean about manipulating and hurting people, and he really didn't like that."

Jesús smiled. "Which could be a good thing. Honesty is powerful. You want to be better, and you are openly working to improve yourself. That's part of your story now. Another thing to consider is that by admitting this to Sean, you made yourself vulnerable. Hiding behind lies and silence is easy and weak. It takes incredible strength to admit your mistakes, to decide to show your vulnerability, and then address your faults head on. You are stronger than you think when you admit weakness."

"How do you come up with this stuff? It makes sense, but..."

"Look at me, Ayanna, and then consider the other Jesus. I feed the hungry, heal the sick, turn the other cheek. He tells the hungry to get a job and the sick to suck it up, and he delights in the pain and blood caused by those who worship him. I am kind, and far too many people call that weak. He is infinitely cruel, and the same people see cruelty as strength. They are wrong. Cruelty is easy, and it comes from weakness—fear, ignorance, and insecurity. Kindness requires strength, love, wisdom, and empathy. Once, long ago, as a Goddess of Love and War, you embodied both cruelty and kindness."

"Even if this crazy idea of yours works, I'm not giving up on war. I respect your dedication to peace. Even more now, actually. But sometimes the bad guys don't allow pacificism to be a realistic option. Plus, if I'm being honest, I fucking *love* punching Nazis."

Jesús sighed. "As much as you get on my case for asking tough questions, you can sometimes bring up your own."

Ayanna grinned at Jesús. "Oh, I like knowing you are jealous of my Nazi-punching skills. Pacifists should get a free pass on punching Nazis."

"I'm so glad that pleases you," he said, his voice dripping with sarcasm.

"Thank you for talking with me. I need to get ready for work. And you just got home from work." Ayanna gave Jesús a friendly hug.

"You're welcome. Any time, and have a good day. And a good date tonight."

Chapter 28

Guilty As Sin?

Taylor Swift

Business was brisk when Ayanna arrived at Brandi's Bitchin' Brews, but Annabelle and Enrique were keeping the queue moving along. Ayanna jumped in a few minutes before the official start of her shift to help them out. She and Enrique prepared the drinks and food in a seamless dance while Annabelle took orders. Ayanna had broken a sweat before the morning rush was through. After the rush, Ayanna gave Annabelle a break while she and Enrique cleaned up and served the stragglers.

She had just finished serving one of those latecomers when a dark van pulled up across the street. Three men got out while the driver remained inside. All three men sported buzz cuts and wore silver crosses. *Hounds.*

"What can I do for you guys?"

"We're looking for Jesús Sanchez."

"There's no Jesús Sanchez here, but maybe you can order something that's actually on the menu. Y'all look like you could use some coffee."

"Who's the guy in there with you?"

"That's Enrique. He's also not on the menu."

"We'd like to see some identification."

"I have a nametag right here. It says Ayanna. We tried putting a nametag on Enrique's little speedo, but it kept poking his huge dick, so you'll just have to trust me. Now, you three, though... You roll up here like cops, but you aren't showing us your identification, which makes me think maybe you're a bunch of militia types who think anyone without pale skin is here to steal your job and your Social Security check."

"Look, ma'am, we just want to know that guy's name."

Ayanna glowered at the insolent idiot. "Don't 'ma'am' me. I've already told you his name is Enrique. I'll add that you're definitely *not* his type. Feel free to order coffee, though. *To go.*"

"Just let us see—"

"Listen up, shithead. Unless I see a badge, you aren't seeing anything. Now, you can show me a badge, you can buy a drink, or you can get the *fuck* out of here. Those are your choices."

"Or what?" His tone was arrogant.

Ayanna gave him her best cheerfully evil grin. "Or we'll beat your asses."

"We?"

"Yeah, 'we.' I mean, I could do it myself, but I'm sure Enrique's boyfriend would love to help." She gestured behind the trio to where Aiden was looming. "And look, he brought friends." The six mechanics from the auto shop were all holding tire irons in their fists, their grease-stained clothing emphasizing that they weren't afraid of some dirty work. The Hounds, outnumbered and flustered, beat a hasty retreat to their vehicle and took off. Ayanna wrote the license plate number down, just in case.

"Thanks for showing up, y'all. Drinks are on the house."

"No problem," Aiden rumbled. "Enrique texted me you might need help and the rest of the shop came along in case I needed backup."

"Thank you again. We appreciate it. Annabelle is coming

back, so give me your drink order, and then go and let Enrique give you a big thank you kiss."

She took Aiden's order along with the rest of the crew from the body shop. Annabelle had called the police, who showed up twenty minutes later, and Ayanna provided them with a summary of the incident, descriptions of the men, and their license plate number. She didn't think the cops would actually do anything, but at least there was a written record of the incident. The patrolman handed Ayanna a business card at the end, telling her to call him if she remembered anything else. He added a phone number on the back, telling her it was his personal cell, just in case she needed anything in the future, *anything at all*. She would have felt better about his offer if his eyes had ever managed to go above her collarbone. The cops hung around for a few minutes, mostly staring at her and Annabelle's breasts before they started toward their car.

Annabelle and Ayanna watched them drive off before returning to work. Annabelle said, "That was weird. Sorry, I thought you were in trouble, so I called the cops."

"What was weird? The three shitweasels badgering Enrique, the cops who kept staring at our tits, or just the whole thing?"

"The whole thing. Why did those guys think someone named Jesús worked here?"

"No idea, but I'm definitely going to have to tell Brandi about this. The police, though— that was irritating."

"Do you think they'll do anything?"

"No. They'll most likely assume we're prostitutes and that those guys were just disgruntled customers, so this report will go to the bottom of the pile. All they see is our tits and asses hanging out, and they figure we're worthless whores."

"That sucks."

"Come here and give me a hug. We could both use it."

Ayanna sent texts to Brandi and Jesús to tell them what

happened. Only Brandi responded, as Jesús was likely asleep. Ayanna soothed Brandi's anger, assuring her everything was fine.

After the incident with the Hounds, the rest of the day was much easier. Ayanna was restocking right before her break when she heard Annabelle call out, "Hi, Sean." Ayanna heard Enrique's snicker as she knocked over a stack of lids in her rush toward the window.

"Hi, Sean! Wait right there." She wheeled toward the door of the cart. She felt Annabelle smack her on the ass, loud enough that all four of them heard it. Ayanna's cheeks colored as she opened the door and came around the side of the cart. Sean was standing there obediently as she slowed down and sashayed up to him. Ayanna placed her arms over and around his shoulders, and kissed him to within an inch of his life.

When she finally let him come up for air, she heard the sound of clapping from the cart, and saw Annabelle and Enrique cheering them on. Ayanna looked back to a red-faced and gasping Sean. "Sorry about that. I *really* missed you."

When he didn't respond, she added, "I should have asked first, I'm sorry. Was that okay?"

Annabelle chimed in, "Okay? It was so damn hot my bikini bottoms were soaked. I think you broke the poor guy's brain."

Enrique added, "*Muy caliente.*"

"Ignore them. Really, though, are you all right?"

"Hiyanna. I mean, hi, Ayanna. Hiyanna, that's funny." Sean was grinning like an idiot. "The kiss was unexpected, but I really liked it."

"You're right, Annabelle. I broke his brain. Hey, can you two stop ogling us and maybe get Sean some restorative energy tea. Ginseng and ginger would work. I'm going on my break."

Spinning back to Sean, Ayanna said, "I liked it, too. Sean, sweetie. Let's go and sit down in my car." She gently led him over to her car, opened the back hatch, and helped him sit. "Let me get your tea for you." She went back to the cart, where Annabelle handed her Sean's ginseng and ginger tea and a lemon tea for her. "Thanks, Annabelle."

"Sorry about earlier." Annabelle said. "I probably shouldn't have said that, even if it was totally true."

"No worries, sweetie. Sean will be fine, eventually." Ayanna winked at her friend. "I'm all wet, too."

Annabelle moaned, "Fuck, that's hot. I'm looking forward to our double date with you two tonight, but first I'm going to text Tanya and tell her to come home early. I am horny as hell right now."

"Get some, girl. I'll be back in thirty minutes, but if Tanya can get off early, then maybe just have Enrique cover for you."

Sean was looking less shocked when she got back to him. After a few drinks of his tea, he seemed capable of rational thought again.

"Is it just me, or was that kiss even better than last night?"

"I definitely think so. I probably should have asked you before I kissed you, though."

"It's fine. More than fine, actually." His idiot grin was back.

"Good. You're early today. I usually don't see you until after five."

"Ah, right. I wanted to talk about something important that's bothering me, but doesn't seem to bother you."

"Oh." Now Ayanna was worried. "What is it?"

Sean's face flushed a deep red. "Sin."

Ayanna realized her facial expression must have betrayed her as she watched Sean recoil.

"Ayanna, I'm sorry. I shouldn't have said anything."

"But you did, and it's obviously important to you or else you wouldn't have brought it up. Honestly, given your... faith and upbringing, this conversation was inevitable. I'm sorry for my reaction. I have some—let's call them challenges—with concepts of sin and morality."

"I guess I'm having some challenges, too. Which is why I wanted to talk with you. I tried talking with Huntress, and while she is a great listener, she's not much help on figuring things out."

Ayanna pictured him discussing sin with a calico cat and laughed. "Okay, go on."

"You know I'm a virgin. I've been saving myself for marriage because that's what I've been taught to do. I've been fine with that for most of my life, until now. Last night, we talked about the possibility of having sex, which is almost certainly a venial sin, but we definitely didn't discuss marriage."

Ayanna snorted.

"Your reaction is what I'm getting at. Are you not concerned about sin? Or going to heaven, or worse, hell? Or don't you believe in an afterlife?"

This is an awkward question. I can't really tell him that my sister, Ereshkigal, presides over the underworld. Well, an underworld. I also shouldn't mention that I died, spent three days in Ereshkigal's realm, was brought back to life, and my faithless husband now resides there in my place. Christians tend to get touchy when you mention how deities dying and being reborn three days later was fairly common back in my day.

"It's complicated. I do believe in an afterlife. I actually think there are a lot of afterlives. You may not know this, but long before Abram left Ur of the Chaldeans, the people there had an afterlife. It was... miserable. Everyone died and spent eternity clothed in feathers, eating clay. Later civilizations did much better. I've always been impressed at just how elaborate the medieval Catholic afterlife was. It's much less fun once they've eliminated Purgatory. Anyway, it's not like there was no concept of right or wrong in ancient Mesopotamia. After all, Hammurabi gave the world the first written code of laws. It's just that everyone ended up in the same place after death."

"Do you know a lot about ancient Mesopotamian religion?"

She raised her shoulders in a quick shrug. "The Epic of Gilgamesh is the world's earliest known literature. Gilgamesh sought eternal life to avoid the misery of the afterlife. Reading it sent me down a bit of a rabbit hole of afterlife study."

"That sounds like an awful fate. So, what you did in life didn't matter?"

"Not really, which was a big flaw. That's why most other civilizations ended up with a binary afterlife choice. Some of it was still pretty stupid. For the Norse, you had to die valiantly in battle to get to Valhalla, which is just dumb for a whole host of reasons."

"Like what?"

"Let's say you are a great warrior, one of the best to ever live, and then you slip on a wet stone after a bath, hit your head, and die. Do you go to Valhalla? Nope, you go to Hel."

Sean chuckled. "Yeah, that is incredibly stupid."

"As much as I despise the innate repression of the Catholics and Orthodox, they did actually set up a fairly decent afterlife, at least in the old days. Major sinners went to hell, minor sinners went to purgatory, and decent people went to heaven. It wasn't ideal, especially the loopholes and corrupt shit like selling indulgences or papal pardons rewarding crusaders."

"What do you mean, loopholes?"

"Baptism, for one. Constantine, the emperor credited with making Christianity the religion of the Roman Empire, was a truly awful person. He went through life betraying and murdering many, including one of his sons, and he had his wife boiled to death. Then, on his deathbed, he was baptized—which wiped away his infinite number of sins. So, that murderer and despot was sent to heaven. Although, I do wonder about that, because

Constantine's baptism was performed by a bishop who was later deemed a heretic."

"That doesn't seem right."

"No, it wasn't. And the system is still horribly flawed. There are all sorts of loopholes which would allow horrible people to get into heaven while condemning good people to hell. I look at all these preachers on television who promise to heal people if their followers send them money—which I know is something Jesus would never do—and then they don't actually heal people because they don't have that power. These assholes somehow are supposed to be in heaven?" Ayanna snorted furiously. "No thanks, I'd rather spend eternity with anyone but those sanctimonious hypocrites."

"Wow... that's a lot."

Poor Sean looks like I hit him with a brick. I'm pretty sure he's never given any real thought to how absurd the idea of heaven and hell or any afterlife is. Now, if I were to ever create an afterlife, I would just make a nice quiet place where decent people could spend eternity. Who counts as decent anyway? Would I even make it? Also, create an afterlife? Ugh, I swear Jesús is getting in my head with all of this reinvention nonsense.

"I don't want to tell you what to believe or what not to believe. Morality is complicated and messy. Humanity has spent thousands of years trying to figure out right and wrong, and it's an ongoing challenge."

"But, God tells us what is right and wrong."

"You mean like the time he told the Israelites to sacrifice every male of a conquered tribe, as well as every non-virgin female, and keep all of the virgin females as rape-slaves? Oh, or how God has rules on how to sell your daughter as a sex slave?"

Sean looked stunned. "Sex slavery is in the Bible?"

"Go read the story of Jacob, where he works for fourteen years to *purchase* two cousins as wives, plus he gets two bonus sex slaves. Think about it. He *purchased* two women at the cost of seven years of labor each." Ayanna shook her head, although she knew Assyrians were no better in their beliefs. "Seriously, you really should read your Bible. Some parts are beautiful and amazing, and others are... let's just say your God was sometimes just as awful as humans too often prove themselves to be. That said, personally, I'm a big fan of Jesus." With a smile, Ayanna added, "The original Jesus, though."

"You're making my head spin."

"Sorry, this might be a bit much."

I managed to do this without telling any lies. I just didn't mention a lot, including the reason I like the original Jesus is because I got to know how good of a person he is. Oh, by the way, he's my housemate and he made us an excellent shrimp scampi.

His expression was bleak. "I really wanted to talk with you about the morality of sex before marriage, and this was way more than I was prepared for. I've really been struggling with the idea of what I should do with you."

"Sean, that's something you'll have to struggle with and decide for yourself. I can't tell you what you should or should not do—what *we* should or should not do. I can tell you I will be willing to listen, to offer advice if you ask, and to support you, no matter what."

"Thank you. I really appreciate that."

"Of course. The other promise I will make, and that I'm going to do my best to keep, is to make sure whatever we do is comfortable and consensual."

"Again, thank you."

"Did you have anything else you wanted to talk about?"

"Not really, you already gave me a ton of food for thought."

"Great. Would you like to make out until the end of my break?"

Chapter 29

Learning To Fly
Pink Floyd

Sean needed to sit for a few minutes once Ayanna's break was over. Between the frenetic kissing and watching her delightful ass as she sashayed back to the cart, his aroused state was very obvious. As it was, Sean was a bit embarrassed to just be sitting there, especially when Enrique exited the cart and proceeded to give him a huge smile and a double thumbs up. Somewhere in the back of his mind, the sixteen-year-old version of himself was screaming something along the lines of, *"Dude, we should have been doing this all along."*

Once he felt capable of walking without a flagpole in his pants, Sean headed for home with his mind abuzz. He didn't actually have much of a conversation with Ayanna. Sean had asked about sin, and that had unleashed a storm from her. It wasn't so much a discussion as a frenzied monologue. She'd clearly put a lot of thought into sin and the afterlife, and Sean realized he really had not. One nice thing about someone just telling you the answers before you even know the questions is you didn't have to spend much effort on thinking. The glaring downside, Sean was just realizing, was that he felt completely unaware of what questions he should have been asking in the first place.

He obviously knew the story of Jacob by heart, but he had never actually thought about it the way Ayanna talked about it. Working for seven years to purchase your wife from her father sounded insane. Then, after being tricked, having to work another seven years to purchase the wife you really wanted was even more insane. The idea of purchasing another human being was morally repugnant to Sean, and his ancestors had fought a civil war to stop it.

After greeting the deliriously happy Huntress, Sean picked up his Bible and laptop, and sat down on his couch. Before he could start anything, Huntress hopped up beside him and head-bonked him insistently. Sean threw a blanket over his lap, which Huntress promptly crawled under and snuggled against him. With a now much warmer lap, Sean did some web searches. He felt a desperate need to verify what Ayanna had said, because as much as he feared she was right, he also desperately didn't want her to be wrong. Once he found what he was looking for on the internet, he opened the Bible and found the relevant passages.

Sean read the laws on selling one's daughter as a slave. She would then become the purchaser's wife, or else he could purchase her to be his son's wife. There was even a rule about how he should treat her if he were to purchase an additional wife. In the next chapter, he read that a girl's purchase price would go down if she was no longer a virgin. Sean tried to wrap his head around the implications, especially as there was no mention of whether she consented or not. She was property.

People owning people is simply wrong. The idea a man could rape someone and then purchase his victim makes my skin crawl. What kind of asshole would make up such evil rules? Realization hit Sean like a piledriver. *Oh. Now I understand the patriarchy. These are all rules benefiting men, particularly wealthy and powerful men.*

None of this fit into the spoon-fed pablum Sean had been

given. Once his brain started looking for holes, he kept finding them.

Why bother to defend the idea of marriage between one man and one woman as being from the Bible when the Bible has laws saying men can simply purchase as many women as they can afford to care for?

Then there are the passages related to some of God's commands for how the Israelites were to treat conquered peoples. In modern parlance, these were war crimes. God even commanded Saul to sacrifice an entire nation. Then God got angry when Saul enslaved them instead. How is genocidal human sacrifice a good thing?

The term *cognitive dissonance* sprung to mind as Sean tried to reconcile the concept of a loving God with that of a genocidal, enslaving God. As he turned to some of his favorite passages, he felt the truth of Ayanna's words—that some parts of his holy book were transcendentally beautiful, while others were horrific nightmares.

There's so much good in here, and so much evil. It's almost like God is... human.

Sean found himself face-to-face with a moral dilemma he had never contemplated—what to do next. He suddenly understood why so many people never questioned their faith. It was so much easier that way. He could still make that choice, possibly. The other option was frightening and dangerous. He could think critically about his faith and find inspiration in what called him to be better. It was this figurative door he chose.

I should probably ask Ayanna for Jesús' phone number. He seems like the sort of guy who would be willing to help talk through some of my questions without the pent-up anger Ayanna clearly feels.

After such a long break, Sean felt guilty about ditching work, but as he tried to actually do his job, he realized his job made him feel guilty, too. Clearly, he had questions to ask in many parts of his life.

Regardless of what else might be going on, having Huntress pressed against him and snoring adorable little cat snores made him feel better. He could sometimes feel her twitch as she dreamed. Sure, his legs were going a bit numb, but it was a price worth paying.

Once six o'clock rolled around, Sean gingerly got up, deeply disappointing Huntress in the process. He worked blood back into his legs as he stumbled to the kitchen to feed Huntress, whose mood recovered with alacrity once she heard the sound of an opening can. As she inhaled her dinner, Sean got changed for his double date.

Knowing his wardrobe needed an upgrade was one thing, but figuring out what to wear was another. The polo and khakis look was easy and generally fit in almost anywhere, but it was also a source of endless amusement for Ayanna, as were his attempts to move away from that look. Tonight, he was going wild with jeans and a newly purchased Iron Maiden t-shirt.

I should actually listen to some Iron Maiden before I go, in case someone asks me about this shirt.

Sean told his virtual assistant to play Iron Maiden, and she (Sean had picked a female voice for the assistant, so he thought of it as 'she') started playing some for him. The immediate effect was jarring. Sean really wasn't a music person, and this was his first intentional foray into rock and roll. His introduction to heavy metal was "The Trooper" and it was mind-blowing. The galloping rhythm mixed with vocals that shifted from staccato to soaring as the singer recounted the final minutes of a soldier. The effect was inspiring, yet unnerving. Sean went to his laptop to get information on the band as the next song started. He read about the history of the band as the hooks of "Run To the Hills" dug into his psyche.

Satisfied he wouldn't make a complete ass of himself if anyone acknowledged the shirt, he put on hiking boots. Sean finished the look with the hat he'd bought with Ayanna and a worn leather bomber jacket he'd found at a vintage shop near the dream reader he had visited a few days prior.

After rechecking the address, he hopped in his car and resumed listening to Iron Maiden. "Fear of the Dark" helped him feel less alone in his recent crisis of faith, a feeling reinforced as "Hallowed Be Thy Name" played next. It seemed incredibly appropriate. Searching for parking while "Wasted Years" played also seemed like a perfect match.

By the time he parked, Sean was disappointed to turn the music off. He got out and walked to the brew pub. He was early, but Ayanna was already there waiting outside. She wolf whistled when she saw him approach. He stopped and gave a little spin to her claps of approval.

When Sean walked up to Ayanna, she reached out and grasped his hands, placing them on her bare waist as she maneuvered in to give him another knockout kiss. As she broke the kiss, Ayanna purred, "Mm, you look good. Here, let me get another look at you."

She nudged him back and eyed him from head to toe. He took the opportunity to do the same. Ayanna wore knee-high boots, a short black skirt, a red crop top, and a black motorcycle jacket.

Sean felt close to drooling. "Wow, you are hot tonight."

She smiled innocently, and responded, "Just tonight?"

He laughed and said, "Yep, only tonight."

Ayanna mock pouted at him. "Fine, well, I'm going to take back my comment then."

"I'm sorry, let me make it up to you." Sean leaned boldly back in and kissed her again.

Sean wasn't sure how long they kissed. It felt like eternity, but also far too short—and then he realized they had an audience.

I can't believe I was so bold. She liked it, though.

Ayanna pulled back and gave the new couple a little wave. "Hi, y'all. This is my boyfriend, Sean."

Annabelle grinned lasciviously at them and said, "Hi, again Super Stud Sean, this is my girlfriend, Tanya."

Tanya was a pretty brunette with a slim girl-next-door look which contrasted with Annabelle's voluptuous frame and boldly plunging neckline. All three women giggled at Sean's title, but Ayanna at least had the grace to mouth "I'm sorry" to him.

"Come on, stop teasing my boyfriend and let's eat."

The two couples walked toward the pub door. Sean held the door for them all and was surprised when it was Tanya who dragged her fingertips across his arm as she entered. Ayanna stuck her tongue out at Tanya, and Tanya giggled in response.

The hostess led them to a table for four, and Sean felt like he had a spotlight on him yet was somehow also invisible, surrounded as he was by three beautiful women. Once seated, Annabelle turned to him and said, "Nice shirt, Sean."

"Thanks. I like the shirt and the band kicks ass, too. Nice shirt as well." He nodded at the fashionably torn AC/DC t-shirt that was currently exposing a generous amount of cleavage.

"Why, thank you."

Ayanna chimed in. "I have to say, I never figured you for a Maiden fan."

He blushed. "I'm a fairly recent fan, but they're really good."

"Oh, I know." Ayanna acknowledged before pointing at her menu. "By the way, the stout mac and cheese with local-made sausage is amazing. Sean, you have to try that."

"I need to trust you again, right?"

"Have I steered you wrong yet?"

"No, you haven't."

They all heard Annabelle say *sotto voce*, "Especially if she steers you into bed." She suddenly sat up straight and exclaimed, "Hey! That hurt—both of you."

Ayanna and Tanya, who flanked Annabelle, both snickered.

Tanya asked Sean, "So, is this a thing for you two?"

"What? The ordering?" Sean shrugged. "Yeah, kinda. I've had a fairly sheltered life, and Ayanna is helping me learn and grow, including trying new foods."

"You've never had mac and cheese before?"

Sean chuckled. "I've eaten a lot of mac and cheese. I mean, a *lot*. But only from a box."

"Wow."

Ayanna inserted herself into the conversation, saying, "I know, right? This poor man had never eaten Indian before he met me."

Tanya gave him a pitying look. "You poor thing."

"It's true. Ayanna has graciously introduced me to many wonderful new flavors. She's like my Goddess of Spicy Foods."

They all focused on Annabelle as she made strangled choking noises. "What? I didn't say anything. Kick him this time. He said it."

Tanya placed her hand on her girlfriend's arm and gently said, "My love, you didn't have to say anything. We could all hear your thoughts." Smiling at Sean, she said, "I apologize for Annabelle. She has an uncontrollably dirty mind."

"I didn't hear you complaining about my dirty mind earlier today."

"Shush." Tanya leaned over and gave Annabelle a loving kiss.

Sean was briefly taken aback as he was rarely this close to a public display of affection, and definitely a first involving a same-gender couple. He was a bit surprised to realize it didn't bother him at all. He looked at Ayanna, finding that she was staring intently at him. "What?" He mouthed at her. Ayanna placed her hand on his arm and smiled as she shook her head at him.

There was a test there, and I think I just passed.

"Ayanna, what are you getting?"

"The meatloaf with garlic mashed potatoes is calling to me."

"Mmm, sounds good. Can I try it?"

"Yes, but only if I can try your mac and cheese."

"Deal."

They all ordered their meals and then chatted while they waited. There was a live band that night, so there was also entertainment during any lulls in the conversation. The food was excellent, as was the company. Sean was feeling really good about the whole experience. He was sipping his root beer, somewhat lost in the music when Ayanna tapped his hand.

"Do you want to split a dessert?"

"Oh, sure. What are you thinking?"

"Does the brownie sundae sound good to you?"

"That sounds delicious."

Each couple ended up splitting a brownie sundae. This was the second time Sean had shared ice cream with Ayanna—he still thought it seemed highly unsanitary, but, given the amount of kissing he had done with Ayanna, he knew it couldn't hurt. Eventually, all that was left was the solitary whipped cream and chocolate-streaked cherry. Sean and Ayanna each eyed the cherry, their spoons circling like sharks.

Which of course created the perfect opportunity for Annabelle to whisper, "I wonder who is going to get that cherry tonight." Sean heard Tanya smack Annabelle's arm. His cheeks flushed furiously.

"It's all yours, Ayanna," Sean said gallantly.

Weirdly, she blushed as well.

Once the check was settled, they all bundled up and headed for the door. Sean found himself walking next to Tanya and said, "It was really nice meeting you. This was fun."

"It was. I was a bit uncomfortable about going on a double

date, but I'm surprised at how fun this was. You seem very nice, and Ayanna is the best. Sorry about Annabelle—"

"Annabelle is great, and you two seem like an amazing couple." Sean suddenly remembered how Annabelle and Tanya had become a couple, and he blushed. "She's really sweet, and I appreciate her ribald sense of humor."

"Good word. I love that about her, even if it's sometimes embarrassing in public."

Sean and Tanya fell silent, which of course was just the right moment to hear Annabelle say to Ayanna, "He's a keeper, girl. Any guy who can pay more attention to you than my boobs is hooked on you for sure."

Ayanna responded, "So that's why you sat across from him."

"Of course. I'm looking out for you. And I mean, Sean definitely looked, so he's not gay, but he didn't stare. Not like when we had dinner with Tanya's brother and his wife. That was *awkward*."

Sean saw Tanya cover her face with her hands, then stop so she could quiet Annabelle with another kiss.

Life with Annabelle must be a roller coaster, but clearly Tanya loves her.

Ayanna took this opportunity to put her arm through Sean's and lean against him. "Do you want to come back to my place for a bit?"

That question nearly broke Sean's brain. He barely managed to stammer out, "Sure."

"Great, let's say goodbye to the girls, and then I'll meet you at mine."

Sean somehow managed to regain enough brain function to bid Annabelle and Tanya a good night. The cool autumn air helped bring his fever down enough to drive somewhat safely, although his mind was still racing. He got lucky with parking and soon found himself at Ayanna's door. He knocked and was a bit surprised to see Jesús open the door. Before he could even say 'hi' there was a blur as a cat darted upstairs.

Jesús said, "Hi, Sean. Sorry about the cat."

"That must be Bast. I guess she's shy around new people."

"Actually, she's extremely friendly most of the time, especially with men. Probably too friendly, really. I guess she's feeling shy tonight."

There was an audible hiss from upstairs.

"Are you looking for Ayanna? She's not... wait, isn't she on a date with you? Oh, there she is, behind you."

"Hey, Jesús. You remember my boyfriend, Sean."

"Of course, welcome in."

Sheepishly, Sean asked, "Thanks. Uh, Jesús, by the way, I've been wanting to ask—this might seem weird, but can I talk to you sometime? I've got some stuff going on and—I'm sorry, it's stupid."

"No, of course. Any time, my friend. Whatever it is, it's not stupid."

"Are you sure?"

"Absolutely. Ayanna can give you my number. I'll leave you two alone."

"Actually, Jesús. Please stay," Ayanna said. "We were going to hang out downstairs, and it would be nice to have some extra company. Maybe we could watch a rom-com."

Jesús gave Ayanna a surprised look, but recovered quickly. "That sounds great. I picked up some organic popcorn a couple nights ago. I'll go make some."

"Make sure to put some organic butter on it this time." Jesús looked hurt.

Ayanna led Sean to their big, 'L' shaped couch and had him lie down with a pillow behind his back to keep him upright. "Want anything to drink?"

"Just water, please."

"Okay, get comfortable." She returned a couple minutes later with two glasses of water, which she set on a low table sitting in the crook of 'L.' Ayanna then proceeded to settle herself down, leaning back against Sean, between his legs.

She felt incredibly warm, pressed against him firmly. Sean quickly became aware of a rapidly developing situation in his pants.

Please don't let her feel my erection pressing into her back.

"Mm, is that for me? I'm very flattered, Sean. Hm." He felt her wiggle against his hardness. "Oh, yes, I suspected I might like it far too much, which is why we are on my couch and not yours."

"Huh?"

"I don't trust myself to be alone with you right now. But I definitely trust myself with Jesús around."

"We could still go—"

"Trust me, Sean, not rushing into things will be better for us in the long run, and I want this to be a long run."

"All right, I do trust you."

"Good, now let me enjoy your hard cock pressed against my ass before Jesús gets back with the popcorn."

I have no idea how to respond.

Jesús saved him from having to speak by showing up with two bowls of popcorn. The bowl Jesús handed to Ayanna filled Sean's nose with a hot, buttery scent. Ayanna settled the popcorn in her lap and pulled Sean's arms around her where he could reach it. When he reached for the popcorn, his arm brushed the side of her breast. Sean murmured an apology and pulled away. He wasn't disappointed when she pulled his arm back. Any subsequent attempts to shift away were met with a similar reaction. Before long, Sean's right arm was still touching one breast, while his left arm was snugly fitted under the other breast with his hand on her well-muscled stomach.

Sean had no idea what they watched as his entire focus was on the gorgeous woman in his arms. Every point of contact tingled. He felt the energy passing between their bodies as they lay on the couch. After the movie was over, Ayanna slowly unentangled herself, and Sean instantly missed her touch. Jesús took the empty popcorn bowls to the kitchen, leaving the two of them standing alone. Sean looked at Ayanna and felt his heart thundering in his chest.

"Ayanna..."

"Sean..."

Fuck it, here goes.

"Ayanna, I think I'm falling in love with you."

Sean nearly lost his balance as Ayanna attempted to shove her tongue down his throat.

Jesús gently coughed behind them.

Ayanna pulled herself off of Sean and said, "Sean, as much as I want you to stay, I think you should go. Thank you for tonight."

Sean drifted out the door and to his car, his mind in a fog.

Chapter 30

Shock The Monkey

Peter Gabriel

"Well, I didn't expect that," Jesús intoned.

Ayanna wheeled to look at Jesús. "I'm a little bit shocked, myself. I really like him, Jesús, and I don't want to make a mess of things."

"So, you are waiting to sleep with him? It's definitely a different choice for you."

"Huh. I would have thought you would approve. You know, given you've waited two thousand years to sleep with the woman you love."

"You make an interesting choice of words there. Are you implying you are delaying sexual gratification with Sean because you love him?"

"Dammit, Jesús. That wasn't what I meant to say."

"Are you *sure?*"

"I... I don't know. I really do like him. A lot. He's shy and inexperienced, but sometimes he forgets and lets this confidence leak out. He is *so* sexy when he lets himself go. And, he thinks he's falling in love with me."

Jesús grinned. "I'm going to take a leap of faith here and say he is definitely in love with you and is feeling his way toward fully telling you. He is also probably trying to protect himself in case you don't feel the same about him."

"Wait, didn't you say you knew how he felt because he is one of your worshippers?"

"True. I could sense how he felt, but he is no longer one of mine."

"Tonight, he called me his Goddess of Spicy Foods. Jesús... you better not be right. I will be so pissed if I'm cursed to forever be Ayanna, Goddess of Curry."

"I suspect you are far more than the Goddess of Curry to Sean. Goddess of Spicy Foods and Tea for sure." Ayanna could hear the grin in Jesús' voice. Apparently, he could read her face and quickly added, "Seriously, though, your relationship is new, but it grows deeper every day. He sees a lot in you he likes. Not just food."

"Thank you. Now, are you done teasing me?"

"Oh no, not at all. Do you know how much teasing I've endured from you since we started living together? Ayanna, I have a lot of payback coming."

"What happened to turning the other cheek?"

Jesús snickered. "Is that what you did when Sean felt your butt?"

Ayanna's face flushed at Jesús' joke, which in turn brought up the all-too-recent memory of pressing against Sean's hardness for ninety minutes. "Okay, I'm sorry I teased you so much. I shouldn't have been so hard on you... Don't say it, Jesús. I can see you thinking it." Ayanna sighed. "You're going to say it, aren't you? Fine, let it out."

"You'd prefer it if Sean's hardon was in you."

"You know, for the Lamb of God, you have an incredibly dirty mind."

"And where do you think I learned that, huh? I've been living with you and Brandi for years now, and the two of you have unfathomably dirty minds."

"Did I hear my name?" Brandi joined them.

"Why didn't you join us? I wanted to introduce you to Sean."

"And how were you going to explain your housemate's pregnancy? Especially if you're still seeing him in a month, and I'm no longer pregnant but there's no human baby, just a litter of kittens."

"You make a really good point. Thank you for thinking ahead."

"My absence wasn't entirely altruistic. You know how horny I get when I'm pregnant. Well, your pheromones are in full force, then add Sean's musk on top, and I've been masturbating for the last hour."

"That's a bit too much sharing, Brandi." Jesús looked very uncomfortable.

"As much as I do enjoy watching you blush, I heard back from Thoth. He is fascinated by Sean's ability to see Inanna's past in his dreams. Any sort of dream communication is rare now, and he is unaware of any human actually having visions of a deity's past in such vivid detail. Thoth is also puzzled how Sean, a Christian, would have such clear visions of Inanna."

"So, Thoth doesn't know anything?"

"No, sorry, Ayanna. He does have some thoughts about this situation. Sean could be a very distant descendent of yours."

Ayanna snorted. "Unlike someone I can name, I don't have a lot of progeny, and I can confidently dismiss this idea."

"I think Thoth would agree with you. His current premise is something he calls the wet clay theory. Essentially, Thoth surmises that Sean is at heart a believer; however, he has never had the inclination or education as a child that would have imprinted faith upon him. Ergo, he is like smooth wet clay, and when he encountered and engaged with Inanna, or more specifically, your identity as Ayanna, you essentially created an imprint. Because of that, he has been having these visions."

"I don't know. Jesús said Sean was one of his worshippers, which would run counter to Thoth's theory."

"Is that true, Jesús?"

"It is. I suppose it is possible Sean's feelings for Ayanna may have overridden the imprint Thoth spoke of, but I feel like this is unlikely. Forgive me, Ayanna, but your power is non-existent at this point."

"No offense taken. You speak the painful truth."

"Thanks for your input. I will take this back to Thoth. Now, let's talk about what is really important... Ayanna, why aren't you and Sean boning?"

"You haven't heard? She's taking things slowly because she's worried she might be in love."

"*Jesús...*" Ayanna's voice was like the soft hiss of a steel blade leaving a scabbard.

"Tell me I'm wrong, Ayanna."

"I met him less than two weeks ago. Plus, I haven't been in love since Athena. I just don't want to hurt him."

"Brandi, what do you think?"

"I think it's very sweet that she cares so much about him. Personally, I would have been on him like a crocodile on a careless waterbearer. Plus, he passed Annabelle's test."

"She texted and told you about that? Ugh. What else did she tell you?"

"Not much. Just that he's smart, and sweet, and you two were adorable sharing dessert. Oh, and you ran out of the cart today so you could kiss him. Your kiss left Annabelle, and I quote, 'hot, wet, and ready to explode.'"

"I like seeing him, and he's a good kisser."

Jesús decided that was a perfect time to add, "And he told you he loves you."

Brandi exclaimed, "He said *what?*"

Chapter 31

Stargazer

Rainbow

Sean woke up late on Saturday morning, not feeling particularly well-rested. His mind kept replaying those last few moments of his evening with Ayanna. His profession of falling in love, her kiss, and then her sending him home— the whole sequence on a seemingly endless loop as his mind tried to determine if this was good or bad. She didn't respond with a profession of love to answer him, which worried him. The one positive of his night once he finally fell asleep was that some of the weirder dreams of Ayanna didn't appear, although they were replaced by a new dream of Ayanna lying naked on a table, but covered entirely in food, and as much as dream Sean tried to eat this buffet, he never could eat his way down to her skin.

Huntress' hungry meowing finally woke him up. He stumbled through the process of feeding her, as always made more difficult by her insistence on sticking her face into the food as he moved it to her bowl. Around the time he finished this process, his phone buzzed. There was a new text from an unknown contact which turned out to be Jesús inviting him out for breakfast. Sean responded affirmatively and a few minutes later was driving down into the Sellwood neighborhood.

Jesús was waiting for him outside of a quirky little diner, smiling at Sean as he walked up. "Good morning, my friend."

"Hi, Jesús. Thanks for the invite."

"My pleasure. I thought you might want to talk sooner rather than later, especially after last night."

"Yeah. Definitely."

"Come on. Let's order, and then we'll talk."

It didn't take long to order, and then Jesús said, "What was it you wanted to talk about?"

"This might sound weird, but yesterday I asked Ayanna about sin, you know, because we've been talking about..."

"Sex. Don't look surprised. You don't think I know what my role was last night? Ayanna brought you home because she figured she was less likely to sleep with you if I was around. It worked, obviously. Also, sex and sin are closely entwined. Let me guess, you asked Ayanna about sin and she went off like a bomb."

"That's putting it mildly. She gave me a lot to think about, but she really seems to have some harsh feelings about Christianity."

"It's not my place to talk about Ayanna's feelings, but let's just say there is some history there. You said you had some things to think about. Like what?"

"Well, I followed up on some things she said, and there's stuff in the Bible that just seems really immoral to me, but other things make so much sense."

"So, you started thinking critically about a religious book, and some of it made moral sense and some of it did not. That, my friend, is part of the great struggle of humanity. What is good? What is evil? Is it just duality... black and white, right and wrong... or is there nuance and gray spaces?"

Oh boy, this is going to be another headache-inducing conversation.

"Exactly, and I'm really confused right now."

"Correct me if I'm wrong, but up until now, someone in a

position of authority has essentially told you what is good and what is bad, right?" Not hearing a correction, Jesús continued on. "Then Ayanna challenged what you've been told, but provided no real alternative, so you feel adrift. That's a challenging place to be, and a very frightening place as well."

"That sums it up perfectly. What do you think?"

"About good and evil?" Jesús smiled. "Are you familiar with the Trolley Problem?"

"The what?"

"Imagine a trolley filled with people, racing out of control and about to crash. Now, imagine yourself standing next to a switch that can change the track. If you choose to do nothing, then the trolley will crash, killing twenty people. If you choose to throw the switch, then the trolley will switch tracks and everyone on board will be saved, but the trolley will hit and kill someone on the other track. What do you do?"

"Throw the switch and save twenty people."

"And deliberately kill one person."

"But I saved twenty people."

"And you feel that is a reasonable trade off, correct? But isn't it murder? You deliberately chose to kill someone."

"I didn't think of it that way. But I did save twenty, which matters, right?"

"Well, what if the one person was Ayanna?"

Sean wasn't sure how to answer. He grappled with the fact he wanted to save the hypothetical Ayanna, but was already on record as saying it was better to save twenty people.

Jesús smiled at Sean's silence. "You don't have to answer. There are infinite variations on the Trolley Problem. One of my favorites is the version where there is no one on the other track but a young Hitler is riding in the trolley. Do you condemn twenty people to death to stop Hitler before he ever gets started?"

"Is there a right answer?"

"To morality? I thought so once. One of my personal favorite sayings is still, 'love your neighbor as yourself.' It's actually a really good guide to living, but over time I've discovered a flaw."

"It sounds perfect; what kind of flaw is there?"

"Let's call it a lack of imagination regarding who one's neighbors are. You might also call it an empathy gap. Are your neighbors your friends and family, or are your neighbors also refugees standing in a frozen river facing a wall of barbed wire while trying to find a safe harbor? What I've discovered is so many people can't imagine someone else's pain or fear until it affects them personally. That's the flaw."

"Wow. That sucks."

"It does. Sean, humanity has been trying for thousands of years to figure this out, and it is still a work in progress."

There is something about Jesús that had been bugging me for a while, and I just figured it out. Jesús almost always seems to be smiling in a way that suggests he knows something no one else does. Normally, that would be infuriating, but for some reason, it isn't in Jesús' case. He's just so kind.

"After thousands of years, there's no answer? That doesn't seem right."

"I'm not saying there are *no* answers. Love your neighbor as yourself, and consider the whole world to be your neighbors. Treat others as you want to be treated."

"The Golden Rule."

"Exactly. The efforts of philosophers and theologians across thousands of years have not been entirely in vain. There is wisdom out there, but you have to be open to it."

"Jesús, I have to ask—and I mean no offense. You're obviously a very smart guy. Why are you restocking groceries overnight?"

Jesús paused and smiled his knowing smile. Finally, Jesús said, "People need these items, so by restocking shelves, I help make their lives better, even though I may never meet them. That brings me joy. At some point, I will move on to something else, but my goal is always to make the lives of others better."

"Has anyone ever told you that you remind them of Jesus, you know—"

"Every so often. I take it as a compliment. Now, let's talk about you and Ayanna."

"Oh, like am I going to... you know—"

"No, Sean. That's not what I'm asking. How do you feel about her?"

Sean laughed nervously, glad he didn't have to answer a question about sex. "Well, I told her last night I think I'm falling in love with her."

"I heard you, and saw her reaction. But do you just *think* you are falling in love with her, or are you actually in love with her?"

Sean was saved from an immediate answer by the arrival of breakfast. Digging into his eggs gave him a chance to think about his answer. After devouring the eggs, he started jabbing at his home fries, but he was ready to answer. "Yes, I love Ayanna."

"I sense some hesitation there, hidden behind your home fries."

"I'm worried, Jesús. I told her I was falling in love with her, and she didn't say anything except to tell me to go home. Does she feel the same about me? Also, have you seen her? She's like a goddess, and I'm a nerd."

"A goddess, hm? A very interesting choice of words." Jesús smiled that knowing smile of his. "Tell me, Sean. What sort of goddess would Ayanna be?"

That's a strange question.

"A Goddess of Love for sure. Oh, and a goddess who pushes you to be better."

"How so?"

"Well, she told me this dark truth about herself, but she recognized her failure and she is working to not make the same mistakes again. She inspires me to do the same in my life. She also inspires me to try new foods and experiences."

"Would that be part of being a goddess?"

Sean laughed. "Yes, definitely a Goddess of Spicy Foods. Oh, and great drinks, too. More seriously, though, a Goddess of Honesty and Self-Improvement. And helping others improve. Actually, speaking of helping others... Ayanna is a total badass. She caught some guy trying to drug a woman's drink, and she kicked his ass. So, she's definitely a badass, but for good."

"She's a Goddess of..."

"A Goddess of Protecting Those In Need. A strong and powerful defender. Like a lioness, protecting her pride." Sean felt a moment of confusion as he wondered where that analogy came from.

"She sounds like a fascinating goddess to me. This Goddess Ayanna you describe seems like she could be interested in a guy like you, nerd and all. She played Dungeons and Dragons with you, so maybe she's a bit of a nerd, too."

"Goddess of Nerds, Bookworms, and Gamers would be awesome, too." Sean thought the idea was funny, yet somehow fitting.

"Seriously, Sean. I believe Ayanna really likes you, and you clearly like her. Don't overthink things, and don't put yourself down. You're a good person at heart, and she sees that."

"Thanks, Jesús. I really needed to hear that."

"I'm glad I could help."

Sean laughed. "Yeah, it's kinda your thing."

"It definitely is. Now we should pay our check and go. It looks like there are some hungry people waiting for an open table."

Chapter 32

Pray

MC Hammer

Ayanna was waiting when Jesús got home from breakfast. "Jesús, where were you just now?"

"Because I want to strangle you," is what she wanted to add.

"Hi, Ayanna. I just had breakfast with Sean. He wanted to talk about some things after your conversation yesterday afternoon."

"Was that all you talked about?"

"Not all, no."

"Jesús... what the *fuck* did you do?"

"I'm sure I don't know what you mean."

"Don't you give me that smile. I planned to have yogurt this morning, and instead I found myself at the store just now getting something completely different. I came back and made chorizo and eggs for breakfast, with seasoned hash browns and a cinnamon hot chocolate. I'm also feeling a sudden desire to read some spicy romance novels."

"None of which sounds like a bad thing to me."

"I'm also feeling something I haven't felt in almost two thousand years."

"What are you feeling?"

"Prayer. There are prayers out there, whispers sent to no one, and they are finding their way to me. Jesús, why am I hearing people pray for good dice rolls?"

"I may have had a discussion with Sean about you, and something came up about a Goddess of Nerds, Bookworms, and Gamers."

"What the—you're serious? Is your crazy idea actually not crazy after all?"

"I am hopeful for you."

"Hopeful Sean changes the essence of who I am?"

"No, that the two of you can reinvent you together. He does love you, Ayanna. Also, while this may be my hypothesis, I have no control. Now might be a good idea to assert some control of your own."

"I *really* wish I could hate you right now, but you're just too nice."

"Thank you, I think. Any chance you will let me go to bed soon? It's getting late for me."

"I told you to stop working nights. Go, get some rest. I'm going to call Sean."

Ayanna was pleased when Sean answered her call. They exchanged pleasantries for a bit before Ayanna got around to asking whether Sean had plans for the day. Being new to the city, Sean was going to visit one of Portland's iconic sites, Powell's Books. Ayanna asked if she could meet him there, which he readily agreed to.

She met him at the Burnside entrance with a big hug. Ayanna felt warm and light in Sean's embrace. As they browsed the new books, Sean asked Ayanna what she liked to read.

"I'm a big fan of mysteries and classics, mostly. Austen, Twain, Hiaasen. I've recently discovered an interest in romance novels," Ayanna said. "What about you?"

"I read a lot of biographies."

"Wow, there's a pretty wide gap in genres between us."

"No kidding."

"Let me give you the full tour of this place," Ayanna said. "Powell's takes up an entire block, so it will take a bit. Then we can either browse together or separately."

"Sounds like a great plan."

They wandered from room to room, floor to floor, until she had given Sean a survey of the whole store. Each massive room was assigned a color and held certain categories, with entire rooms dedicated to children's books, history and sociology, or travel and self-help. Fiction was large enough to be broken into two rooms. He asked Ayanna, "Which section are you heading to?"

"I'm thinking of going to the romance or fantasy sections. What about you?"

"You know what? I think I'll stay with you. If that's okay with you?"

"I would love to have you with me. Come on, to the Gold Room we go." Ayanna took Sean's hand and headed for the stairs. They spent over two hours browsing, during which Ayanna selected a small handful of books to purchase. As they browsed, she convinced Sean to get the first book in the Harry Dresden series.

"So, what did you think of the most dangerous place in Portland?"

"Dangerous?" Sean looked confused.

"Yeah... to your wallet."

Sean laughed. "I liked it. I've never seen a bookstore that big. It's easy to see how someone could spend all day there."

"I've done that."

"The little cafe in there looked nice. We should try it next time."

"Definitely."

"Ayanna... want to come back to my place to read? Maybe later we can grab dinner?"

"Like take out?"

"Yeah."

"I have a better idea. I'll meet you at your place, but I'll grab some groceries on the way. Then, we can make dinner together. You do have cooking stuff, right?"

"Yes, and that sounds great."

Chapter 33

Get It On (Bang A Gong)
The Power Station

"Perfect." Ayanna gave him a quick kiss and walked away. Sean stood there, watching her go. He was certain she was adding some extra sway to her steps. As she waited for the light to cross the street, she looked back at him and smiled. He waved to her, and she waved back before joining the crowd in the crosswalk.

Once back home, Sean petted Huntress and then made sure his place was tidy and nothing embarrassing was lying around. He felt a pang of uncertainty about the secrecy required by his job and how he would handle being honest with Ayanna while also hiding what he did for a living. Shelving that problem for later, Sean opened up the Monterey Aquarium website and put on the otter cam.

Before too long, there was a knock at the door. Sean opened the door and Ayanna walked in with a full bag of groceries. He helped her put the refrigerated items away, and then gave her a hug. Their hug quickly transitioned into a kiss, which Sean enjoyed immensely. He fervently hoped Ayanna couldn't feel just how much he enjoyed their kiss, but as usual, those hopes were quickly dashed.

Ayanna broke their kiss and gently pushed him back. "Ahem. You invited me over to read, so let's read." She grinned as she gestured toward his crotch. "I see Big Sean might have other ideas, but let's just keep it to reading for now."

"Yeah, sorry about... ah, Big Sean."

"Don't be sorry. I'm very flattered. Oh, you have the otter cam on. They are so adorable. Did you do that for me?"

"Yes, but I like to watch them, too. The blonde otter over to the side is Ivy. She's my favorite."

"The gentleman prefers blondes?"

"Uh, no, it's just that she is very active and playful."

"I'm teasing you. Let me grab a book and I'll join you on the couch."

Sean did as he was instructed. Ayanna joined him a minute later on the other end of the couch, and Huntress jumped up on her lap.

"Aw, Huntress. Thank you for joining us. Maybe you should go and lie down in Sean's lap. I think he would appreciate a nice warm *pussy*... cat." Ayanna snickered at her own joke while Sean's cheeks colored.

He really didn't have a good response, so instead he opened his book. Sean was barely through the first sentence when he felt Ayanna's feet touch his side. She looked comfortable, stretching out a bit with a book in one hand, while her other hand idly scratched a curled up Huntress in her lap.

She looked up at him over the top of her book and asked, "What?"

"You're very beautiful. I like seeing you relaxed and happy."

"Aw, thank you. You're quite handsome yourself. Now get comfortable and read your book."

That's exactly what they did for the next hour or so. They each stole glances at each other, sharing happy smiles as they read. Huntress just napped, as cats are wont to do. Over time, their bodies molded together, each stretched out comfortably to fully occupy all of the space on the couch. Sean slowly and subtly twitched the hand not holding his book, so he lightly stroked Ayanna's bare ankle. A raised eyebrow indicated Ayanna was quite aware of exactly where his hand was and what he was doing, but she said nothing.

Ayanna's skin feels warm and soft. I like this slow flirting we're doing.

And so they read their books, content to spend time together. Sean felt the same sort of peace he'd experienced at the Gardens. Eventually, Ayanna broke the silence.

"Since your hand is already down there, could you rub my feet?"

Sean blushed at the acknowledgement that his subterfuge had failed, but agreeably said, "Of course." He put his book down and reached both hands for her feet.

"Okay, sweetie, you're going to have to put my feet in your lap."

"Ah, sorry. This is actually my first time ever—"

"I figured. Do you mind if I guide you through this?"

"That would be great. I want you to enjoy this, so please tell me what makes you feel good."

"Wow. You want to please me and are willing to accept instructions? You might be the perfect man."

Sean laughed and blushed as he lifted Ayanna's feet into his lap. Huntress gave a startled squeak as the movement caused her perch in Ayanna's lap to shift. She gave a frustrated little cat huff, but used this opportunity to stand up and shift her position before settling back down in her new favorite lap. Once positioned, he started to gently rub Ayanna's feet.

"That's very nice, Sean, but I'm not made of glass. You can dig in there, but don't hurt your hands."

Sean increased his pressure, shifting to the bottoms of her

arches and digging his thumbs in. This elicited a happy groan. From there, he shifted up to the balls of her feet, but couldn't get the same amount of pressure, so he experimented. Using one hand to hold a foot, he made a fist and dug in with his knuckles. The groaning from the other end of the couch intensified. Sean alternated from one foot to the other, eliciting more contented noises.

"Mm, you're doing so well. My heels and ankles are feeling left out, though."

Sean took the hint and shifted his focus. As he poked, prodded, and rubbed, he felt where her feet were tense and tried to focus there. He learned to alternate his pressure and style, making use of his whole hand to try different ways of relieving her tension. Over time, Ayanna's groans became moans, which then transitioned into murmurs. From time to time, he glanced up to see her lying back, eyes closed, and smiling blissfully.

His hands were tiring, but he persisted, not wanting to disappoint her. Before he reached his breaking point, Ayanna gently called out to him. "Sean, thank you. My feet feel really good right now."

"Are you sure you don't want more?"

"Oh, trust me. I would love it if you did this forever, but I suspect your hands are getting tired."

"A little."

"Then you should stop. Thank you again."

"You're welcome."

"Are you hungry?"

"Not yet, but probably soon."

"Let's start making dinner. We'll probably be hungry by the time we finish." Ayanna leaned forward. "All right, little Huntress, I'm sorry, but I'm going to have to stand up." Huntress was highly offended by Ayanna's movements. She tried to clamber up on Ayanna, looking to maintain a purchase in order to find a new resting place, but her attempts were in vain once Ayanna stood up. Huntress gave another annoyed squeak and stalked off with her tail twitching in irritation.

"So, what is on the menu tonight?"

"Spaghetti and meatballs, and we're going to make the meatballs from scratch."

"Sounds great."

"Another time we can make sauce from scratch, too, but for tonight we'll keep it simple. Now, why don't you turn on the oven while I get the ingredients?"

Ayanna set out the ingredients, bowls, measuring cups, and a parchment-lined baking sheet. She guided Sean through the various steps until he had to actually mix and form the meatballs. He had his hands deep in the cold mixture when he felt her slip behind him, and her hands snaked down into the bowl along with him. Sean felt her breath on his neck and cheek and her soft hair touching his skin. She used his hands to mix and mold.

"Don't be shy, Sean. Get in there like you did with my feet earlier. Get everything thoroughly mixed... Good... Now, you're going to take some of the mixture, and you're going to shape it into a ball. Not too much, but not too little. Gently caress it like one of my breasts, round and smooth."

Sean's knees went weak at her analogy. As he staggered, Ayanna deftly hooked her arms, holding him upright. This maneuver had the unfortunate, or perhaps fortunate, side effect of pressing her aforementioned breasts into his back, further distracting him.

"Oh, my. Did I compare these firm and spicy meatballs to my breasts? That was very silly of me. I'm sorry, Sean."

I definitely heard a flirtatious tone in her voice, Also, I suspect there was no mistake, and that wasn't a real apology. Somehow, I don't mind. Instead, I'll exaggerate the smoothing and caressing of the meatballs to make it more sensual. Two can play this game.

It took longer than necessary, but the meatballs were finally finished and in the oven. After thoroughly washing their hands, Sean and Ayanna started on the rest of the meal, timing everything to be ready at the same time. They danced around each other, touching casually and chatting idly about their books. Sean took some time to feed a grateful Huntress before the human dinner was ready. Feeding Huntress was easier than normal as Ayanna petted and distracted her.

Sean and Ayanna sat down to eat, plates piled high. The meatballs were a bit spicy, but they were good, and they went well with everything else.

Plates empty and hunger satisfied, Sean rose to clear their plates and clean up. As he stood up from loading the dishwasher, he felt Ayanna's arms wrap around him from behind. Her embrace felt good, and he relaxed back into it. Ayanna's lips touched his ear, followed by her teeth. Her fingers gently pulled his head around so she could gently nibble on his earlobe, her tongue probing along the lower edge of his lobe.

"Oops. I forgot to get us dessert, and now I'm needing something to nibble on."

"Uhng." Sean couldn't stop the groan from escaping his lips.

"I guess it's okay if I continue to nibble on your ear, then?"

"Uh huh," he moaned.

"You know what I think? I think we should have dessert on the couch. Doesn't that sound nice?" He felt her pull away from him. She looked back over her shoulder and extended a hand, which he took. Sean followed Ayanna mindlessly to the couch, where she sat him down. He felt excited, elated, and above all, overwhelmed.

"Ayanna, I need a minute."

In an instant, the flirting was gone, and he read only concern on her face. "Did I go too far? I'm so sorry."

"No... this is amazing. You. Are. Amazing. I just need to let my brain catch up."

"Too much blood going somewhere else?" Ayanna asked lasciviously.

"Something like that."

"Seriously, thank you for saying something. I want you to be comfortable with anything we do."

"Speaking of what we were doing, I recall you mentioning dessert."

"Mm, yes, I did." She pulled him into a kiss. As their tongues danced, Ayanna continued to pull him until he was partially on top of her. This prompted a break in their kiss until they could reposition themselves, at which point, Sean resumed his tongue's examination of her teeth.

Sean's experience with kissing prior to Ayanna was limited to a few brief and awkward pecks, so being in close full-body contact with a woman was very unfamiliar territory. As their tongues dueled, his brain struggled to determine what to do with his hands. Ayanna's hands were sliding up and down his sides and back, so Sean began to mimic her motions. They went on like this for an enjoyably long time, until Ayanna pushed him back, interrupting their make-out session.

He looked down at her and asked, "Is everything all right?"

"Oh yes, very all right. But I would like to try something different, if you are interested?"

"This is exciting, but different sounds fun, too."

"Great, let's do this." Ayanna sat up and reached for the bottom of his t-shirt, slowly pulling it upward. "Are you good with this?"

"Yes."

Ayanna's fingertips brushing his abdomen sent tendrils of electricity to his brain. *Very, very good. I can't believe this is happening.*

"Mm..." Ayanna purred as she pulled his shirt over his head and off. "Now, I'm going to do a little show and tell. Tell me what feels good, and remember what I do so you can do the same to me later, all right?"

"Uh huh."

With his assent, Ayanna pushed him backwards until he was prone on the couch. She climbed on top of him and kissed him, her hands resting on his bare chest. The kiss was brief as she pulled away and down. Sean started to protest, but then felt her lips and tongue on his jawline. Ayanna left a trail of kisses up to his ear, which she gently suckled and nibbled. Sean struggled to remember what she was doing for later as the sensations over-whelmed him.

He groaned as Ayanna went from his ear, down to his neck, kissing, licking and gently biting her way down. He felt her hands moving as well. One of her hands was now bracing herself on the couch while the other was now playing with a nipple. Sean moaned softly as her mouth continued its explo-ration to his collarbone, then proceeded further to his other nipple. She stopped there, once more suckling and nibbling. Sean could feel her tracing circular patterns with her tongue, alternating with more kisses and sucking. Ayanna's hair felt like a silk curtain on his skin. He groaned again as she left one nipple and trailed her tongue across his chest to the other one. Sean was practically panting when Ayanna lifted her head and looked him in the eye.

"How did that feel?"

"Amazing, incredible, so hot, wonderful, sexy—"

"I get it. All right, lover boy, are you ready to use what you've learned on me?"

Sean gulped audibly.

"I'm going to warn you, you'll be doing this to me for much longer than I was doing that to you."

"That doesn't sound fair."

"I'm the woman, and those are the rules. If you want access to *these...*" Ayanna ran a finger slowly along her cleavage. "...then that's just what you need to do. Would you like to try?"

"Yes. Very much yes."

"Good," Ayanna purred. "Now, would you like to take off my shirt, or should I take it off for you?"

Sean's brain locked up, along with his capacity for speech.

"I'll assume your silence means I should take off my shirt for you." She stood up in a long and languid motion. Sean watched as Ayanna slowly and sensuously unbuttoned her shirt. Her motions kept the shirt mostly closed, but each button gave a hint of what lay beneath. She shifted strategically, allowing the shirt to fall off of one shoulder but still leaving her breasts covered. Sean's pants felt incredibly constrictive as Ayanna undid the final button. He watched as she held the shirt up with one hand and beckoned him with the other.

Sean stood up and grasped her beckoning hand. Ayanna drew him in, embracing and kissing him. Sean could feel her hands on his back. The skin of Ayanna's waist felt warm underneath his own hands. They ground together as they kissed, and Sean felt her shirt slowly fall away and then his skin was pressed against hers. Something about the full contact of their chests drove Ayanna into a frenzied onslaught. Sean felt Ayanna forcefully grab the back of his head and press his lips into hers, almost as if she was trying to kiss her way through his head to reach her hand.

As her frenzy waned, Sean felt himself being dragged back onto the couch, on top of Ayanna. She pushed him up, staring at him with eyes aflame with lust. "Come on, my love. Show your teacher you've learned your lesson well."

"I will, but first, let me look at you." Sean took a minute to admire the breathtaking view. He scanned down her bronze body, from tousled hair and flushed face, to her glorious, heaving breasts, to her taut and well-muscled stomach, to her skirt now bunched up near her waist, a hint of black underwear teasing what lay beneath, and finally to her long and athletic legs. "You are a goddess, and I must worship you."

Sean dove forward, burying his face in Ayanna's neck. He kissed and nipped and suckled as she had. Ayanna's moans were a symphony in his ears. Her fingernails dug furrows up his back as he teased and tormented her earlobes. Sean felt her heart as he licked down past her collarbone. It pounded with a beat that would do Iron Maiden proud. Finally, he reached his Promised Land, his chin moving up one orb as his kisses followed. Sean devoured Ayanna's perfect globes like a man possessed.

Back and forth with the regularity of a pendulum, savoring the taste of her sweat in between. With his fingers, lips, teeth, and tongue, Sean exalted Ayanna's breasts. His ears were filled with her groans of pleasure and heated whispers of guidance and encouragement. "Pull my nipple, yes, just like that. A little more teeth, oh, that's perfect." Ayanna writhed under him, forcing her peaks into his hands and mouth. She keened, whimpered, and cried in pleasure.

Eventually, Sean felt her hands gently grasp the sides of his face. Ayanna pulled him up for a contented and gentle kiss. "Thank you," she breathed. "Do you like my boobs?"

"Yes, very much."

"I'm sorry my tits aren't nearly as big as Annabelle's."

This is the first time Ayanna has expressed even a hint of insecurity about her body. It must be important to her that I appreciate her for herself.

"Yours are perfect. Absolutely perfect. The most perfect... tits the world has ever seen."

"Thank you." Ayanna looked at him through her eyelashes.

"No, thank you. Really, thank you very much."

"Mm, you are so welcome. As much as I'm enjoying this, I think I should be going."

"You don't have to go. We could do more."

I sound like I'm begging. Okay, I'm definitely begging.

"Sean, my love, do you remember earlier when you needed a minute to let your brain catch up?"

"Yeah."

"Let's give your brain some time to process this, okay?"

"You're probably right."

The logic makes sense, but Big Sean definitely wants more. Probably best if he isn't making the decisions.

"Can I use your bathroom?"

"Ah, sure."

Ayanna grabbed her shirt and put it on as she sashayed toward the bathroom. She was in there for about a minute before emerging with her hair mostly back to normal and her skirt pulled down and smoothed out. Ayanna stopped to put her shoes back on.

"Thank you for a great day and an exceptionally good evening."

Sean blushed. "Thank you for being the best teacher I could ask for."

Sean held out his arms for a farewell hug and kiss, which Ayanna accepted with enthusiasm. He felt her hand go into his pocket before she released him.

"Okay, I'm going now. Good night."

"Good night."

As the door closed, Sean reached into his pocket. He felt something warm and wet. Sean pulled it out to discover Ayanna's black panties. Just then his phone buzzed with an incoming text. "Oopsie. I forgot something at your place. I guess I'll have to come back to retrieve my panties soon."

Chapter 34

Holding Out For A Hero

Bonnie Tyler

Ayanna drove home with her windows down, but that didn't help cool her off. Brandi was lying on the couch when she opened the door. Ayanna tried to rush past, but Brandi's stern voice brought her to a screeching halt. "Okay, spill."

"What?"

"I can smell you from here." Brandi heaved herself up and walked over, sniffing the air. "I can smell Sean all over you. Your hair is a wreck and you missed a button on your shirt... Did you fuck him?"

"No—"

"*No*? Why not? You are definitely in heat."

"That's partially why we haven't done it yet. I want him to learn how to enjoy all of this, not just skip to the main event."

Brandi's expression shifted from lustful to sappy in an instant. "Aw, you're really sweet. I can't believe you held out, though."

"Trust me, it wasn't easy."

"Oh, so he's good? Do tell."

"Tonight we... Actually, for once I'm not going to kiss and tell.

We went to Powell's and had a nice time there, then we made dinner together, and that's all I'm going to say."

"Spoilsport." Brandi stuck her tongue out at Ayanna. "I'm impressed, though. You must have strong feelings for him."

"I do. It's strange. For some reason, he just does it for me."

Brandi sighed. "You're adorable. You still need to go out with me sometimes, though. Jesús is not an acceptable wingman."

Someone is calling. It's faint. Whoever it is, it's urgent.

Ayanna laughed. "Fine... Hang on."

"What?"

"I need to go."

"Where?"

"Out. Sorry, Brandi." Ayanna spun and ran for the door.

These cries for help aren't in my ears—they're in my head. Someone nearby is praying for help. They aren't praying to anyone, but I hear them. Maybe that's why it's so faint.

Ayanna raced through the wet streets of Portland, shifting direction whenever the prayer grew weaker, hoping she would get there in time. The prayer was still faint when she found herself stopped on a street near some bars and restaurants. Whichever direction she traveled, the prayer weakened. Ayanna looked closely at the cars and buildings nearby. There was a man sitting alone in a parked pickup truck, which seemed suspicious.

Ayanna walked up to the truck and peered in the window. The man's eyes were closed, and he wasn't alone. He was holding another person's head in his lap, forcefully moving it up and down. *Asshole.* Ayanna knocked on the driver's side window.

The man opened his eyes and angrily rolled down the window.

"What? I'm busy here."

"It doesn't look like you're doing anything at all."

"You ain't a cop, so get the hell out of here and leave us be."

"I don't like your attitude."

"You're a pretty bitch, aren't you? Maybe you'd like my attitude more after sucking my dick for a bit." The man released his hold on the other person, who sat up. It was a young woman, her face streaked with tears.

I found the source of the prayers. This jackass needs to be taught a lesson.

"Yeah, I don't think so," Ayanna sneered.

"If you aren't going to put your lips to good use, then fuck off."

Ayanna punched him through the open window, then reached down and opened the pickup's door.

"God damn it, bitch. I'll teach you a lesson."

"Nope, the lesson is yours, and class is in session." Ayanna backed up to give him space. "Bring it, asshole."

The man swung at her clumsily, trying to punch with one hand and zip up his pants with the other. Ayanna easily caught his swing and smoothly added her momentum to his while redirecting his punch into the side of his pickup. He screamed as his fist hit metal with an audible crunch. Ayanna slammed him face first into the truck, and then punched one of his kidneys. While he was stunned, she looked into the vehicle to check on the woman.

"Are you okay?"

"I can't open the door."

Ayanna popped the master lock on the driver's side, allowing the girl to get free.

"Thank you so much."

Holding the limply groaning man against his truck, Ayanna asked, "What happened?"

"I had a few drinks in the bar and he seemed nice, but then when we got in his truck, he got really aggressive."

"So, you didn't consent to sucking his dick?"

"No. He hit and threatened me."

Ayanna punched the pig in the kidneys again as he struggled to stand up. "I'm not done with you yet."

Referring to the young woman, she asked, "How old are you anyway?"

"Twenty-one."

Ayanna snorted. "Bullshit. Really, how old are you?"

After a pause, the girl answered, "Fifteen."

"Are you fucking kidding me? Take this as a lesson and make better choices in the future."

"How did you find me?"

"You prayed for help, and I came."

"God sent you to help me?"

"No, God didn't do shit. You prayed, and I answered. Now, do you have any lipstick?"

"Yeah, why?"

"Give it to me."

"Oh, okay."

As the girl fumbled for her lipstick, Ayanna dragged the whimpering man to his feet. With ease, she ripped his shirt off. She idly punched him again and then told him to take his shoes and pants off. He protested until she kneed him in the balls. Shortly thereafter, he was standing in the street wearing nothing but socks, holding his injured hand and trying vainly to cover his exposed genitals.

As the girl handed over the lipstick, Ayanna asked, "What's your name?"

"Heather."

"Heather, do you have a safe place to go?"

"No. Not really."

"Not even home?"

"Hell no. My mom's boyfriend is a fucking creep who touches me whenever she isn't looking. Then she yells at me and calls me a liar if I tell her what he does."

"Any other family?"

"No. My dad is a drunk asshole who lives in Idaho."

"I'm really sorry. You can crash on my couch tonight if you want. As for you..." Ayanna focused her attention on the cowering man. She used lipstick to write the word 'rapist' across his chest. Ayanna forcefully flipped him around and slammed him against the pickup truck. She wrote the words 'I don't believe in consent' across his back.

Ayanna fished his phone out of his pants and made him unlock it. She dialed 911 and told the dispatcher the location where the police could find a publicly intoxicated man exposing himself to minors. Ayanna hung up and threw the phone into a sewer, then got into his truck and rolled the window most of the way up. Getting out, Ayanna locked the pickup and then threw the keys inside through the small gap in the window.

Turning to Heather, Ayanna said, "Let's get out of here."

"You can't leave me like this," the man wailed.

"Watch me."

Ayanna walked Heather back home where she introduced the girl to Brandi, who immediately took over her care. While Brandi got Heather tea and a washcloth, Ayanna went and knocked on Mortimer's door. As vampires go, Mortimer was unusual, as they much preferred being a club DJ to the usual undead professions. They were ready to leave for a gig when Ayanna knocked and asked them for help. Unsurprisingly, they knew just the right lawyer to help Heather get her life sorted out. Ayanna called that lawyer who agreed to help and also advised Ayanna to not punch Heather's mom's boyfriend's teeth in.

Ayanna checked in on Heather and made sure she was comfortable in Brandi's capable hands. The poor girl was already drunkenly snoring. Ayanna thanked Brandi and wished her a good night before going to bed herself. Between Sean getting her wound up and then the adrenaline rush of saving Heather, Ayanna needed to masturbate to three orgasms before she could fall asleep.

Waking up and feeling refreshed, Ayanna went downstairs to find Brandi and Jesús keeping an eye on the still sleeping Heather. She greeted her friends, although only Jesús responded verbally. Brandi had assumed her cat form to make it easier to watch over Heather in the night without being creepy, so she responded to Ayanna with a tail twitch.

Jesús handed Ayanna a steaming mug of coffee, and they sat down at the table for a whispered conversation. "What happened last night?"

Ayanna recounted the night's events from when she got home to Heather's presence on their couch.

"You really heard her prayer for help?"

"I'm as surprised as you are. Wait... you aren't surprised, are you?"

"I am." He didn't look very surprised.

"Jesús, what aren't you telling me?"

"Remember yesterday when I had breakfast with Sean?"

"You mean the breakfast where I somehow became the Goddess of Nerds and Gamers? That's been super annoying, by the way. Do you have any idea how many people pray for good dice rolls on Saturdays?"

"I'm guessing a lot. Don't forget, Goddess of Bookworms, too."

"Well, now I know why I had such a good time at Powell's yesterday."

"You mean, besides being there with Sean?"

"Jesús, stop distracting me. What happened at breakfast with Sean?"

"I may have asked Sean what attributes you might have if you were a goddess."

"*May have?*" Ayanna was clearly struggling to keep her voice at a whisper.

"All right, I asked him, and one of his responses was that you are a badass for good. A goddess who protects people in need."

"Are you kidding me?"

"Of course not. He said you were a strong and powerful defender, like a lioness, protecting her pride."

"What else, Jesús?"

"Sean said you were a Goddess of Love. Also, honesty, self-improvement, and helping others improve themselves."

"And war?"

"No, no mention of war. But you are a defender and protector."

Ayanna sighed. "I can live with badass defender. Your stupid reinvention idea worked, and apparently it worked well."

"As you know, I'm existentially on the side of the peacemakers, but as much as I hate to admit it, sometimes that has its limitations. A badass goddess who stands up to defend others isn't a bad thing."

"No, it isn't. Honestly, it's better than being a Goddess of War. I've done and seen horrible things. Being a protector is an improvement."

"See, Goddess of Self-Improvement."

"You're pushing your luck, Jesús."

Jesús was saved from further threats by a meow from Brandi. They spun to see Heather groggily sit up.

"Good morning, how did you sleep?"

"Pretty good. This couch is surprisingly comfortable."

"It is. Heather, this is my housemate, Jesús. Do you mind if he gives you a brief check up? He was a medic, once upon a time." *It's a generally true statement.*

Jesús looked briefly startled, but he quickly smoothed his expression and nodded in assent.

"I guess so, sure. Just... Promise to stay here with me. I don't feel comfortable being alone with a guy right now."

"Of course, I will stay with you, sweetie. And don't worry.

Jesús is definitely the nicest person you will ever meet in your life."

Heather still looked leery, but she allowed Jesús to give her a brief examination. After pronouncing her fit, Jesús started talking with Heather. Ayanna took this opportunity to get Heather some tea.

"Here, drink this. It's Jesús' special medicinal blend. It helps, trust me."

"Oh, thank you."

As Heather and Jesús talked, Ayanna texted Sean to say good morning. They texted back and forth. He seemed disappointed she was busy, but he graciously said he understood. She silently observed the conversation in front of her. Heather was relaxing and unburdening herself while Jesús gently guided her toward healing her internalized struggles. Eventually, Jesús drew Ayanna into the conversation so she could talk with Heather about the options she learned about from the lawyer the previous evening. The two of them helped Heather come up with a plan. The next few years of her life were going to be tough, but they knew she had the strength to not just endure, but thrive.

Chapter 35

In My Dreams
Dokken

Sean had a lot to process after Ayanna left. That was, without question, the best night of his life. Just as important, he felt Ayanna had been pleased with the evening and his performance. Sean appreciated everything she had demonstrated for him. Not only had it felt really good for him, but it meant he didn't have to work so hard to figure out what she wanted from him.

Even better, he had seen boobs for the first time. Besides on a screen, of course. Thinking of all of this was not helping with the hard problem in his pants. Before he could get to sleep, he had to take this problem in hand, as it were. Outside of a few years ago when he had very guiltily watched porn for the first and only time, Sean hadn't masturbated because it was a sin.

I guess I'm past that now. Actually, why would God even care what I do with myself? Shouldn't He be dealing with wars and famines and stuff?

With that decided, Sean slowly stroked himself, as he recalled just how he felt with Ayanna. Once he finished, he suddenly felt exhausted. Sean cleaned himself up and crawled into bed, joined soon after by Huntress, who curled up behind his knees.

In the morning, Sean felt refreshed and revitalized. His dreams were the pleasant dreams of Ayanna, now with the new addition of her clad in form-fitting leather and chain armor, prowling the streets of Portland, protecting the innocent.

After feeding Huntress, he bustled about the apartment, tidying up and feeding himself. His phone buzzed, and he saw a message from Ayanna wishing him a good morning. They chatted, and she told him there was a situation she needed to tend to. He responded to say he understood and would really like to see her again soon.

With his morning free, Sean skipped church and walked over to Brandi's Bitchin' Brews for a late morning tea. Annabelle and Enrique were there, and Sean chatted with them while they prepared his tea. He mentioned how much he'd enjoyed the double date with Annabelle and Tanya on Friday.

Annabelle's shift was ending, and she suggested hanging out for a bit. Sean waited while she threw on sweats and a jacket. They walked to the nearby bridge, chatting pleasantly.

"So, when you aren't making coffee, what do you do?"

"I'm an artist. Mostly paintings and drawings."

"Wow, really?"

"Yeah. I've done a lot of natural scenes, flowers, gardens, and things like that. All of my tattoos are designed by me. I also like to showcase the human body."

"Like nudes?" Sean asked nervously.

Annabelle laughed at his blushing question, answering, "Yes, some. Did you want to model for me?"

Sean was all-out blushing now. "I don't really have the body for it."

"Of course you do. The human body is amazing and comes in so many shapes, sizes, and colors. Look at me. I'm obviously not your typical supermodel build, but that's okay with me. Some people like my body, and some people don't. Tanya likes it, and her opinion is what matters most to me."

"I get that. Accepting yourself is a healthy outlook—one I'm still working on."

"You obviously don't have to pose, but I would be happy to use you as a model. Clothes on or off." She waggled her eyebrows suggestively as she added, "I've never drawn any couples, but I would love to draw you and Ayanna if you two are interested."

"Wow, that's very flattering."

"It's an open invitation, so no pressure."

"Can I see some of your work?"

"Yeah, I have some on my phone. It's not the same as seeing the pieces in person, of course." They stopped on the bridge and Annabelle opened up a photo gallery on her phone.

Sean was not an art critic by any stretch, but he thought Annabelle's work was amazing. She had a lot of beautiful land-scapes and sketches interspersed with uncomfortably detailed human bodies. As he viewed her later works, he saw how she used natural backgrounds for some really pretty and sometimes sexy fantasy scenes involving faeries.

"Now you're getting to my most recent stuff."

Sean scrolled forward and almost dropped Annabelle's phone in the river. There on the screen was a painting of a bloodied half-orc version of Ayanna wearing a chain mail bikini, leaning wearily on a greatsword. He had seen this exact image in his dreams. The next image was of Ayanna in a bikini, swimming in a pool-sized cup of coffee. The image after that was of her as a barista with a battle axe. All exactly as he had dreamed of them.

"These last few are interesting," Sean said cautiously.

"Oh, I'm sorry. It's probably weird that I'm making art featuring your girlfriend. I didn't mean to upset you."

"No, it's fine. Where did you get the inspiration for these?"

"I don't know. I sat down, and it's like the images just flowed out of my hand."

"You didn't dream about them first?"

"No, why?"

"Because I did. I have seen each of these images in my dreams."

"That's strange and kinda creepy."

"Tell me about it."

"Have you had any other dreams like this?"

"Yeah, like the one where she is a vampire dressed all in black. Oh, there's the one where Ayanna is naked on a table, covered in spicy foods."

"Hang on. I painted this last night but haven't added it to the gallery yet." Annabelle switched to a different photo gallery and there was the image of Ayanna on a table, covered in food. "Okay, I'm getting one of those supernatural feelings. How long have you been having these dreams?"

"Some for a couple of weeks. The food dream was new as of a couple days ago. When did you start drawing these?"

"Yesterday. I felt like my arm was going to fall off when I went to bed last night."

"You haven't done any paintings of Ayanna as some kind of ancient goddess, have you?"

Annabelle looked puzzled. "No, why? Wait... you don't think maybe she is some kind of goddess, do you? Because a goddess wouldn't be working at a coffee cart in Portland with her tits hanging out, would she?"

She might, actually.

Sean kept his face as neutral as he could. "No, that wouldn't make sense. Have you ever drawn or painted religious art or anything? Not just random goddesses."

"I haven't. My parents weren't religious, and I grew up agnostic. Religion was never part of my life. You?"

"My parents didn't really do church, but they had very harsh moral views. In college I became Catholic."

"No wonder you almost broke your eyes not staring at my jugs the first day I saw you at the cart."

"Sorry." Sean couldn't help the reflexive rush of shame burning his ears.

"It's cool. I'm glad you can look at my girls now but still don't gawk at them. It shows maturity and respect. I mean, when I'm wearing a bikini in the cart, it's almost insulting if you don't look."

"I didn't think of it that way."

"Sean, you really are a sweet guy, and you can always ask me if something is uncomfortable. I'm very happy for you and Ayanna. You two seem so good for each other."

"Thank you. You and Tanya are a great couple, too."

Annabelle looked awkward. "I'm not sure if I should—"

"Tell me you slept with Ayanna? She already told me. I'll admit it bothered me a bit at first, but at this point, I am totally fine with it. Ayanna is... pansexual, I think she called it, and let's be honest, you and Tanya are beautiful women, so I get why she slept with you."

"Oh, wow. Have you thought about a three—"

He shook his head vigorously. "Nope, I'm not going there. Like I said, you are beautiful; however, I happily have my hands full with Ayanna, and she is more than enough for me."

"I bet you have your hands full..."

Sean grinned. "I walked into that, didn't I?"

"Yes, you did. Speaking of my beautiful girlfriend, I'm going to go home to her now. Thanks for walking with me, Sean. Maybe I'll draw more of your dreams."

"Yeah, this was fun, Annabelle. Say hi to Tanya for me."

"Will do. Later!"

After Annabelle left, Sean fell deep into thought. If he were anyone else, then he would probably chalk up his dreams matching Annabelle's art to some kind of weird coincidence, but he was a Diviner, and Diviners examined weird coincidences for a living. That, combined with his discussion with Jesús, made Sean suddenly very suspicious. Protocol required he draft a report with all available information and let the Hounds decide if it was worth following up. But Sean wasn't going to follow protocol.

Sean: "Are you still busy?"

Ayanna: "A bit, why?"

Sean: "We need to talk. ASAP."

Ayanna: "Okay."

Sean waited a few minutes for any further response.

Ayanna: "I can meet you."

Sean: "My place in an hour?"

Ayanna: "C U then."

Chapter 36

Who Are You

The Who

Ayanna was nervous when she arrived at Sean's place. Heather was in good hands with Brandi while Jesús slept. The poor girl was handling this well, especially for a fifteen-year-old with a terrible childhood. Ayanna was happy she didn't have to worry about Heather for the moment, although thinking of Heather's situation was a welcome distraction from Sean's dreaded four words. "We need to talk" was the death knell for many relationships.

Sean opened the door when she knocked, closing it behind her. His mood was somber, and there was no 'hello' kiss.

"Have a seat, please." His tone was grave.

Ayanna sat on the couch and said, "What's up?" as pleasantly as possible.

Sean sat down and looked her straight in the eye. "There's no easy way to ask this question, so I'll just say it. Ayanna, are you a goddess?"

Ayanna was stunned by the question.

How could he know? What gave me away? Why can't I lie? What is happening?

She tried to play it off by saying, "I knew last night was good, but I didn't think it was *that* good."

"I'm serious, Ayanna. Very serious. Are you a goddess?"

Ayanna struggled to lie, but somehow she couldn't.

Goddess of Honesty and Improvement of Self and Others. He did this to me. They both did. Sean and Jesús. I am so screwed right now.

She was horrified as a single word escaped her lips. "Yes."

Sean's face was an unreadable mask, his voice cold. "Yes, you are a goddess? As in an ancient being of unimaginable power?"

"Yes and no."

"What does that mean? Who are you, really?"

Ayanna answered reluctantly, "My name is Inanna, and I am over six thousand years old. I am so old that I don't truly remember how old I am. I have had many names over the years, including Ishtar." The final words came out in a rush that Ayanna couldn't stop despite her best efforts.

"The Goddess of Love and War. You cast some kind of bewitchment on me, didn't you?" Sean looked angry, furious even. "You tricked me into falling in love with you."

He's in love with me.

"No. It has been a very long time since I was the Goddess of Love and War. The last of my worshippers died out many centuries ago, and I have been powerless ever since. I don't age, and I am immune to many of the perils of mortality, but I have no power over mortals."

"So, you claim there is no bewitchment on me?"

"Sean, I don't claim that—I state it with complete honesty."

"Uh huh. You say you're honest, but a six-thousand-year-old goddess must be wily beyond belief."

"You might be right in most circumstances, but in this case, you are wrong. You are wrong because I am no longer Inanna or

Ishtar." Ayanna stood up. "I am Ayanna, Goddess of Honesty and Improvement of Self and Others."

"What the fuck does *that* mean?"

There was heat in Ayanna's voice now. "It's what *you* made me. I am also Ayanna, Goddess of Love, Goddess of Tea and Spicy Foods, Goddess of Nerds, Gamers, and Bookworms, and Badass in a Good Way Who Protects Those Who Need It."

"What do you mean, *I* made you? I can't create a goddess."

Ayanna laughed wildly. "My dear, sweet, Sean. How do you think deities came to be in the first place? We didn't create you in *our* image, you created us in *yours*."

She watched as Sean absorbed this knowledge.

"So, God didn't create the world? He didn't even exist when it was created?"

Ayanna snorted. "Please. I remember when Abram slunk out of Ur with his jealous and fearful God. If I had known the future, then I would have destroyed them both then and there. I was at the height of my power and it would have been easy."

"My dreams. I saw you as a goddess."

"Yes, and that terrified me. I barely remember those days now, and you saw me at the height of my power." Ayanna's voice lowered to a whisper. "You saw me as I was brought low, forced to kneel before Alexander and his gods."

"That was Alexander the Great I saw in my dream?"

She grunted. "Alexander the Over-entitled Asshole if you ask me."

Realization continued to dawn on Sean's face. "Wait... Jesús said you met in Rome. When? When did you meet him?"

"I met Jesús during Diocletian's reign."

"Are you telling me—"

"Jesús is Jesus Christ. Well, one of him anyway."

Sean was reeling at this point. Ayanna could see how every

new revelation was a shock to his system. "What do you mean, 'one of them?' Are there multiple Jesus Christs?"

"Two, as far as I know. You've met Jesús, obviously. He is the kind and gentle Christ everyone knows and loves. He feeds the hungry and heals the sick. Jesús blesses the meek and the peace-makers. He loves his neighbors and considers the whole world his neighborhood. You don't ever want to meet the other Jesus."

Sean's face was ashen. "Why?"

"Because the other Jesus is a monster. Christians who accumulate vast wealth in his name are his followers. So are the Crusaders who made the streets of Jerusalem run knee-deep in blood. The Inquisition that burned thousands at the stake, and the Conquistadors who brought death to millions, all followed the other Jesus. Today, the Christians who cheer when refugees drown in barbed wire in the Rio Grande or hound trans kids until they die by suicide—they follow the horrible Jesus."

"But Jesus is supposed to be good."

"Jesús is good—the best, really. But humanity is complex—for better or worse, we are your creations. Humans give us our attributes and spheres of influence, so we are often more focused with distinct traits, but some of us have multiple incarnations. After Constantine, the cruel and vicious Jesus became ascendent. He created the Godkillers, humans trained to hunt gods, and we've been running from them ever since, including Jesús."

Sean looked sick.

"What? No questions about the Godkillers? You questioned everything—oh, *fuck me*..." Realization came crashing down on Ayanna now. She wanted to vomit, to scream, to run and never stop running.

"You wanted to know about my mysterious job. I'm a Godkiller." Sean's face strained with grief, and his voice dripped with contrition.

After all of the shocks I delivered to Sean, I suppose it makes sense that the worst shock of all comes back to me.

"No, no, no. Sean, please tell me you're lying."

He stood up and reached for her. "It's true, and I'm sorry. I'm not going to tell anyone. I swear on it on my life. I love you, Ayanna, and I would never let anyone hurt you. Or Jesús for that matter. Wait, what about your cat, Bast? Is she..."

"Actually Bast."

"And Mortimer?"

"They're a vampire."

He looked confused. "You said they weren't."

"That was before I became the Goddess of Honesty."

"Oh."

"Sean, as the Goddess of Honesty, and Love, I'm going to tell you something—something I haven't said to anyone in over sixteen hundred years. I love you."

Even with all of this, it feels amazing to say those words.

"Thank you." His smile was brilliant. "I love you, too. Can I ask who the last person was?"

"You can. It was Athena."

"As in..."

Ayanna shrugged. "Yes, that one."

Sean cackled ruefully. "Quite a downgrade from a literal goddess to me."

"You sell yourself short, Sean. You're a really great guy."

"Hang on, who is Jesús' girlfriend?"

"Mary Magdalene, of course."

"No shit," Sean uttered breathlessly.

"Yeah, no shit. Before you ask, yes, his mom is hanging around as well. I don't know where. Most of us who are left keep our heads down to avoid... well, you."

"I'm putting in my two weeks notice tomorrow."

"Are you sure? Not that I want to screw a Godkiller, but

would it look suspicious if you just quit two weeks after arriving in Portland?"

"Are you going to screw me?"

"I love you, Sean," Ayanna chortled fondly. "We're discussing gods and Godkillers and *that's* your takeaway?" Ayanna laughed and kissed him. Sean kissed her back with equal passion.

Chapter 37

Do You Wanna Touch Me (Oh Yeah)
Joan Jett & the Blackhearts

As they kissed, Sean's old nemesis, guilt, reared its ugly head. He grudgingly broke the kiss, pushing Ayanna back. "I need to ask you something. You said you're the goddess of all these things because of me, right?"

"Honestly, I'm not completely sure. Jesús came up with this theory, and so far, it seems to be correct. It makes sense, given what I remember of my past."

"Does this mean I'm controlling you now? You talked before about consent, but how can you really consent if I'm the one who makes you goddess of whatever?"

"That's a tricky question I don't entirely know the answer to. I can say I had feelings for you before you decided I was still a Goddess of Love. I also believe my prior love life was linked to my worshippers' beliefs about me. The god I was married to, the men and gods that I slept with, the son I had, none of that was really my choice. I really don't want to go back to being a pawn."

"You shouldn't have to. Ayanna, I want you to be free and in control of your life, even if it means you don't love me anymore."

They both paused, waiting for some sort of profound change to occur.

Sean broke the silence and asked, "Do you feel any different?"

"Let's try something." Ayanna kissed him again, hesitantly at first. As the kiss continued, the passion ramped up quickly to a full-blown game of tonsil hockey. Panting, they pulled apart. Ayanna gasped, "I'm still hot and bothered for you."

"But do you still love me?"

"Definitely."

"What if I'm not your only worshipper now? Would that change things?"

"Who?"

"Annabelle. We talked and she showed me her art. She's been drawing you—drawing the images in my dreams even though she knew nothing of my dreams before today."

"Really? Fascinating. Annabelle is incredibly talented, but dream reading seems an unlikely talent to have."

"I don't think it's dream reading because we never talked about any of this. Are you sending out signals or something?"

She sniffed. "That's not how prophecies work. This is something different—something new." Ayanna's face lit up. "Which gives me an idea. I'm going to call Annabelle. While I do that, why don't you get a pen and paper and draw me?"

"Draw you?"

"Trust me, okay? Let me get my phone while you get what you need."

Sean heard Ayanna call Annabelle while he found a pen and something to write on.

"Hey, Annabelle." Pause. "I have a strange question for you. Do you think I should date or screw whomever I want?" Pause. "No, ah, things with Sean are great. Amazing, actually." Pause. "He is really sweet. That's actually why I called you." Long pause. "As incredible as a threesome would be, or foursome, I didn't call you for sex. I guess I just wanted to check with a friend before Sean and I... you know." Pause. "That's great, thank you. I think you and Tanya are a fantastic couple, too." Pause. "What? Really? Of course, I won't tell her." Pause, then Ayanna squealed. "Seriously, that's amazing, Annabelle, and I am really excited for you. I want you and Tanya to both be happy in life and with each other." Long pause. "Wow. That would be a huge step. If that's something you want and Sean doesn't mind, then maybe the foursome idea isn't off the table after all." A laughter-filled pause. "Thank you for talking with me. Say hi to Tanya for me, and I wish you both the best."

"What was that about? A foursome?"

"Again, that's your takeaway?"

They both laughed.

Ayanna continued, "Annabelle thought I was hinting at a threesome at first. She didn't want to have one because she thinks you're a great guy who loves me and only me, and a threesome wouldn't be fair to you or her, for that matter. You heard my response, I'm sure. Then, she told me how much she's fallen for Tanya and she's thinking of proposing to her."

"Wow, that's really fast."

"Yes and no. They've known each other for years and get along great. Now their relationship is on a new level, and apparently Annabelle wants to take the next step."

"What was the foursome bit at the end?"

"Annabelle wants kids, and I... uh... well, you heard. But, you know, only if you wanted to, of course. Annabelle laughed at the idea, but she didn't say no either."

"Um, that's really flattering and all, but we still haven't done it. I could be bad at sex."

Ayanna responded with a feral leer. "I guess we'll find out soon. First, though, let me see what you've drawn."

Sean showed Ayanna what he drew.

"Sweetie, please don't take this the wrong way, but it looks like Picasso dropped acid and tried to paint with a broken arm."

"Yeah, I thought so, too. Were you trying to see if maybe Annabelle had made you into a Goddess of Art?"

"That's exactly what I was checking. Clearly not, although being a Goddess of Art would be really nice. I think I would like that."

"Why don't you decide to be a Goddess of Art, then? For thousands of years, you were molded by your believers. Maybe you always had the power to choose but just didn't know you even had that option."

"I wonder if I can also not be certain things, like the Goddess of Nerds, Gamers, and Bookworms."

Sean's face must have betrayed his feelings, because Ayanna continued, "Oh, sorry. You must like that one."

"I do. I'm sorry. You don't have to be that goddess if you don't want to."

"No, it's okay. Those folks need a goddess, too. I want to be there for them."

Sean was feeling better now, his initial anger now fully subsided. "Ayanna, I'm sorry for how I reacted and for accusing you of manipulating me."

"You don't have to be sorry. It was a very valid concern."

She's being very understanding, even about my job.

"I'm also sorry about, you know, making you the goddess of stuff. I didn't know."

"Sean, it's okay. Like you said, you didn't know."

"I just want you to be the goddess you want to be. I love you and trust you, and I know you will be a great goddess."

"Thank you, I appreciate you saying that."

"What does it mean for us, though? You've already lived for thousands of years and are immortal. I'm not."

"I don't know, Sean. I really don't. What I do know is I want to be with you as long as possible."

Sean embraced Ayanna and they simply held each other for a

while. She felt comfortable in his arms. He worried about how much time they would have together, but he was looking forward to every minute of it.

As the embrace lingered, holding each other slowly shifted into exploration with their hands, followed by their lips. Sean pulled back and said, "There's another thing I need to confess."

"Go on, although I'm not one for confessions."

"Last night, after, you know, all the things we did... I touched myself."

"You masturbated, thinking about me?" Ayanna's eyes danced with lurid glee.

"I did. Was that wrong?"

"Did it feel wrong?"

"Yes... No... I felt like I should feel guilty because of what I had been told all my life, but yet it didn't, because maybe masturbation doesn't matter."

"How many times?"

"Just once, I swear." Sean felt a rush of panic.

Ayanna chortled. "Would it make you feel better if I told you I got myself off three times last night thinking of you?"

"Three? Now I feel bad I only did it once."

"You definitely should have done more, then." Ayanna teased.

Inspired by Ayanna's revelation, Sean remembered something from yesterday and decided to move outside of his comfort zone. He wrapped one hand in the hair at the back of Ayanna's neck and firmly pulled, exposing her neck and an ear. Sean attacked her ear with his lips and teeth, eliciting a throaty groan from Ayanna. As he gently-yet-assertively nipped at her earlobe, Sean murmured, "I'm only mortal, and we should make good use of my limited time, don't you think?"

"Mm, you wicked mortal," Ayanna sighed. "Such temerity to insinuate such things of your goddess. You do make a good point, though." She wrested control back from Sean by putting her hands on his chest and marching him backwards until he hit the couch and sat down with a surprised grunt.

Sean was still a bit stunned when Ayanna pounced on him. She straddled his legs and pulled him upright just enough to haul his shirt over his head. Once Sean's torso was bare, Ayanna attacked his mouth, neck, and ears. In the midst of this frenzy, she grunted, "Shirt. Off."

"It is," Sean panted.

"*Mine.*"

Sean worked to open the buttons of Ayanna's blouse, a task made significantly more difficult because she continued to maul his ears and neck, which was very distracting. Her writhing further complicated things, but he did eventually manage to get her shirt off. Once they were both bare from the waist up, Sean made good use of his access to Ayanna's breasts.

He was enjoying the rhythm of their combined motions, Ayanna's mouth on the sensitive skin of his ears and jawline, and her warm, soft orbs in his hands. Just as he was getting used to what they were doing, she firmly planted her lips on his. Ayanna rose up as her tongue invaded Sean's mouth. He felt her hands moving sensuously and purposefully down his chest. Keeping her mouth firmly attached to his, Ayanna lifted up and started tugging at Sean's pants. He tried to help her, their fingers dueling as they both tried to get his pants undone.

With the button finally undone and the zipper down, Sean lifted his hips. Ayanna stopped kissing him long enough to ask, "Are you good with this, and can I go further?"

"Goddess, yes. Don't stop."

"Perfect. Tell me if anything changes." She resumed kissing him passionately while pushing at his pants. "Fuck it," Ayanna snarled. She stood up and yanked his pants and underwear down to his ankles, then pulled them completely off, along with his socks. "You're not wearing only socks for this," she muttered.

For the first time since infancy, Sean was completely naked in front of a woman, and she happened to be a goddess. He fought the urge to cover himself as Ayanna ogled him from foot to head. Sean was pleased when she uttered a single word, "Nice." With a wicked grin, Ayanna pounced on Sean again, kissing him fiercely while her hands grasped at his cock. She stroked him slowly as she kissed her way down his chest.

Sean watched the top of her head as Ayanna descended until she was kneeling between his legs. His head lolled back, and Sean nearly fainted when he felt a gentle kiss on the head of his stiff member. Ayanna's tongue swirled around the crown and trailed down his shaft. He felt her caress his balls as she reached the base. Sean looked down to see Ayanna's eyes blazing with passion as she looked back at him. She licked her way back up and then engulfed him in her mouth. Their eyes stayed locked as she drew him further in, working on him with her lips, tongue, and hands.

The heat and wetness of Ayanna's mouth was intense beyond anything Sean could have imagined. As she bobbed her head, he felt an explosion building. "Ayanna, I'm... Oh, goddess, I think—" Ayanna stroked his balls with one hand and took him even further inside. Sean erupted, filling her mouth. He nearly blacked out from the pleasure. Ayanna kept her mouth on him, suckling until the final spurt before raising her head and visibly swallowing.

She sat beside him, gently caressing his cheek, before asking, "Did you like that?"

"Oh, my goddess... You are amazing. I've never felt anything like that. Thank you. Thank you so much."

"Can I kiss you now, or would you prefer if I—"

"Fucking kiss me, please."

"Mm, good boy," Ayanna cooed.

Sean could slightly taste himself in her mouth, but really didn't care. All he cared about was this incredible woman. As they kissed, he instinctively slid a hand lower, down to her thighs. With a groan, Ayanna guided Sean further up her thighs and under her skirt. At the top of her leg, his fingers felt a hot wetness.

Ayanna leaned back and said, "Oops, you still have my panties."

Sean chuckled as he responded, "Maybe I should never give them back."

"Oh, you're very naughty. Are you ready for your next lesson?"

"Yes, definitely."

"Let's get this off of me and we'll do some show and tell." Ayanna perched precariously on one leg, and Sean put his hands in the waistband of her skirt while simultaneously trying to suck one hanging boob. "I admire your desire to multitask, but I'm going to need you to focus for a minute."

Once Sean shimmied her skirt off, Ayanna fell back, naked with her legs spread before him. Sean thoroughly admired the view. Ayanna took one of his hands and placed it on her pussy. "Let's give you a little geography lesson. Do you feel this hard nub? That's my clitoris, and unlike what you may have read on the internet, it is very real. Playing with this is a lot like playing with your penis. It feels really good. A little down is where I pee. There are some good nerve endings there, too. Does that bother you?"

"Uh." Sean hadn't thought of that before.

"Recall where my mouth was a minute ago. Now think about your answer."

"Doesn't bother me at all," Sean responded quickly.

"Good answer. Down below, let's call these my other lips. There are lots of nerves down here, too. It's easy to forget them between the clit and what comes next." Ayanna took hold of two of Sean's fingers and pressed them through her outer folds into her hot, wet core. "And this is the vagina, the promised land. You can do a lot for me with all of these places, so don't neglect any of them. Now, would you like to get your tongue down here?"

"Yes," Sean said with immense enthusiasm. He practically dove in headfirst.

"I'm going to let you explore, but I will also give you some guidance and instruction, okay?"

Sean gave her a thumbs-up as he ran his tongue from bottom to top. He felt a bit awkward with his nose buried in what she called a "landing strip," but he persevered. Sean wasn't exactly sure what Ayanna tasted like—musky, but he liked it. He lapped at her lips and clitoris with his tongue, eliciting pleased moans. At Ayanna's suggestion, he did some nibbling and sucking in those areas as well. Sean experimented with getting his tongue inside of her, before resuming licking and nibbling. Ayanna encouraged him, teaching him different ways to use his tongue. At one point, she was compelled to say, "Lover, when I tell you to keep doing that, you should keep doing exactly what you're doing and not something completely different." Sean took the hint.

His mouth started getting tired, but he pressed on, heartened by her whimpers and moans. Ayanna started crying out, and Sean redoubled his efforts, to be rewarded as her hips bucked. Sean latched on with his mouth and held on for dear life as Ayanna came hard.

As Ayanna's orgasm subsided, Sean wearily made his way up her body, resting his head on her heaving chest. Her panting subsided, and Sean asked, "Did you like that?"

"Oh, yes."

"So, I did well?"

Ayanna murmured, "Very well. Are you sure you've never eaten pussy before?"

"I'm positive."

"I give you five stars, and I would *definitely* ride that ride again," Ayanna said with a satisfied leer.

Sean asked shyly, "Can I kiss you?"

Ayanna answered Sean by pulling him into a ferocious kiss.

Chapter 38

Pour Some Sugar On Me

Def Leppard

They snuggled together on the couch, gently kissing, touching, and fondling each other. The skin-to-skin contact soothed any lingering feelings from their earlier discussion and grew their bond. A comfortable make-out session got them both worked up again when they were rudely interrupted by Huntress, who hopped up on them. They both stared at her as she tried to find a comfortable place to curl up; however, their bare skin seemed to make her nervous. Huntress' paw pads and claw tips felt strange on their sensitive skin.

Ayanna finally sat up to pick up the mewling cat. "I'm sorry, little sweetie. This isn't the best time for you to be here. Your daddy and I have some business to take care of right now, but I promise we will provide you with plenty of love and affection later." Huntress seemed mollified by this and consented to being placed on the floor.

"It really seems like you can speak to cats."

"Brandi can, but she's a cat goddess. We are both lioness goddesses, so cats can kind of understand me. I can't understand them, though. I can communicate with doves, though."

"Doves and lionesses? That seems like a strange pairing."

"No argument here. You could ask why, but the people who could answer are long dead, I'm afraid."

"Lions seem to be a common theme from your era. I mean, older days, uh..."

"You're cute when you stumble over things."

"To be fair, not many guys have a six-thousand-year-old girlfriend."

"Never discuss a lady's age, my love."

"Sorry."

"To answer your question, yes, lions were the ultimate apex predator in those days, so they show up a lot in art and writing."

"Cool." Sean leaned in; his voice eager. "So, you mentioned unfinished business."

"Right, where were we?" Ayanna returned to kissing and fondling with renewed energy. She could taste herself on Sean's mouth, and she loved it. He really had done very well for his first time.

Not as good as Athena, but he'll get better. I'm going to really enjoy coaching him.

As much as she was enjoying this, she felt like she needed to check in. "Hey, Sean. Are you good with everything so far?"

"Yes, I am. What about you?"

"Very good. I just want to make sure I haven't broken your brain again."

"You came close when you, you know."

"Gave you a blow job?"

"Yes, that."

"Sean, you are going to have to learn how to express yourself and talk about these things. What happened after I gave you a blow job?"

He looked nervous. "I ate your pussy?"

"You did. We each went down on each other. And what is it called if we go down on each other at the same time?"

"Sixty-nine?"

"Good boy."

"Are we going to sixty-nine?"

"Not tonight, lover. If you want to, there's something else we can do tonight."

"Uh..."

"We're going to bang like a screen door in a hurricane, Sean."

"Um."

"I'm going to ride you like a gold medal equestrian."

"We're going to get it on?"

"That lacks a certain expressiveness, but it's a good start."

"We're going to plow like a..."

"You'll get it. But yes, if you want to, of course."

"Um, I'll be your show pony if you want to ride me."

Ayanna roared with laughter at Sean's awkward but heartfelt attempt. "Now you're getting it. And soon you'll definitely be *getting it*." Ayanna ended any further discussion by giving their lips something better to do. The kissing and fondling ramped up quickly to a full-on make-out session with heavy petting. Once Ayanna got to a place where she felt very ready, she forcefully maneuvered Sean into a prone position with his back on one arm of the couch. Ayanna straddled Sean and kissed him, reaching down to rub the tip of his cock along her labia. "Are you ready?"

"Yes," he said, voice hungry with desire.

With Sean's consent, Ayanna slowly lowered herself down, feeling him slowly fill her. Once she had him fully engulfed, she stopped and held still. "How do you feel?"

"I thought your mouth was incredible, but this is far beyond that."

"Thank you. Just take a minute to let Big Sean get used to his new home."

"Um, Ayanna, I know I'm new to this and all, but shouldn't we, you know—"

"Use a condom? One of the side benefits to being a goddess is that I can't get or give diseases, and another benefit is, for the most part, I can't get pregnant unless I want to."

"Oh, good to know. What does 'for the most part' mean?"

"It's not always true. Brandi—well... Bast—is a fertility goddess. She gets pregnant all the time. Condoms are a must for her, at least until she inevitably gets pregnant. Then she fucks anything that moves."

"That's a little too much information."

"You're right. Now where were we..." Ayanna started to shimmy. She watched Sean's facial expressions as she slid all the way up and then came hurtling back down. Ayanna was pleased he had the decency to feel her tits while she rode him. The extra sensations were doing good things for her. As Ayanna rode Sean, she worked her own fingernails down his chest. He grabbed her hips and followed her motions, now meeting her descents with upward thrusts. Ayanna kissed Sean fiercely, rewarding his vigor.

Ayanna continued pistoning on his shaft until sweat was pouring off of both of them. Sean was the first to give out, spasming beneath her. Ayanna strummed her clitoris as she felt his seed explode inside of her. Sean fell limp underneath her as her own orgasm rocketed through her body. As the waves of pleasure diminished, Ayanna collapsed on top of Sean, both of them panting like racehorses, still joined together.

"Was it good for you?"

"Oh, dear... I don't have... words... Deer are nice..."

"Deer are nice, my love. It was good for me, too."

Exhausted, they both drifted off to sleep.

Chapter 39

I Wanna Be A Cowboy

Boys Don't Cry

Sean didn't sleep for long. He was in a weird position already, and Ayanna was heavy. The struggle to breathe pulled Sean roughly from slumber, and he found himself wondering exactly what to do.

Sex is a lot of fun, but it's messy, and right now I feel very damp. I wonder if I can get myself out from under her without waking her up.

Sean tried to gently push Ayanna off of him while simultaneously sliding the other way. This process turned out to be futile due to Sean's lack of both strength and leverage, Ayanna's weight, and the fact that they were still physically attached. His efforts did succeed in waking her up.

"Mm, I'm sorry I fell asleep on you. I bet you're uncomfortable."

"A bit, but it's no problem," Sean lied.

"You're lying, but I appreciate the effort. As much as I would like to go for round two, I'm going to get cleaned up instead. You made me very messy."

"Oh, sorry—"

"I'm teasing you, Sean. You did really well, and making a mess is kinda the point. While I'm cleaning myself up, why don't you feed Huntress and then meet me in your bed?"

"Okay, sure." Sean heaved himself up and staggered over to the kitchen, where he fumbled his way through the process of feeding Huntress. As he walked to the bedroom, Sean debated putting on some clothes. He felt shy, having never walked around naked in front of someone else. When Sean reached the bedroom and saw Ayanna standing naked next to it, he felt as though he'd made the right choice. He watched as she slipped under the covers, leaving him a space next to her.

Sean wasn't really sure what to do next, so he asked, "What now?"

"Let's just hold each other. No sex, no fondling. Let's just comfortably enjoy our skin against each other."

And so that's what they did. Sean and Ayanna cuddled, exchanging the occasional murmured words until they both fell asleep. Sometime late in the night or perhaps early in the morning, Sean woke to find Ayanna dressed next to the bed.

"Are you leaving?"

"I need to be at work soon, and you do, too. Thank you for last night."

"Thank you. You are the best teacher ever."

"Aw, you're welcome." Her smile warmed his heart.

"I love you, Ayanna."

"I love you, too, Sean." She kissed him gently on the forehead and then left. He watched her, and she stopped at the doorway to look at him and give a small wave before she exited his apartment.

Sean woke again a few hours later, ravenously hungry.

I hope yesterday wasn't a dream. Oh, I'm naked. Not a dream, then. Holy shit, I'm dating an actual goddess. Sean bolted upright as the reality of the situation pierced the lingering fog of happiness from the previous night. *Oh, wow, I'm totally screwed. How do I cover this up so that no other Godkillers find out there is a goddess alive and well in Portland? Right... two goddesses, a vampire, and Jesus Christ, the good one. This is so bad.*

Chapter 40

True Colors
Cyndi Lauper

Ayanna slipped quietly through the door and past Heather's sleeping form. She was happy to have saved the girl, but having an unaware mortal in the house could get tricky. Ayanna opened her bedroom door and saw a cat sitting on her bed.

"You're slinking home late," Brandi said. "You smell like sweat... and cum. Ayanna, please tell me you and Sean finally did it."

"Um."

Brandi's voice was filled with pride. "You magnificent slut. Tell me everything."

"Nope, I'm not going to."

"At least tell me if it was good."

"It was... perfect."

"*Damn it.*"

"What?"

"I owe Jesús twenty bucks."

There was a light knock at the door. Ayanna opened it, and Jesús asked, "May I come in?"

Brandi snickered. "Too late, Sean already came in her."

"*Really?* Ayanna, I'm very happy for you."

Brandi choked in shock at Jesús' reaction.

Jesús snickered. "Hairball?"

Ayanna was similarly shocked. "Jesús, how come you aren't disgusted and telling us to be better?"

"This is too much fun. I should have learned to do this a long time ago. Oh, and Brandi owes me twenty bucks."

"What were you two betting on?"

"Brandi bet that Sean was just a passing phase, and I bet that it was true love."

"I love him, but there's a problem. He's a Godkiller."

"*What?*" Brandi exclaimed.

And Jesús said, "I know."

"*You know?*" both goddesses shouted.

"Yes, and I trust he knows the truth about you, Ayanna?"

"He figured it out, and I confirmed it."

"You told him you're a goddess?" Brandi's voice was rising dangerously.

Ayanna made soothing gestures. "Hear me out, and then we'll get to you once I'm done, Jesús." Ayanna took a deep breath and started, "Yesterday, Sean asked me if I was a goddess. I tried to lie, but I couldn't, because Sean and this meddler here—" she gestured at Jesús "—made me into a Goddess of Honesty. Then Sean accused me of manipulating him, and I explained I couldn't. Then, I told him the truth about gods, which blew his mind, and then we made up and I sucked his cock. After that, I taught him how to eat pussy, and we had wonderful sex. Also, he knows that you're Bast, that you're the good Jesús, and that he's basically working for the bad Jesús."

Brandi looked stunned. "Wow. That's a lot. Presumably we aren't going to have Hunters at our door today?"

"No, he's planning to quit his job. On to you, Jesús. You knew Sean was a Godkiller, and you let me date him anyway?"

"I could see into his heart. He's a good and caring person. In my defense, it worked out well for you."

"We discovered something important. *I* can decide what I am a goddess of. *I* can decide my own fate. We don't have to be bound by what our worshipers believe."

"Are you saying I don't have to be pregnant all the damn time?"

"Yeah, I think so."

Brandi changed from cat to human to give Ayanna a huge hug. Ayanna looked at Jesús over Brandi's shoulder. "Any chance you can do an accelerated pregnancy miracle for her?"

He shrugged. "I've never tried it, but I can give it a shot."

Brandi was crying by now. "Thanks, Jesús. I just want to finally have control over my own fertility."

"I want that for you, too, my friend," Jesús said kindly.

"All right, get out of my room, you two."

After they left, Ayanna lay down and rested, mentally reviewing the last day. Her reminiscing came to an end when the alarm went off. As Ayanna went to get a shower, she could hear the mewling of newborn kittens from Brandi's room. Smiling with hope for her friend, Ayanna washed herself, wistfully wishing she could be clean while still having Sean's smell on her skin.

Ayanna's phone buzzed with a text from Bridget informing her that her chainmail bikini would be delivered later that day. Even seeing a long line at the cart couldn't dampen her mood. She entered the cart and stripped down to her bikini before joining Annabelle and Enrique in action.

Time passed quickly in the blur of the morning rush. Once the rush subsided, Annabelle focused on Ayanna and said, "Okay, spill."

"What?"

"You are glowing."

"It's just adrenaline from the rush."

"Enrique, back me up. Something's going on with Ayanna, right?"

"*Sí.*"

"I'm just in a really good mood this morning."

"It's Sean, isn't it? Please tell me you rode the bone roller coaster, made the two-backed beast—"

"All right, all right. Yes, we, uh, made sweet and passionate love. And it was wonderful. Are you happy now?"

"Happy for you," Annabelle squealed as she gave Ayanna a massive hug. Enrique joined in, making Ayanna feel very cared for and supported.

The sound of gravel crunching under the foot of an approaching customer brought their reverie to an end, and they returned to work. Ayanna noted Annabelle eyeing her nervously throughout the morning.

Once Enrique was on a break with Aiden, Ayanna addressed the redhead, "Now, it's your turn to spill."

Annabelle said shyly, "I have something to confess. I've been drawing you lately."

"Sean told me."

"He did? Was that when you were fighting yesterday?"

"How did you know we were arguing?"

"I drew the two of you arguing. Ayanna, what's going on?"

"You wouldn't believe me if I told you." *That's an honest answer, if not the one Annabelle wants.*

"Try me. I shouldn't tell you this, but somehow I feel like I have to tell you and only you. Last night, Tanya and I talked about marriage. She told me we can't because she's a *witch*, like an actual spell-casting witch, and it would be too dangerous for me."

"Annabelle, I'm sorry."

"Don't be. I told Tanya I don't care because I love her and would risk anything and everything to be with her for the rest of our lives. She wants me to think about it, though. Something about men who hunt people like her."

"Godkillers."

"She didn't have a name for them. Wait, how did you—"

"Because they hunt me, too."

"You're a witch?"

"No, I'm a goddess."

"I mean, yeah, just look at you... Oh, wait, you're serious. Like an *actual* goddess—holy shit, I slept with a goddess. Does Sean know?"

"He figured it out, thus the fight. Oh, and he's a Godkiller."

Annabelle looked shocked. "Wow, you've got that whole Romeo and Juliet thing going on, don't you?"

Ayanna sighed. "I hope not. I'd really prefer a happier ending."

"Seems like you got a happy ending last night." Annabelle's lurid sense of humor helped reset the mood, which was good since Enrique was returning.

By mid-afternoon, Ayanna was once again alone in the cart when her phone buzzed. There was a text from Sean. "Hounds are coming, along with a Hunt team. Someone put something on social media about praying for help and being saved by a goddess."

Heather. Of course she told the entire world.

"What do they know?"

"Nothing yet. I'll do my best to throw them off the scent."

"Thank you. Please be safe."

Sean didn't come to the cart that day, and there were no further messages. Ayanna felt distracted as she served the final few customers and closed up the cart.

I hope Sean is all right. He's playing a dangerous game, and I suspect he doesn't realize just how dangerous this is.

After work, Ayanna went over to Sean's apartment. She slipped quietly up to his door and listened. Inside were two voices.

One was clearly Sean's, and he sounded stressed. The other voice was deep and sharp, a voice used to command obedience. From the sounds of it, Sean wasn't being as obedient as the other man wished.

Don't do anything stupid, my love. Play the game, and let me worry about me.

Ayanna slipped back to the stairwell, where she could observe Sean's door unseen. She hoped Sean's neighbors used the elevator today, as lurking there was clearly suspicious. Luckily for Ayanna, she didn't have to wait long until Sean's door opened. A solidly-built man of slightly above average height emerged. He had dark hair and olive skin, and wore an outfit which could best be described as paramilitary casual. The man gave Sean a terse order and swung around toward the elevator. Ayanna stifled a gasp when she saw his face.

Whatever I could have imagined, this is definitely worse. We are all so screwed.

Ares, the God of War, was in Portland—and apparently working for the Godkillers.

Chapter 41

Highway To Hell

AC/DC

Sean's day started with a series of angry messages about his gross incompetence and lack of communication. A Diviner in Seattle had flagged something on social media yesterday. This young woman named Heather claimed that she'd prayed for help while being assaulted, and that a woman had answered her prayers. Not God, but a woman. While Sean was sleeping, this overzealous Diviner had found a police report verifying the young woman's story.

The brief was in Sean's email along with a written warning, which he found to be grossly unfair since all of this happened on a weekend. He read through the brief, especially the police report. The description in the report matched Ayanna.

What did you do? More importantly, why? You drew attention to yourself. Oh no, this is my fault. Badass goddess who protects people. It's all my fault, and I have to fix this.

Sean did his best to debunk the lead, but by early afternoon, he knew he'd failed. Word came in that Hounds were en route from Seattle and a hunt team was flying in from Boise. The Lord Hunter was a former mercenary named Eric Marsh, and his resume was largely redacted. Sean did some research on the parts of Africa and Latin America where he could surmise this Marsh person might have been, and the tales he read were brutal. Because of the redactions, he couldn't be sure if his guesses were correct, but it seemed likely Marsh was a monster.

As much as Sean could use some calming tea, he decided to avoid the coffee cart. He didn't want to risk leading Marsh or the Hounds to Ayanna. A loud pounding on his door didn't help Sean's nerves.

Sean's heart sank when he opened the door. Eric Marsh pushed his way into the apartment uninvited. Marsh proceeded to harangue Sean relentlessly about his incompetence and lack of actionable intelligence. The man finally left, ordering Sean to provide immediate updates if he found new information. Sean could tell by the look on Marsh's face that Marsh clearly expected nothing useful from him.

Not long after Marsh left, there was another knock on the door, a much softer knock. Sean opened the door to see Ayanna, who looked terrified.

"Come in, quickly. What are you doing here?" Sean whispered frantically.

"I was worried about you, so I came to check on you."

"You shouldn't have come. There was a Hunter here a few minutes ago. Not just a Hunter, a Lord Hunter."

"I know, I saw him." Fear was written across Ayanna's face. "Sean, listen. Your hunter is Ares."

"Impossible. There's no way a god could infiltrate the Godkillers, especially not as a Lord Hunter."

"I would recognize his face anywhere. Believe me, that is Ares."

"I want to believe you, but it's impossible. No one could forge the paperwork necessary for that."

Sean studied Ayanna's face as she silently reflected on his

words. He watched as whatever puzzle pieces had been bothering her fell into place. She did not look happy.

Ayanna pulled out her phone and made a call. "Brandi, who forged the Jesús Sanchez identity?" Sean heard Brandi's voice but couldn't make out the words. "That bastard set us up. Brandi, Ares is in town, and he's working for the Godkillers. Hang on." Ayanna turned toward him. "Sean, do you know if the Godkillers employ any forgers to create identities and travel papers for Hunters?"

"Uh, I think so. I never got one, obviously, but I think it's a couple of brothers who do the work." Sean frowned as he struggled to recall that bit of gossip. "Yeah, the Swift brothers. They create false news stories and social media to cover up successful hunts."

"The *Swift* brothers? Those assholes are Hermes and Mercury. I *knew* Ares wasn't smart enough to come up with the idea of infiltrating the Godkillers."

Sean nodded. "That's how Ares could get in. They would have forged his paperwork to give him a legitimate birthdate and history, and then if they were asked to evaluate it for legitimacy, then they would obviously say it was."

Ayanna directed her attention back to the phone call. "Brandi, anything you have from them is now suspect. We all need to be ready to run." Pause. "I hope so, too. I like Portland, and I really don't want to leave." Ayanna hung up.

"What did she say?"

"She wants to wait this out, keep our heads down, and hope this blows over."

"That's really dangerous."

"When you've been hunted constantly for seventeen hundred years, you almost get used to constant danger."

"I'm really sorry. I thought I was doing a good thing, and now I know I wasn't." Sean felt miserable.

"You didn't know, and you're making a change for the better," Ayanna said soothingly.

"Thank you. I can't quit now, though, not while I can feed you information."

"Be careful, Sean. Ares is unpredictable and unfathomably vicious. The Greeks have enough latent veneration to ensure he is still powerful. I worry about you."

"You're being hunted, and you're worried about me?"

"Of course. I love you."

"I love you, too."

"As much as I would like to spend some quality naked time with you, we both know that's not a good idea right now. If I'm lucky, then I'll see you in your dreams." With a quick kiss, Ayanna headed out the door. Sean watched her go, wondering who he could pray to for her safety.

Sean would have loved to meet Ayanna in his dreams, but that would require him actually sleeping. He tossed and turned all night, his anxiety making sleep nearly impossible. Whatever sleep he managed was shallow and troubled. Sean drank three cups of coffee as he showered and dressed.

His nerves were shot as he sat down at his computer. Less than ten minutes later, a message flashed on the screen. The Hounds had an address. Sean immediately picked up his phone and called Ayanna.

"Ayanna, you have to run now! They know where you live!"

No sooner had Sean finished his sentence when his door crashed open. Eric Marsh strode in with a full breach team. The smile on Marsh's face was pure evil.

"Look here, boys. Security was right, we do have a mole."

Sean's phone fell from his shaking hands as he stared at the wrong end of multiple gun barrels. He could hear Ayanna's voice dimly as she begged him to tell her he was all right.

Right before a sadistically grinning Ares crushed the phone, the god said, "Take him. He'll make fine bait."

Chapter 42

The Trooper

Iron Maiden

Annabelle cooed over Ayanna's brand new chainmail bikini. With all of the tension and danger in her life right now, her friend's praise helped settle her nerves. That brief respite was shattered when her phone rang.

Ayanna heard Ares' words before the call ended, and she felt ice cold fear grip her heart. Her mind raced as she thought of how to save Sean and her friends. She discarded ideas as fast as she thought of them, until one stuck.

This is a terrible idea, yet it's somehow the least stupid idea so far.

"Annabelle, I gotta go."

"Now?"

"Sorry."

Ayanna raced across the street to the body shop. "Aiden, can I borrow a big wrench, or metal rod, or something?"

He handed her a tire iron. "Do you need help?"

"I appreciate the offer, but I have to handle this myself."

"Go get 'em, Ayanna."

"Thanks, Aiden."

Ayanna returned to the cart, dashing to the head of the line.

She called out to Annabelle, "I need you to put something on your social media."

"What?"

"Just get your phone."

The line in front of the coffee cart stalled as Annabelle activated her camera's video. A few of the patrons also turned on their phone cameras because there's nothing people love more than a spectacle. Even in Portland, a woman wearing a chainmail bikini and wielding a tire iron definitely counted as a spectacle.

"I'm ready," Annabelle said.

Ayanna took a deep breath, and then bellowed, "Ares, come and face me, you coward. You couldn't defeat me at Gaugamela. Only Athena was strong enough. You couldn't beat me on the field of battle, and you couldn't get me into your bed, but Athena did both. I always knew your *spear* was as weak and pathetic as the rest of you. Face me, Ares the Coward. I challenge you to fight me. Come and find me on the Morrison Bridge. I will give you the beating you deserve."

Finished, she sprinted off, racing for the bridge, hoping the magic of social media would bring Ares to her. She knew her chances of survival were negligible, but she hoped to buy her friends enough time to run, and if she was lucky, to save Sean.

Six thousand years is a long time. When I die, I'm not coming back from this one. It's ironic that for the first time in centuries, I have something to live for, and yet I'm running toward my death. I just have to sell my life dearly enough to save my loved ones.

As Ayanna sped through the streets, her video spread across social media, from Annabelle and those patrons who had filmed her as well. As Ayanna hoped, the video soon reached the eyes of Eric Marsh, who ordered a change in direction to the Morrison Bridge. The video also reached other Hunters, and soon multiple plain work vans were speeding for the bridge.

A nearly naked woman running through the streets drew

attention and a lot of curious onlookers. A small collection of cyclists and joggers gathered in her wake as she raced west toward destiny. Ayanna slowed as she turned onto the bridge, her pace dropping to an easy jog. She stopped at the center of the bridge and waited, hoping her mad plan had worked. The small crowd that stopped to watch the seemingly insane woman wearing a metal bikini on a cold autumn morning was just starting to get bored when two plain work vans screeched to a halt, each disgorging a half-dozen men armed with guns. As most of the gun barrels leveled at Ayanna, more phones came out. Some called the police, while most started live-streaming. Three more vans pulled up, two of which carried Eric Marsh, his teams of Hunters and Hounds, and Sean, dragged along in Marsh's grasp.

Tensions rose rapidly as armed and anxious men pointed guns in many directions. Catholics, Orthodox, and the myriad variations of Protestantism all had their own Godkillers, and those hunters had hunted each other many times over the centuries. Now, four teams of well-armed and high-strung men were eyeing each other and Ayanna. The Catholic team consisted entirely of Marsh's hand-picked men, utterly loyal to him. The Baptist, Orthodox, and Pentecostal teams had seen Ayanna's message and were anticipating the opportunity to eliminate two gods at once and give the Catholics a black eye.

It was Marsh who broke the impasse, shouting, "I brought your spy. Or maybe he's more than just a spy to you. Either way, come and get him." Marsh kicked Sean, who stumbled forward and nearly fell. As Sean regained his footing, Marsh shot him twice in his back.

"No!" Ayanna's scream ripped through the chill air, echoed by the screams of stalled motorists and random onlookers, who suddenly realized the danger was all too real. Ayanna sprinted faster than a human could, closing the distance to Marsh. One of his men loomed in front of her, and she swung the tire iron with all of her might. His skull shattered with a sickening crunch at the same time as the first bullet caught Ayanna in her flank, spinning her around. Bullets flew in a storm as the Hunters fired at her and each other.

Seeing a nearby target, Ayanna shifted into a lioness and leapt, tearing the man apart as she landed. She lost sight of Marsh, but there were plenty of Hunters who needed killing if she were to protect her friends. Ayanna shifted between woman and lioness, tears streaming from her eyes as she killed men and mourned Sean.

The battle took its toll on her body as more bullets slammed into her. Ayanna bled from more than a dozen wounds, roaring in pain and fury as another Hunter died under her claws. This time, her roar was echoed by a second lioness, sleeker and darker than Ayanna, who tore the throat out of another Hunter.

As blood flowed on the Morrison Bridge, Jesús walked calmly through gunfire toward Sean's body. No bullet would touch him, and he knelt by Sean's dying form and placed his hands upon Sean's back. The bleeding stopped, and two spent bullets tinkled on the ground as Jesús healed Sean's wounds.

News helicopters and camera-equipped drones were circling the raging battle on the Morrison Bridge. A few exceptionally stupid onlookers continued their live streams. Those lenses caught Sean's rasping breath as Jesús brought him back to life. A dozen cameras bore witness to the return of the final combatant. Ares emerged from a bullet-scarred van, no longer clad in modern tactical gear, but now in ancient bronze armor. The plume on his helmet was as red as the blood spilled on the street. His bronze spear and shield gleamed in the morning sun.

"Go," Bast snarled at Ayanna. "I've got the Hunters."

Ayanna needed no further encouragement, leaping to block

Ares' path to Jesús and the still-prone Sean. From the corner of her eye, she saw a Hunter take aim at her and then drop his gun as a dark cloud of stinging insects enveloped his head, blinding him.

That tiny black cloud means a witch has joined the battle. Perhaps it's Tanya. I'll thank her if I live.

Ayanna shifted her focus to the bronze spearpoint leveled at her chest. She danced from side to side, and the spearpoint followed her.

Ares was a skilled opponent, and Ayanna was already gravely wounded. Her time was running out, and she knew it. Blood and gore streaked her heaving flanks, too much of it her own. Ayanna's focus was slipping further away as each beat of her heart sent more precious blood coursing from her wounds.

This wasn't the plan. I was supposed to save Sean, and my friends were supposed to run. They weren't supposed to be here. Ares toys with me now, knowing I grow weaker with each breath. I can feel the end coming, and my remaining time is measured in seconds. I have to find a way past his spear, and I have to find it now.

Ayanna heard a voice, faint with pain and blood loss. Sean's voice. "I love you, my badass protector."

She darted toward Ares' spear, shifting into human form to knock it aside. The wicked blade sliced open her thigh before Ayanna shifted back to a lioness. Now past Ares' spear, she raked her claws into the gap above his greaves. His scream of agony ripped the air. Ayanna felt tendons snap under her claws, and Ares collapsed as she shredded his thigh muscles. Ayanna drove her muzzle toward Ares' throat, but he blocked her with his arm. He screamed again in agony as her jaws crushed down. She felt his bones snap in her fangs. Ayanna released his arm and again dove downwards, trying to finish him. As her teeth tore out Ares' throat, she felt his dagger pierce her side.

Ares' breath rattled from his ruined throat, his hands dropping lifeless to the ground. Ayanna rolled off of Ares' corpse, his dagger clattering to the pavement as she became human one final time. Just before Ayanna's eyes closed, she saw Sean crawling toward her, tears streaming down his face. With her final breath, she whispered, "I love you."

Chapter 43

Alone

Heart

Sean crawled over to his fallen love, taking her hand. He couldn't feel a pulse, and her chest was still. "No, no, Ayanna, no. Jesús, help her. Do something, please."

Jesús laid his hands on Ayanna's still form as the last sounds of combat faded. His gentle face showed the strain of his concentration, followed by tears and disappointment. "I'm sorry, Sean. I cannot raise a goddess from the dead."

From behind him, Sean heard a high-pitched wail as Brandi realized her friend was dead. Brandi tore off the arms of the last Hunter standing, then raced to Ayanna's side. Falling to her knees, Brandi screamed, "*Osiris!* Osiris, please help her."

A hole opened in the air, and through tear-stained eyes, Sean observed a tall, bronze-skinned man dressed all in white step out from a lush landscape and onto the concrete bridge. Osiris embraced the cat-headed goddess while a dozen cameras recorded. He intoned, "Bast, she is not one of ours. The *Duat* is closed to her."

The weeping goddess responded, "Please, Osiris. There must be something you can do."

"There is little I can do for her, Bast. For your sake, I will do what I can." Osiris released Brandi and walked over to the fallen Ayanna. With a flick of his wrist, another hole opened in the air, this time to a featureless white void. Sean staggered backward as Osiris gently picked up Ayanna and placed her in the void, closing the hole in the air with another flick of the wrist. "Bast, I have done all I can do for your friend."

Sean asked, "Where is she now? What did you do to her?"

Osiris placed a gentle hand on Sean's shoulder. "She is elsewhere now." Sean shuddered as the black eyes of the Judge of Souls delved into his inner being. "Mourn her for three days, Sean of Portland." The Lord of Death swung round, stepping through the portal from whence he came. As it closed, Osiris warned, "Bast, war is coming."

The air seemed still after the furious chatter of gunfire, the silence broken by the whimpers of wounded onlookers. Jesús began moving from one wounded person to another, healing as he could. The sound of approaching police sirens pierced the unnatural stillness on the bloody bridge, but it was an intrepid reporter who arrived first, a reluctant cameraman in tow.

The reporter stared at Brandi, not sure what to make of a nude woman with the head of a cat. Brandi saved him the trouble of figuring out what to say by transforming into a cat and darting off under a car. This left the weeping Sean as the only person to talk to.

"What happened here? What is your name?"

"She's dead."

"Who? Who is dead? Where is she?"

"Osiris sent her somewhere."

"Did you say Osiris? Like the Egyptian god?"

"Not *like* the Egyptian god—the *actual* Egyptian god. The Lord of the Dead. Osiris sent Ayanna somewhere."

"Who is Ayanna?"

"She—" Sean choked up. "She was my—Ayanna is a goddess, once known as Inanna or Ishtar."

"A goddess? Living in Portland? Why?"

"She was hiding from Venatores Falsorum Deorum, also known as the Godkillers." Sean indicated the scattered corpses of the many gunmen. "They've been hunting her and others like her since the time of Emperor Constantine."

The reporter seemed stunned by this revelation. "The catwoman and the other man... he healed you, didn't he?"

"Yeah, that was Jesus, the good one." Sean felt shock giving way to anger at the incessant questions.

"As in Jesus Christ? What do you mean the good one?"

"He's hiding from the bad Jesus and the Godkillers."

"There is no bad Jesus. Are you sure—"

"I used to think that, too. I know better now."

"If Ayanna was fighting Godkillers, then what was this guy doing?"

"She fought Ares. He infiltrated the Godkillers with the help of Hermes and Mercury." Sean noticed the streamers who were standing nearby with their phones, sending his words out to whomever was watching.

He spun away from the irritating reporter to address the onlookers and their audience. "I want to tell you about Ayanna. She is a protector and a lover. I am... I *was* a Godkiller—consider this my resignation—and she loved me despite that. Ayanna came to this bridge and made herself a target. I'm certain she did it to buy time for her friends to escape, although instead, they came to her aid, because they love—*loved*—her so much." Sean's voice caught in his grief-stricken throat.

"Ayanna enjoyed quiet gardens and spicy foods. She introduced me to the wonderful world of tea. She was six thousand years old, but lived and loved to the fullest. Ayanna made mistakes —we all do—but she was learning and growing. She helped me learn and grow, too. I love her and miss her."

The police finally showed up and cordoned off the area, brusquely detaining any and all witnesses they could find. They never did find the cat, or the man who healed the wounded. The police questioned Sean relentlessly about the events of the day until he was thoroughly exhausted. Once released by the police, Annabelle and Tanya met Sean outside the precinct and took him home. They stayed and talked with him as he fed Huntress.

Sean felt an urge to return to the Morrison Bridge, back to where Ayanna had died. Annabelle and Tanya understood, offering to feed Huntress for him. Sean agreed and gave them his spare keys, then left. Once he arrived at the center of the bridge, Sean sat down on the sidewalk and cried for his lost love.

A figure wandered an empty white void. Every step was the same, as nothing changed no matter which direction the figure went. The figure had no memory of anything except the void.

Sean fell asleep on the bridge. He woke to discover that someone had covered him with a rough blanket in the night. Shortly after Sean rose, Brandi arrived with breakfast and coffee. They sat together for hours, talking at times, but mostly just mourning silently.

The figure walked and walked. Never tiring, never stopping. No matter where the figure went, nothing changed, but the figure knew nothing different than the void.

Sean stayed all day, only taking breaks for bodily needs. He knew it was stupid and pointless, but he couldn't think of anything else to do. Annabelle and Jesús joined Sean that afternoon with tea for him, and they sat together for hours, holding hands, crying, and talking. Tanya joined them in the evening, sitting down next to Sean. They stayed like that for a while, until

Annabelle and Tanya left for home, and Jesús left for work. Before they left, Tanya cast a protective charm on Sean to see him safely through the night.

He spent another night on the bridge, but not alone. Mortimer visited and watched over Sean as he slept. The two had only met briefly, but they shared a mutual bond through Ayanna.

There is no time or space in the void, and the figure neither knew nor cared how long it wandered. Those wanderings were interrupted, though, by something new. It was almost imperceptible against the background of endless white, but there was now a white gravel patch. The figure pondered this change.

Sean awoke to find Brandi and Jesús and a small crowd of onlookers. The two deities sat with Sean, and they mourned together. Sean focused on Brandi and asked, "Why did Osiris tell me to mourn for three days?"

"Numbers and numerology were very important in our glory days. Three had numerous meanings and portents attached to it. For gods, it was a sometimes-critical number."

"Critical in what way?"

"Ask him."

Sean pivoted his head. "Jesús?"

"You know my story, although my three days were... let's just say, very technical."

"What do you mean?"

"I died on Friday afternoon, right before dusk and the beginning of a new day. I was dressed and buried on Saturday. On Sunday, before dawn, I rose."

"That's what, thirty-six hours maybe?"

"Like I said, technical. Anyway, Ayanna died once before, and three days later came back from her underworld. There were other gods who died and were reborn on the same cycle. Death and rebirth in three days was a common theme."

"Does that mean Ayanna is coming back?"

Brandi shrugged ruefully. "I don't know. Neither of us does. Osiris admitted he doesn't know, but he feels this is the right thing to do for Ayanna."

As the figure contemplated the white gravel, new shapes and colors appeared. Soon there were islands of green in the white gravel. A border appeared, fixing the size of the gravel. Outside of that low border, trees appeared, then a stream full of fish. The figure wasn't sure where the words to describe the scene came from, but the words' meanings were clear.

The videos of the Battle on the Bridge, as it was now commonly known, had been viewed millions of times. The discovery that gods were real and numerous sent shockwaves through much of the world. Talk shows and news articles sought to further the conversation or debunk the idea, depending on the leanings of the editors. Sermons thundered from pulpits condemning this new heresy while friendships developed as strangers discussed Ayanna's last stand in coffee shops.

None of this was relevant to Sean, though. Throughout the day, a small crowd of onlookers remained, although the size ebbed and flowed. Sean's vigil had become a minor spectacle. Some people laid flowers down, or left small mementos to their own lost loves. As the day wore on, more people engaged with Sean. A few were cruel and mocking, but most were pleasant. Sean talked with them about grief, their loved ones who were gone, and about Ayanna. The care and kindness of strangers didn't lessen his mourning, but it helped make it more bearable.

A few of the people Sean talked with wanted to know more about Ayanna and what she was like. Many more people asked about Jesus, especially about Sean's understanding of the existence of a kind and loving Jesus, as well as a cruel and brutal Jesus. Late in the afternoon, Sean engaged in a long conversation with a group of professors from the nearby universities who spent more time arguing with each other than speaking with Sean.

The figure studied the newly formed terrain from a prominent height. It... no... she could see a river coursing through green fields below forested hills. In the far distance was a lush plain sandwiched between other rivers, with brown desert on the sides. This reminded her of something, but the memory kept slipping away. She couldn't remember her name, but she knew she had one.

As evening fell, Annabelle and Tanya returned, this time with Krystal, Enrique, and Aiden. They sat and ate with Sean, sharing stories from the coffee cart and their memories of Ayanna. He felt the warmth of their friendship as they talked, laughed, and cried. The group expanded their circle to include any willing onlookers, creating a feeling of camaraderie.

Enrique, Aiden, and Krystal left after sunset, as they all had to work early the next day, but Annabelle and Tanya stayed. The people they sat with became less like strangers as the evening wore on. They shared stories and hopes over take-out food and bottled water. Sean eventually drifted off to sleep, resting his head on Annabelle's shoulder.

Sean woke up around dawn with his head still on the shoulder of the now sleeping Annabelle. He noticed that the crowd had grown during the night. Jesús was deep in conversation with two women, while Brandi was handing out coffee to people and taking orders from others. On the other side of Annabelle, Sean saw Tanya talking with a man that looked a lot like Osiris and another woman.

Annabelle stirred as Sean looked around, and he apologized for waking her. Brandi noticed they were awake and walked over. She asked, "Would you like some coffee or tea? I'm sending orders to Enrique and Krystal. He should be here soon with a delivery."

"A caramel latte would be wonderful," Annabelle purred groggily.

"Tea for me. Um, I'll let you pick what kind of tea for me. Are you doing good business this morning?"

Brandi shook her head. "I'm giving out drinks for free, so no." She winked at him. "But I'm hoping I'll make some new customers. Let me introduce you to some people."

Brandi indicated the couple talking with Tanya. "Sean, you briefly met Osiris, and this is his sister and wife, Isis."

"Hi, uh. Sorry, did you say sister?"

Isis shrugged. "Genetics don't really apply to deities, and there aren't all that many of us. As Ayanna probably explained to you, we didn't have any choice in the matter, either. That said, the incest thing is pretty common among gods—which again, says more about our worshippers than us. Anyway, it's good to meet you. Bast has told us much about you."

"Good to meet you, too. Sorry if I said anything wrong."

Osiris waved it off. "We understand how disconcerting our relationship is in this era. We are wishing you the best today."

"Thanks," Sean responded warily. Before he could ask what Osiris meant, Brandi dragged him over to Jesús.

"Sean, these two are Brigid and Athena. Brigid and Athena, this is Sean."

"Hi, good to meet you," Sean said with some trepidation.

Brigid gave him a big hug and said, "Hello, you can call me Bridget," with a strong Irish accent.

Athena gave Sean a coldly appraising look. For his part, Sean was feeling incredibly inadequate. It was one thing to know that his girlfriend's ex was an actual goddess, but it was quite another to be standing right in front of her—especially when it was someone as tall, athletic, beautiful, brilliant, and downright badass as Athena. He was starting to sweat when Brigid leaned over, kissed Athena on the cheek, and whispered in her ear. Athena's frown wavered, and she stepped over to embrace Sean. "Thank you for being good to Ishtar. I appreciate the care you've shown for her."

"You're welcome, Athena. I miss her, too."

"I know. I didn't want to believe it... to believe she loved a mortal, but I'm glad she found love again."

"Me, too, and I'm forever grateful it was me. You aren't mad that Ayanna killed your brother?"

"Ares has always been an asshole, so she did us all a favor. Unfortunately, there's enough belief left for us, so he will be back. Honestly, I feel more powerful today than I have in centuries. All thanks to Ayanna."

Sean heard a gentle cough and looked over to see a lanky young Indigenous man with golden eyes and a mischievous grin standing behind Athena. Brandi shrugged, as if to say she didn't know him.

"Hi," Sean said.

"Hello, my name is Coyote. Good to meet you." Coyote's voice had a tone of subtle amusement, as if he knew a joke no one else did. "I'm here to pay my respects to those who defeated so many Godkillers."

"Welcome, Coyote." Sean felt a heavy dose of guilt because he knew very well how many hours he'd spent seeking signs of Coyote and other native deities in the many reservations dotting the Pacific Northwest.

Seeming to read Sean's mind, Coyote grinned, adding, "Don't worry, Sean. You never would have found me."

Before they could say more, Osiris stood and intoned, "It is time."

The crowd observed a thin, gray disc coalesce in the cool morning air. The disc elongated until it was taller than a human. The gray faded from opaque to translucent, showing hints of green beyond. The green came into focus, revealing trees and flowering bushes dotted with brilliant white, red, and purple blossoms. On the far side of a raked white gravel floor stood an onyx-haired woman with bronze skin, dressed in flowing white linen. Ayanna. She stood, frozen in place.

Dozens of cameras recorded as Jesús stepped forward and spoke, "Ayanna, honest goddess who seeks to improve herself and aid others as they work to improve themselves, we ask you to step into this world." Ayanna appeared slightly closer now.

Next to Jesús, gray-eyed Athena lifted her arm to beckon someone behind Sean and said, "Ayanna, the lover—Goddess of Love and Intimacy, we ask you to step into this world." Ayanna was now standing on the gravel, leaving it mysteriously undisturbed.

Brigid gently kissed away the tears now streaming down Athena's face before adding, "Ayanna, Goddess of Arts, we beg you to join us in this world."

A wily grin on his face, Coyote called out, "Come now, Ayanna. This world needs your laughter and joy." She now stood on a small island of green within the gravel.

Brandi was the last in line, crying out, "Ayanna, the protector, we call you forth to battle, to be shield and spear for those who must be defended. We require your aid to defeat cruelty and injustice."

There was silence, then Annabelle stood up, saying, "Hi, I'm not a goddess, but Ayanna, you're my friend, and I miss you." Tanya reached out to grasp one of Annabelle's hands as Brandi took the other. "You helped me meet my true love, and you are simply the best. Please join us." Ayanna was more than halfway across the gravel now.

Tanya spoke, her voice deepening into a contralto, "My name is Tanya, and I am a witch. A practitioner of mystical arts whose family has been hunted for centuries by the ignorant. Step forth, Ayanna—guardian, giver, and if you are willing, Goddess of Magic."

A slight figure pushed out from the crowd. A teenage girl jogged up to join the file of deities and humans. "My name is Heather. You answered my prayer when no one else would. You saved my life, and I think I cost you yours. I'm so sorry. Answer my prayer again and come back to us."

Sean was about to speak when a hand grasped his shoulder. Enrique and Aiden walked up to the line, where Enrique spoke. "Ayanna, thank you for accepting me and bringing true love into my life." The two men held hands as he continued. "You are a Goddess of Acceptance and Tolerance, something this world desperately needs. Please come to us, my goddess."

Osiris inclined his head. "Sean, this is your time." The God of the Dead extended his hand toward the portal where Ayanna stood, unmoving on the other side.

Sean stepped up to the shimmering surface of the gateway. He inhaled deeply and stepped through. "My love, my goddess, I'm here for you."

Tears drizzled down her cheeks from sparkling eyes. Her voice echoed in his mind and soul. "I've missed you, Sean. My heart. You waited for me."

"Always, Ayanna. I will wait for you for eternity." He laid a gentle palm on her cheek, feeling the warmth underneath the dampness. The moment his skin contacted hers, Ayanna sprang into motion. She melted into him, his lips tasting the salt of her tears as they kissed.

"Are you sure, Sean? This is paradise and here we are both immortal. You can be by my side forever here."

"I want nothing more than to spend the rest of time with you, Ayanna. But people beyond this gateway *need you*. They need their goddess. What I want isn't as important as your duty. Come with me and be the goddess you were always meant to be."

Ayanna beamed at him. "I love you, Sean. You are strong and brave in ways I never imagined possible when I first met you. Lead on, my hero."

Sean took her hand and stepped forward. Time stretched for a moment and then they stood on the pavement of the bridge. He turned his head to find Ayanna no longer dressed in white. Her vestments were the color of blood underneath plates of gleaming bronze. In her other hand, she held a massive spear, tipped with wickedly serrated bronze. Ayanna squeezed his hand. "The Godkillers are coming, my love. The Protector of Innocents awaits them."

Acknowledgments

A huge thank you to my wife for not thinking I'm crazy for trying this whole author thing. Your support is always greatly appreciated.

I'd also like to thank my parents for their support and for instilling a love of books.

Big thanks to Steve Davala for saying, "Dude, you should write a book," and then not taking no for an answer.

Stacey Pizzitola, thank you for beta reading. The book wouldn't have been as good without you. I'm excited to read your book!

Francesca Varela, thank you for editing. As always, any mistakes are mine.

Jaycee DeLorenzo, thank you the cover design and layout and for not strangling me over email when I wanted to change something... again.

Thank you to Lady Starlight, Merlin, and our dearly departed Francesca. All of our cats make a little appearance in Huntress' purrsonality.

Thank you to independent authors and bookstores everywhere! Shop local whenever you can. A special thank you to my independent sci-fi/fantasy writer's community here in Portland and our meet-ups at the Rose City Coffee Co. Another *huge* thank you to my independent romance author community on Instagram. Y'all are Lovely Hilarious... you know.

Also, thank you to Bikini Girls Coffee. I am certain that absolutely nothing I wrote about the coffee cart is accurate, but y'all make great drinks.

Thank you to the Rose City Rollers community for their continued support.

About the Author

Chris Walters is a romance author living in Portland, Oregon with his wife and two cats. When not reading, writing, or working, he is a roller derby announcer for the Rose City Rollers. He self-published his debut novel, No One Like You, in June 2024. His next novel, Make It Real, will be published later in 2024.